WITHDRAWN

Yury Trifonov

The EXCHANGE
& OTHER STORIES

ARDIS, ANN ARBOR

Ardis Publishers
2901 Heatherway
Ann Arbor, Michigan 48104

Library of Congress Cataloging-in-Publication Data

Trifonov, IUrii Valentinovich, 1925-1981

The exchange and other stories / Yury Trifonov.
p.   cm.
Contents: The exchange — The long goodbye — Games at dusk —
A short stay in the torture chamber.
ISBN 0-679-73442-2
1. Trifonov, IUrii Valentinovich, 1925-1981 —Translations, English.
I. Title.
PG3489.R5   1991
891.73'44—dc20   90-27440
CIP

Distributed by Vintage Books,
a division of Random House, Inc.

CONTENTS

INTRODUCTION

Yury Trifonov's early career gave no indication that he would become a controversial writer. Born in Moscow in 1925, he began publishing in 1947, and received a Stalin Prize for his novel *Students* in 1951. He wrote a number of well-received works: a novel, *The Quenching of Thirst* (1963), about the construction of a canal in Turkmenia; four books of short stories; a documentary work, *Reflection of the Fire* (1965); and the scenario for a movie (*The Hockey Players*, 1965). All of this established him as one of the leading Soviet writers. However, a qualitative change in his writing and his career took place when he published "The Exchange" (1969), quickly followed by "Taking Stock" (1970) and "The Long Goodbye" (1971), all in the leading Soviet literary review *Novy Mir (New World)*. Widely reviewed in the Soviet press, these novellas were seen by some critics as an attack on the intelligentsia as a whole—by one of their own. Other Soviet critics complained that the author was too objective, too alienated from the characters, that he was showing only the ugly side of contemporary life. Maybe this was realism, but it was not, by ordinary definitions, socialist realism.

Trifonov's reputation grew. He continued to write in what readers perceived as a new style—prose which combined relentless and accurate observation with psychological and moral analysis.

In 1973 Trifonov published the historical novel *Impatience*, written for the series Ardent Revolutionaries, about Andrei Zhelyabov of the People's Will Party. The transformation of Zhelyabov from naive optimist to committed terrorist is credited to impatience: "History is moving too slowly." Despite the fact that this historical novel has no apparent connection with the material of the Moscow novellas, the themes of moral and ethical compromise connect the novel to his later works, and it may be seen to mark the beginning of his examination of the political betrayals which dominate his contemporary historical novels, culminating in his last novel, *Disappearance*.

Trifonov returned to the world of contemporary Moscow with the novella "Another Life" (1975), written in much the same key as the trilogy. *The House on the Embankment,* Trifonov's most famous work, appeared in 1976. It was a sensation in Russia due to its treatment of the purges, but suffers from self-censorship, since Trifonov was not free to accurately describe the political atmosphere of the times, something essential for this particular work. In a sense, one had to already know everything to understand the subtle allusions to the purges. Russian readers were amazed that the censorship had passed this work during what was an increasingly difficult time for literature, but this was typical of Trifonov's career. It may have had something to do with his personality: he was calm, slow-talking and immensely deliberate. He appeared very much the former athlete that he was, but his will was powerful and patient, and time after time he was able to publish material other writers would not have dreamed of submitting.

The "house" of the title is a Moscow apartment building that faces the Kremlin. Inhabited by the elite (including Trifonov's own family until his father's arrest in 1937), the house's ever-fluctuating residency graphically symbolizes the rise and fall of a given career, as the relationship between two very different young men is carefully developed—a structure Trifonov will be drawn to again.

The last work to be published while Trifonov was alive is *The Old Man* (1979). The story of Pavel Letunov, an Old Guard Bolshevik who fought in both the Revolution and Civil War, but who also experienced arrest and exile, functions as a short course in Soviet history. Letunov's efforts in the 1960s and 70s to rehabilitate the reputation of a Cossack commander, executed by order of a revolutionary tribunal in 1919, raises essential issues: the erosion of civil liberties and personal freedom is traced not only to the years of the Great Terror, but also to the revolutionary period itself. Typical of the new generation, Letunov's son remains untouched by his father's passionate idealism.

Yury Trifonov died in March, 1981 at the age of 55, as the result of complications after a routine operation.

Time and Place. A Novel in Thirteen Chapters was published in censored form six months after the author's death. The novel, as the subtitle underscores, is composed of a baker's dozen of short stories that can be read independently, but are united by a common setting (Moscow) and a shared history. The highly autobiographical novel, which spans the period from 1937 to 1980, traces the life of two Russian writers.

The process of work on Trifonov's final posthumous work, the novel *Disappearance* (1987), bridges more than twenty years. *Disappearance,* which the author's widow Olga Trifonova-Miroshnichenko has compared to a notebook or diary, was therefore written concurrently with the Moscow novellas, *The Old Man* and *Time and Place,* and shares many of those works' themes and concerns. However, the thorough depiction of the 1930s and the purges (missing from *The House on the Embankment)* marks a radical departure from Trifonov's previously published writings. In *Disappearance,* Igor Bayukov, a resident of that same house on the embankment, loses most of his family to the purges. Clearly written "for the drawer," *Disappearance* could not have appeared in the Soviet Union before the recent introduction of glasnost. The English translation is scheduled for 1991.

Like Balzac, Trifonov is interested in the specifics of existence: his characters are so firmly embedded in their social milieu that it is hard to imagine them alone, as individuals, without their relatives, friends and co-workers. What they have for breakfast, where they go on vacations, what they do with their money—all of these things go into the characterization of a Trifonov family. In these novellas the world of the middle-class professional is subjected to the somber, unblinking observation of the moralist. For all his ethnographic description—many readers have been convinced that he knew their families—Trifonov's real interest lies not in excoriating the vices of his class, but rather in examining the precise moment when a man takes a wrong turn in his life, the moment of moral betrayal. This is the real subject of Trifonov's later work, and through all of the catalogue of Moscow life he never loses sight of it for a moment.

"The Exchange," for example, is firmly grounded in Moscow life; and its plot is based on the eternal housing shortage in Russia. What may seem unclear to a non-Russian reader is miserably familiar to Russian readers: due to the chronic shortage of "living space," especially in Moscow, many people try to exchange different rooms for one apartment where an entire family can live together. Otherwise one must wait for years to get into a decent apartment, or spend a great deal of money to buy into a cooperative apartment house as it is being built.

The moral conflict in this novella seems simple at first glance: Dmitriev's aggressive wife Lena sees a chance to get a larger apartment by inviting her mother-in-law, whom she dislikes, to move in with them, exchanging both her old room and theirs for a real apartment. Lena's real motive, of course, is that she knows that her mother-in-law is dying, and will thus leave them with an extra room in the apartment they could not get otherwise—Soviet law allotting space on the basis of how many members there are in the family. From all of this it appears that Dmitriev's wife is the villain of the story. She is indeed unlikeable, but in Trifonov's world nothing is quite so black and white.

Dmitriev's mother is a cultivated woman who looks down on her daughter-in-law, also an educated person, because she is not of the intelligentsia, that nebulous category of people who find ideas more interesting than money. Lena and her family, the Lukyanovs (who in some ways symbolize the crassness of the future, something like the Snopes family in Faulkner), represent those who "know how to live," know which strings to pull to get the things they need and want. Despite his mother's views, Dmitriev himself sees that the Lukyanovs have their value: his father-in-law, for example, is the only one able to get the dilapidated Dmitriev dacha fixed, and Lena is aggressive about helping her husband and child, not just herself. Dmitriev sees that his mother is proud of not knowing "how to live"; many of her good deeds are done so that she can think well of herself. Lena's contention that her mother-in-law is something of a hypocrite is not without foundation.

Dmitriev is caught in the middle, torn between the noble ideas of his family and the practical views of his wife, who is ready to do whatever is necessary to help her family—even if it means hurting someone else. Dmitriev's wife is in favor of the exchange because she knows that her daughter and husband will benefit, and is almost blind to the reprehensible aspects of the plan. Dmitriev, however, is aware of everything. Just as he has rationalized so many things in the past, he rationalizes this, even though he knows it to be wrong. Dmitriev wills himself to forget the fact that he will profit from his mother's death, using various arguments to make himself as blind as his wife is by nature.

A less obvious, but equally important theme here is the tension between the intelligentsia and the rising middle class. Dmitriev's mother and sister perceive Lena as coming from a background which we would call bourgeois, and they censure her for her materialism. This conflict is the basis of the funny and terrible fight between Dmitriev's cousin and wife about Picasso, phoniness, and philistinism. The fading of the intelligentsia is also embodied in Dmitriev's relationship with his grandfather, a highly educated former revolutionary whose moral code is uncomfortably rigid. Dmitriev sees this man as irrelevant—to the life he is leading, at any rate. Dmitriev's generation is unheroic, too young for World War II, and too far removed from the events of the Revolution to feel their influence. Dmitriev is tired; he just wants to live his life comfortably without all the in-fighting between his family and his wife's. In the end he gets what he wants, but at the end we see that he has paid dearly for his decision.

"The Long Goodbye," the most complex of these works, is ostensibly about a protracted love affair between an actress and a writer, but once again the evaluation of life is central. Here the hero, Rebrov, is a failure, but he is still young; life may give him a chance to be successful—the evaluation is taking place too early.

The moral choices in this story are so tightly bound up with character and psychology that it is impossible to separate them: do these people make the choices they make because of their sense of morality, or because of their essential personalities? The narrative point of view shifts from the actress to her lover and back again, making easy answers impossible. We can understand both sides.

There are two careers: Lyalya, the actress, becomes a great success during the course of the story; but her lover Rebrov is unable to get anywhere in his career as a writer. Lyalya is a woman of instinct, a consoler—not unlike Dmitriev's mistress Tanya in "The Exchange." But the difference is that she is young and beautiful, and capable of consoling anyone who sufficiently arouses her sympathy. The portrait of a woman who needs to be needed more than she needs to be loved is masterful. For all her living by instinct, Lyalya is capable of decisiveness once things become clear to her—her affair with Smolyanov depends on his being weak, and once she sees that he is actually strong she leaves him, telling him that weak men don't do despicable things or hurt people. Smolyanov tells her that this is not true, something that she will discover herself when her weak lover Rebrov leaves her. Like the heroines of the other works, Lyalya is ready to do almost anything to help those she loves. She goes as far as asking Smolyanov, her lover, to help Rebrov, the lover she lives with.

But it is Rebrov who brings down these things upon himself. He will not commit himself to Lyalya by marrying her, preferring to wonder if she is having affairs. Rebrov takes part in humiliating scenes with Lyalya's lover—to help his career, just as she sleeps with Smolyanov in the first place to help *her* career. By the end a chain of circumstances leads to his decision—she has finally told him about all of her lovers, he is in trouble for not having a certificate of employment, which means he can lose his room and permission to reside in Moscow, and he sees that she will never be free of her mother, whom he hates. But the refrain in "The Long Goodbye" is that life is long, meaning that one cannot judge a life, as Rebrov does so hastily, until all of the evidence is in. The end of the story shows that many of the characters did indeed get the lives they deserved.

Both novellas share certain submerged themes. One is the changing face of Moscow, Trifonov's main geographical setting. The locations in Trifonov's stories are all real—restaurants, bars, cafes, parks, regions, streets—his work reflects all the physical realia of Moscow life as well as the spiritual atmosphere. In "The Long Goodbye" the lilac bushes on the first page are more than just local color: they foreshadow the theme of the destruction of nature (Lyalya's father and his garden), which is to be supplanted by much needed apartment houses. Beauty, as so often in Trifonov's world, gives way to practicality.

In "The Exchange" this process is exemplified by the new cement embankment which borders Dmitriev's beloved river, and the new buildings which have changed the face of the countryside into something not necessarily worse, but very different.

The novellas are joined by a somber style, deliberately prosaic in its imagery. Trifonov's heroes do not reach for poetic metaphors when they are happy or sad, they use concepts and objects from their everyday life, their ordinariness is emphasized. Which is the point about these people—they are not better or worse than others, they are ordinary, but they have serious problems, enjoy moments of euphoria when they feel that life has promise; in a word they are *human,* a category that comes up several times in the stories, when it is affirmed that whether a man is an intellectual or not is not important—but whether he has humanity is. In these works humanity is often denied, but the characters have their memories of happier times, usually in their childhood, and these memories can be both consoling and saddening.

In addition to his longer works of prose fiction, Trifonov published a number of collections of short stories. A tennis player in his youth and an avid soccer and hockey fan, Trifonov also frequently covered sports events as a journalist, both at home and abroad. In fact, during the early 1960s he was perhaps better known for his sports writings than as a Stalin Prize laureate. The two examples of Trifonov's short fiction included in this volume utilize this sports background—the first story "Games at Dusk" (1968) provided the title of a collection brought out by a publishing house that specializes in physical education and sport.

The narrator of "Games at Dusk" recalls the prewar summer when he was eleven years old and he and his friend would religiously go to the tennis courts to watch the grownups play. The narrator remarks that they could have had the court all to themselves during the day, "but the empty court and the empty benches didn't suit us—we wanted the public, noise, passions, struggle, beautiful women—and we wanted to see it all, as in a theater." The theater of sport gradually gives way to the changes that take place on the court—a microcosm of Moscow life: "After this, life on the court somehow began to quickly and irretrievably change. Some people completely vanished, stopped coming, others moved away. New people came. Many new ones." The purges and the war as seen by a young boy are conveyed in his own terms: the disappearance of familiar players.

The Overturned House, a cycle of six short stories appeared in 1981, four months after the author's death. The seventh story, "A Short Stay in the Torture Chamber," was not published until 1986, most likely due to censorship, and then included with the other six stories in Trifonov's *Collected Works* the following year. The entire cycle is set abroad and reflects Trifonov's own travels to Europe and the United States in the 1960s and 70s. The stories, however, are not travelogues or exercises in ethnography.

The narrator in "A Short Stay in the Torture Chamber" has traveled to Switzerland to cover the 1964 Olympic Games, as Trifonov himself had done. But the story's focus is not the Swiss landscape or the Olympics: "Who won there, who lost, I don't remember. All that nonsense has been forgotten." In a situation analogous to *The House on the Embankment,* the narrator meets a former friend from his schooldays who presents a contradictory interpretation of an incident which ended their friendship. The narrator, who had concealed the fact that he was a son of "enemies of the people" on his entrance application, was threatened with expulsion. The narrator's friend, N., was summoned to testify. According to N.'s version of the events, he saved the narrator, who was not expelled but merely reprimanded, whereas the narrator remembers only N.'s villainy. The conflicting views of their common past point to the larger difficulties of determining a nation's history, where eyewitness accounts and collective memory are often ambiguous or fallible.

Trifonov's works give us the texture of everyday life, with the interlocking worlds of family, career and conscience; but he provides no solutions, makes no conclusions that can be used. He is content to state the problem clearly, and show us that there are no heroes, no real villains. This is the gray blur of adult moral compromise, not the black-and-white photograph of childhood conceptions of honor. But Trifonov's characters long for the consoling sharpness and clarity of those early beliefs.

Ellendea Proffer and Ronald Meyer

The EXCHANGE
& OTHER STORIES

THE EXCHANGE

In July Dmitriev's mother, Xenia Fyodorovna, became seriously ill. They took her to Botkin hospital where she spent twelve days suspecting the worst. In September they operated on her and the worst was confirmed, but Xenia Fyodorovna, thinking that she had ulcers, felt better, began to walk soon after, and in October was sent home weighing more and firmly convinced that things were on the mend. It was at that moment, after Xenia Fyodorovna came back from the hospital, that Dmitriev's wife began the business about an exchange: she had decided to move in as quickly as possible with her mother-in-law, who lived alone in a nice twenty-by-sixteen room on Profsoyuznaya Street.

Dmitriev himself had raised the idea of moving in with his mother many times. But that had been long ago, at a time when the relationship between Lena and Xenia Fyodorovna had not yet assumed the form of such hardened and solid enmity that it had now, after the fourteen years of Dmitriev's marriage. He had always run up against Lena's firm opposition, and the idea had come up less and less over the years. And then only in moments of irritation. It had turned into a portable and comfortable *handy object*, a weapon in minor family skirmishes. When Dmitriev wanted to get Lena for something, accuse her of egotism or callousness, he would say: "And that's why you don't want to live with my mother." When Lena felt the need to taunt or to hit a sore spot, she would say: "And that's why I can't live with your mother, and never will, because you are the very image of her, and one of you is enough for me."

At one time all this had bothered and tormented Dmitriev. On account of his mother he had harsh words with his wife, as Lena's malicious witticisms evoked extreme hostility; on account of his wife he let himself in for a painful "clearing of the air" with his mother, after which his mother didn't talk to him for several days. He stubbornly tried to throw them together, reconcile them, settle them together at the dacha, and once he bought them both vouchers for the Riga seashore, but nothing ever really came of it.

Some barrier stood between the two women, and they could not overcome it. Why it was like that he did not understand, although he'd often thought it over in the past. Why two intelligent women, respected by all—Xenia Fyodorovna was the senior bibliographer of a major academic library; Lena translated English technical texts, she was an excellent translator, everyone said, and she had even taken part in the compilation of some special textbook of translation—why had two good women who dearly loved Dmitriev, also a good person, and his daughter Natashka, stubbornly cultivated a mutual hostility which had hardened over the years?

He was upset, amazed, racked his brains, but then he got used to it. He got used to it because he saw that the same thing had happened to all of them—they had all gotten used to it. And he soothed himself with the truism that there is nothing wiser or more valuable in life than peace, and that one must protect it with all one's strength. Therefore, when Lena suddenly began to talk of an exchange with the Markusheviches—it was late in the evening, supper had long been over, Natashka was sleeping—Dmitriev was frightened. Who were the Markusheviches? Where did she find them? A two-room apartment on Malaya Gruzinskaya. He understood Lena's simple secret thought, and this comprehension made fear pierce his heart; he grew pale, then bent over, unable to raise his eyes to Lena.

Since he was silent, Lena continued: they would be sure to like his mother's room on Profsoyuznaya; the location would suit them because Markushevich's wife worked somewhere near Kaluga Gate, and they would probably have to add a premium for their own room. Otherwise you wouldn't get them interested. One could of course try to exchange their room for something more worthwhile, that would be a third exchange, nothing so terrible about that. You act energetically. Do something every day. The best thing would be to find an agent. Lucy knew an agent, a little old man, very nice. True, he couldn't give anybody his address or telephone number; he would just suddenly appear out of nowhere, such a conspirator, but he was supposed to make an appearance at Lucy's soon, she owed him money. That's the rule: never give them money in advance....

As she was talking, Lena made the bed. There was no way he could look her in the eye: he wanted to now, but Lena stood first sideways, and then with her back to him, but when she turned and he glanced straight into her eyes, which were nearsighted, with enlarged pupils from the evening's reading, he saw—resolution. She'd probably been preparing for this conversation for a long time, maybe since the first day she'd found out about his mother's illness. Then it had come to her. And while he, terror-stricken, was running around to the doctors, calling the hospitals, making arrangements, being miserable—she had been considering, mulling it over. And now she'd found some Markusheviches. Strange that he felt neither anger nor pain now. Only something flashed by—about the ruthlessness of life. Lena wasn't to blame, she was a part of this life, a part of the ruthlessness of life. Besides, does one get angry at a person who is deprived, for example, of an ear for music? Lena had always been distinguished by a certain spiritual—no, not deafness, that would be too strong—by a certain spiritual imprecision, and this characteristic was further intensified whenever another even stronger quality of Lena's came into action: the ability to get her own way.

He latched on to what was handy: why did they need the agent if the apartment on Gruzinskaya had already been found? The agent's needed if it's necessary to change rooms. And to speed the whole process in general. She wouldn't pay him a kopeck until she had the order in her hand. It doesn't cost so much, a hundred rubles, one hundred fifty maximum. That's how it is! She assessed his gloominess in her own way. Such a refined soul, such a little psychologist. He said that it would be better if she'd waited until he'd started this conversation himself, and if he didn't, it meant it wasn't necessary, it was wrong, that this wasn't the time to think about it.

"Vitya, I understand. Forgive me," said Lena with an effort. "But...." (He saw that it was hard for her, but that she was going to get it all out.) "In the first place, you already began this conversation, didn't you? You started it many times. And second, this is necessary for all of us, most of all for your mama. Vitka, dearest, I understand you, I feel for you like no one else does, and I say: it's necessary! Believe me...."

She embraced him. Her arms hugged him tighter and tighter. He knew: this sudden love was genuine. But he felt irritated and he pushed her away with his elbow.

"You shouldn't have started it now," he repeated sullenly.

"Well, all right, so I'm sorry. But I'm not worrying about myself, really, really...."

"Be quiet!" he almost screamed in a whisper.

Lena went over to the ottoman and continued making the bed in silence. Out of the chest at the head of the ottoman she took the thick, plaid tablecloth which usually served as a pad under the sheets, but which was occasionally used for its proper purpose on the dinner table;

on top of the tablecloth she lay the sheet which had puffed up and didn't lay very evenly, so Lena bent over, stretching her arms out in front, to reach the far side of the mattress—her face reddened from it, and her belly hung down very low and seemed very big to Dmitriev— she smoothed out the tucked under corners (when Dmitriev made the bed he never smoothed the corners), then she threw two pillows on the bed in the direction of the chest, one of which had a case that was less fresh than the other, and which belonged to Dmitriev. Taking the two blankets out of the chest and putting them on the mattress, Lena said in a trembling voice:

"It's as if you're blaming me for tactlessness, but word of honor, Vitya, I was really thinking of all of us.... Of Natashka's future...."

"Oh, how can you!"

"What?"

"How can you talk about it at all right now? How can your tongue work? That's what amazes me." He felt that the irritation was going to grow and erupt. "For God's sake, you've got some kind of spiritual defect in you. A kind of underdevelopment of feelings. Something, forgive me, *subhuman.* How can you? The thing is that *my mother* is sick and not yours, right? And if I were in your place...."

"Speak more quietly."

"In your place I would never first...."

"Quiet!" She waved her hand.

They both listened. No, everything was quiet. Their daughter was sleeping behind the screen in the corner. Behind the screen there stood a little desk at which she did her homework each evening. Dmitriev had played carpenter and he'd hung a bookshelf over the desk, and put in electricity for the lamp—he had made a special little room behind the screen, the "cell" as it was called in the family. Dmitriev and Lena slept on a wide ottoman of Czechoslovakian make, luckily purchased some three years before, which was an object of envy among their acquaintances. The ottoman was by the window, separated from the "cell" by a carved oak buffet which had come to Lena from her grandmother—a ridiculous thing which Dmitriev had many times suggested selling, Lena was for it, too, but his mother-in-law had objected. Vera Lazarevna lived close by, two buildings from them and came to Lena's almost daily on the pretext of "helping Natashenka" and "making things easier for Lenusha," but in fact only with one aim— to shamelessly interfere in other people's lives.

In the evening when they were lying on their Czech bed—which turned out to be not very durable, quickly getting rickety and squeaking with every move—Dmitriev and Lena always listened a long time for sounds from the "cell," trying to figure out whether their daughter had gone to sleep or not. Dmitriev would call, checking, in an undertone: "Natash! Hey, Natash!" Lena would go up on tiptoe and look through the crack in the screen. Some six years earlier they'd gotten a nurse who had slept on a cot here in the room. Their neighbors, the Fandeyevs, had objected to her sleeping in the hall. The old lady suffered from insomnia and was possessed of the keenest hearing; all night long she would mutter something, groan, and listen: a mouse was scratching, a cockroach was running, someone had forgotten to turn off the faucet in the kitchen. When the old lady left, something like a honeymoon began for the Dmitrievs.

"She was doing physics till eleven again," said Lena in a whisper. "We'd better get someone.... Antonina Alexeyevna has a good tutor."

The fact that Lena had shifted the conversation to Natashka's problems and had submitted to all of Dmitriev's insults, let them pass by—which was not like her—signified that she definitely wanted to make up and bring things to an end. But Dmitriev didn't want to make up yet. On the contrary, his irritation grew stronger because he suddenly realized what was Lena's chief tactlessness: she talked as if everything were predetermined, and as if it were also clear to him, Dmitriev, that it was all predetermined, and that they understood each other without words. She talked as if there were no hope. She had no right to talk that way!

It was impossible to explain all that. Dmitriev jumped up from the chair with a jerk, grabbed his pajamas and towel, and without saying a word, practically ran out of the room.

When he returned after a few minutes, the bed was ready. There was a smell of perfume in the room. Lena was combing her hair, in an unbuttoned robe, standing in front of the mirror, and her face expressed indifference, and if you please, even well-screened resentment. But the smell of the perfume gave her away. This was a call, an invitation to a truce. Holding the flap of her robe with one hand at her chin and the other at her stomach, Lena, with a quick businesslike step, and not looking at Dmitriev, walked past him into the hall. He again remembered the lines of poetry he'd been muttering all the time these past days: "O Lord, how perfect are thy deeds...." Closing his eyes, he sat down on the ottoman. "He thought, the sick man...." He sat that way for several seconds. He knew that in the depths of her soul Lena was satisfied, the most difficult thing had been done: she'd spoken. Now to lick the wound—it wasn't a wound though, but a small scratch which it had been absolutely necessary to make. Like an internal injection. Hold on to the cotton pad. A little painful, but it's so that later everything will be fine. It's very important that *later everything be fine.* But he didn't shout, didn't stamp his feet, he just blurted out a few irritated words, went into the bathroom, washed up, brushed his teeth, and now he would sleep. He lay down in his place near the wall and turned his face toward the wallpaper.

Lena came back quickly, clicked the lock on the door, swished her robe, rustled a fresh nightshirt and turned out the light. No matter how hard she tried to move lightly and be as weightless as possible, the mattress began to crack under her weight, and Lena, on account of this crackling, started to whisper with something like drollness, even:

"Oh God, what a nightmare...."

Dmitriev was silent, he didn't move. Some time went by and then Lena put her hand on his shoulder. It wasn't a caress, but a friendly gesture, perhaps an honest acknowledgment of her guilt even and a plea to turn over. But Dmitriev didn't stir. He wanted to get to sleep right away. With a vindictive feeling he was enjoying the fact that he was sinking into immobility, into sleep, that he didn't have time to forgive, explain in whispers, turn over, show generosity, he could only punish for insensitivity. Lena's hands began to stroke his shoulder gently. The final surrender! With shy touches she was sorry for him, she begged forgiveness, made excuses for her callousness of soul, for which one could find justification, however, and appealed to him for wisdom, goodness, and that he find in himself the strength to pity her. But he didn't give in. Something unsettled in him kept him from turning and embracing her with his right arm. Through the approaching drowsiness he saw the porch of the wooden house, and Xenia Fyodorovna standing on its highest step, wiping her hands with a crumpled waffle-weave towel, and looking slowly and directly into Dmitriev's eyes, past the light brown head, past the blue silk dress, and he heard the muffled voice: "Sonny, have you given it careful thought?" Muffled because it was from far away, from an icy May day when everyone was very young, Valka went to swim, Dmitriev lifted a 70-pound weight, Tolya rushed off on his Wanderer for wine, wrecked a fence on the way, the police came, and later, on the cold veranda with the light of a lantern wavering in its glass, Lena cried, was miserable, embraced him, whispering that never, no one, it was for life, that it didn't matter at all. In the morning his mama got on the motorbike, hung a little milk can on the wheel and went to the station for milk and bread. Her misfortune: to say exactly whatever came into her head. "Sonny, have you given it careful thought?" What could be more ineffectual than that absurd and pitiful phrase? He couldn't think about anything. May with its icy winds tearing off the tender barely born leaf—that's what they were breathing then. Mama was studying English, just for herself, so that she could read novels, and Dmitriev was getting ready for graduate school, so they both studied with Irina Evgenievna together and suddenly stopped when Lena appeared. Mama tapped the veranda glass with the umbrella tip—it wasn't late, about seven in the evening: "Get up! Irina Evgenievna's waiting!" Dmitriev and Lena, hiding under the roomy quilt, pretended they were sleeping. The umbrella tapped indecisively two more times, then cones crunched under shoes—Mama left in silence. She didn't want to study English any more herself, and had lost interest in the detective novels. Once she heard Lena, laughing, mimic her pronunciation. And from that, from that country veranda with the small-paned windows, began what it was now impossible to set right.

Lena's hand displayed persistence. In fourteen years that hand had also changed—before it had been so light, so cool. Now, when her arm lay on Dmitriev's shoulder, it pressed down with no little weight. Dmitriev, without saying a word, turned over on his left side, embraced Lena with his right arm and moved her closer, sleepily suggesting to himself that he had the right to, he'd already been asleep, had had dreams, and maybe he was even still asleep. At any rate, he said nothing, his eyes were closed, just like those of a man who was really sleeping, and during the moments when Lena really wanted him to say something to her, he continued to be silent. Only later, when he'd really fallen into a deep sleep, at about two in the morning, did he mumble something inarticulate in his sleep.

Dmitriev had turned thirty-seven in August. Sometimes it seemed to him that everything was still ahead.

Such surges of optimism came in the mornings when he suddenly awoke fresh, with inadvertent cheerfulness—the weather had a lot to do with it—and, opening the vent window he would begin to wave his arms in rhythm and bend and straighten at the waist. Lena and Natashka got up fifteen minutes earlier. Sometimes Vera Lazarevna would appear early in the morning to walk Natashka to school. Lying with closed eyes he heard how the women shuffled, moved around, exchanging words in a loud whisper, clattering the dishes, and Natashka would grumble: "Kasha again! Don't you have any imagination?" Lena reacted with her usual morning wrath: "I'll show you imagination! Sit up straight!" And his mother-in-law would growl: "If other children had what you have...." That was a deliberate lie. Other children had the same things and a lot more even. But on those mornings when Dmitriev awoke, gripped by that incomprehensible optimism, nothing irritated him. From the height of the fifth floor he looked out onto the square with the fountain, the street, the column holding the trolley schedule, and a dense crowd around it, and further on, the park, the multi-storied building against the horizon and sky. On a balcony of the next building, very close by, twenty meters away, a young unattractive woman in glasses appeared in a short, carelessly tied robe. She squatted down and did something with the flowers which stood in pots on the balcony. She touched and stroked them, checked under their leaves, lifted up some of the leaves and sniffed them. Because she was squatting, her robe opened and her large bluish-white knees became visible. The woman's face was the same shade as her knees, bluish-white. Dmitriev watched the woman as he did his exercises. He watched her from behind the curtain. Why was inconceivable—he didn't like the woman at all—but the secret observation of her inspired him. He thought about how all was not yet lost, thirty-seven—that's not forty-seven or fifty-seven, and that he still could achieve something.

Pattering down the hall in confusion, accompanied by Lena's cries: "Did you take your bags? Don't run across the street! Attention, children, attention!..." Natashka and the Fandeyevs' Valya, a sixth-grader, left the house at 8:30. The staircase shook under their jumps. Dmitriev slipped into the bathroom, locked himself in, and in three minutes a light knock interrupted his meditations: "Viktor Georgievich, today's Friday, I've got to do laundry, I implore you—hurry up!" This was the voice of their neighbor Iraida Vasilievna, whom Dmitriev's mother-in-law didn't speak to, and with whom Lena maintained chilly relations, but Dmitriev tried to be proper, protecting his objectivity and independence. "All right!" he answered through the noise of the water. "I'll finish up!" He shaved quickly, turning on the water heater and rinsing the brush under the hot stream, then washed his face over the old yellowed washstand with the broken corner—it was supposed to have been replaced a long time ago, but the Fandeyevs didn't give a damn what kind of washstand they washed up over, and Iraida Vasilievna begrudged the money—and soon, gently whistling, carrying the papers which he had managed to get from the box on his way to the bathroom, he returned to his room. The table was still loaded down with the dishes after Natashka's and Lena's recent meal. Now Lena was hurrying: she left ten minutes after Natashka, and his mother-in-law took upon herself the morning service of Dmitriev. Dmitriev didn't especially like it, and his mother-in-law waited on him with little enthusiasm—it was her little matutinal sacrifice, one of those inconspicuous feats which make up the entire life of the toilers who have the self-abnegating nature of Vera Lazarevna.

Sometimes, Dmitriev noticed, Lena just tried to act like she didn't have any time, but in fact she would have had plenty of time to make his breakfast, but she purposely relinquished this mission to her mother: so that Dmitriev be in some way, if only for a minute, obliged to his mother-in-law. She was even capable of whispering in his ear in passing: "Don't forget to thank Mama!" He thanked her. He saw through all these subterfuges in the regulation of family ties and, depending on his mood, would either pay no attention to them or quietly get irritated. Vera Lazarevna always responded in her usual way to quiet irritation—with the tenderest malice. "My, how quickly Viktor Georgievich freed the bathroom! What a hero!" she said smiling, and wiped a place on the oilcloth for Dmitriev with a damp kitchen towel. "Which means our neighbor asked you to." Lena cut her off decisively: "What does our neighbor have to do with it? Vitya always washed up fast." "That's what I said, a hero, a military style hero."

On that early October morning there was dark blue beyond the window, the room filled with the light reflected by the yellow bricks of the building opposite, and the voice of Vera Lazarevna was not audible. At first glance, having barely unglued his eyes, Dmitriev unconsciously—because of the sun and the light—felt joy, but in the succeeding second remembered everything, the blue darkened, and beyond the window a relentlessly clear and cold autumn day had set in. Before breakfast neither he nor Lena said anything to each other. But after Dmitriev had called up Xenia Fyodorovna—he called his sister Lora's at Pavlinovo, where his mother now lived, and Xenia Fyodorovna related in a cheerful voice that late yesterday Isidor Markovich had come by, found her condition fine, pressure normal, suggested that she go into some sanatorium in the Moscow area by the first snow, and then followed questions about Natashka, how were her eyes, had she improved on her C in physics, were they giving her raw ground carrots, the most effective food for eyes, and what was happening about Dmitriev's business trip—he experienced sudden relief, just like an ebbing of pain from his head. All at once it seemed as if maybe everything would turn out all right. Mistakes can happen, the most incredible mistakes. And with this insignificant joy and the minute of hope, he returned to the room after the telephone conversation—Natashka had already run off, and Lena was hurriedly sewing something, half dressed in a skirt and a black slip with naked shoulders—and passing Lena he lightly slapped her on the bottom and asked amiably:

"Well, how's your mood?"

Lena abruptly answered dryly that she was in a bad mood.

"What's the matter with you?" said Dmitriev, affected by the fact that his amiability was answered so dryly. "How come?"

"As far as I'm concerned, I've got more than enough reasons. Mama's sick."

"Your mother?"

"You think only yours can get sick?"

"And what's wrong with Vera Lazarevna?"

"Something very serious with her head. She's been on her back for two days, I didn't tell you yesterday, but this morning she called.... Some kind of brain spasms."

Lena finished the sewing, put on the blouse and went over to the mirror, looking at herself superciliously. The blouse was short-sleeved, which wasn't attractive—Lena's arms were heavy at the top, her summer tan had gone, her skin had little white bumps showing through. She should only wear long sleeves, but it would be imprudent to tell her that. Such restraint—not a sound about her proposal of yesterday! Maybe she was ashamed, but more likely there was a certain arrogance in it: she had been accused of tactlessness, of a lack of delicacy, those very traits, as it happened, which she found most unpleasant in other people, and she had swallowed this injustice, had even asked forgiveness and somehow abased herself. But now she'd be silent. Why always be in the wrong? No, now you'll start asking—you won't get anything. Besides that, her mind's not on that, she's worried about her mother's illness (Dmitriev was ready to bet a hundred rubles to one that his mother-in-law had her usual migraine. Lord, he'd learned to read that book till he was blind!). But Dmitriev didn't have enough time to enjoy that last thought full of smugness before Lena stunned him. Completely prosaically, peacefully, she said:

"Vitka, I'm asking you—talk with Xenia Fyodorovna today. Just warn her that the Markusheviches may look at her room, and the key has to be gotten."

After a silence he asked:

"When do they want to look at it?"

"Tomorrow or the day after, I don't know exactly. They'll call. And if you go to Pavlinovo today, don't forget, get the key from Xenia Fyodorovna. Put the kefir in the refrigerator please, and the bread in the bag. Or else it'll dry out from you leaving it out all the time. Bye!"

Waving in a friendly way, she went out into the hall. She slammed the entrance door. The elevator buzzed. Dmitriev wanted to say something, some vaguely anxious thought had dawned on the threshold of his consciousness, but didn't quite dawn, and he, having made two steps after Lena, stood in the hall and then returned to his room.

There was not a trace left of the early dark blue. When Dmitriev went out to the trolley stop there was a fine drizzling rain, and it was cold. The last few days had been rainy. Isidor Markovich was right, of course—he's an experienced surgeon, an old hand, they invite him for consultations in other cities—his mother must be taken out of the city, but not during such influenza dampness. But if he advises a Moscow area sanatorium that means he doesn't see any immediate threat—that's it! And for the second time this morning Dmitriev timidly thought that maybe everything might turn out all right. They would make the exchange, receive a good separate apartment, would live together. And the sooner the exchange was made the better. For his mother's well-being. Her dream would be realized. It would be psychotherapy, the healing of the soul! No, Lena was sometimes very wise, intuitively, in a female way—suddenly something dawns on her. Really, that's possibly the only brilliant means of saving a life. When the surgeons are powerless, other forces come into play.... And that's what no single professor could do, no one, no one, no one!

Dmitriev could think of nothing else standing at the trolley stop in the drizzling rain, and later, making his way inside the car, among the wet raincoats, briefcases which knocked against the knees, the coats smelling of damp cloth, and he thought about it running down the dirty subway steps, slippery from the rainy slop brought in by thousands of feet, and standing in the short line for the cashier to change a fifteen-kopeck piece into five kopeck pieces, and again running down even further along the steps, and throwing the five into the slot of the turnstile, and walking along the platform ahead with quick steps so as to get a seat in the fourth car, which would stop exactly opposite the archway leading to the stairway to the connecting passage. And he was still thinking about it when the shuffling crowd carried him along the long hall where the air was stifling, and it always smelled of damp alabaster, and when he stood on the escalator, squeezed himself into the car, looked over the passengers, the hats, the briefcases, bits of newspapers, plastic envelopes, the flabby morning faces, the old man with the household bags on his knees, going to shop in the city center—any one of these people might be the saving variant. Dmitriev was ready to shout at the whole car: "Who wants a good room, twenty by sixteen?...."

At a quarter of nine he got out of the underground and onto the square, at five of he crossed the alley and, overtaking the cars standing by the entrance, entered a door beside which hung, under glass, the black plaque "IOGA."

On this day they were deciding the question of the business trip to Golishmanovo in the Tumenskaya district. The trip had already been confirmed back in July, and none other than Dmitriev was supposed to go. Pumps were his domain. He alone was responsible for this business, and he alone really understood it, unless you counted Snitkin. Dmitriev had started a conversation with him the week before, but Pasha Snitkin, a cunningly wise operator (in the office they called him "Pasha Snitkin-with-the-world-on-a-string," because he had never done one single job on his own, but was always able to fix it so that everybody helped him), said that unfortunately he absolutely could not go— also due to family reasons. He was probably lying. But it was his right. Who wanted to go in bad weather, in the cold, to Siberia? It was awkward for Snitkin to refuse, and he burst out with irritation: "Didn't you say that your mother had gotten better?"

Dmitriev didn't start to explain, he just waved his hand: "How, better...." And Pasha had always inquired about Xenia Fyodorovna's health so attentively, gave the phone numbers of doctors, in general expressed his sympathy, and Dmitriev was for some reason completely sure of his agreeing. But why? Why should he be? Now it was clear that this sureness had been stupidity. No, they're not pretending when they express sympathy and ask with moving care: "Well, how are things at home?"—it's just that that sympathy and care have sizes, like shoes or hats do. You should never stretch them too much. Pasha Snitkin was transferring his daughter to a music school, and the only one who could deal with this troublesome business was he himself—not the mother or the grandmother. And if he went away in October on a business trip, the music school would definitely fall through for this year, which would cause a deep trauma in the girl and the moral destruction of the whole Snitkin family. But my God, can one really compare them—a person is dying and a girl is entering music school? Yes, yes. One can. They are hats of approximately the same size—if a stranger is dying and your very own daughter is entering music school.

The director was waiting for Dmitriev at 10:30. Cocking his head to one side and looking Dmitriev in the eye with a sort of shy wonder, the director said:

"So what are we going to do?"

Dmitriev answered:

"I don't know. I can't go."

The director was silent, touched the skin of his cheeks and chin with his wide white fingers, as if checking to see whether he'd shaved well. His glance became thoughtful. He was really thinking very hard about something and even began to hum a tune unconsciously.

"Mm yes.... What to do, Viktor Georgievich? Um? And if it's for about ten days?"

"No!" said Dmitriev abruptly.

He understood that he could stand like a rock and they couldn't budge him. Only he shouldn't explain anything. And the director, after thinking it over, said the name of Tyagusov, a young fellow who'd finished the institute a year ago, and who, it seemed to Dmitriev, was a complete booby.

Not long ago Dmitriev would have started to protest, but now he suddenly felt that all this had no significance. So why not Tyagusov?

"Of course," he said. "I'll spend two days with him and explain everything to him. He'll manage. Bright guy."

After he got back to his room on the first floor, Dmitriev worked an hour and a half without letting up, preparing the documentation for Golishmanovo. Even though earlier he had not believed that they'd make him go, the thought of the trip had weighed upon him, had been just one more little weight added to all his other burdens, and now when they'd removed the weight he experienced a relief. And he thought hopefully that today, maybe, would be a lucky day. Like all people who are oppressed by fate, Dmitriev cultivated superstition: he noticed that there were lucky days when success followed success, and on those days you had to try to deal with as many things as possible, and there were bad luck days when not a damn thing went right no matter what you did. It looked like a lucky day had begun. Now to borrow money. Lora had asked that he bring at least fifty rubles. On Isidor Markovich alone they'd spent—four times fifteen—sixty rubles this month. But where to get it? Such a crummy thing—borrowing money. But he had to do it today, since today was already a lucky day.

Dmitriev began to think of who he could hit up for it. Almost everyone, he remembered, had complained that they had no money, that they'd used it up over the summer. Sashka Prutyov had gotten a cooperative apartment, and was totally in debt himself. Vasily Gerasimovich, the colonel, partner in games of preference and fishing trips, Dmitriev's constant rescuer, had suffered a tragedy—he'd left his wife, and it was awkward to ask him. Dmitriev's friends at the CSM (Club of the Semi-Married), to whom Dmitriev turned in moments of despair when he fought with Lena, were people of few resources—their fortune

consisted of someone with a car, with a motorboat, a camping tent, bottles of French cognac or White Horse whiskey, bought by chance in
Stoleshnikov and kept on the bookcase for any special occasions of the
house—and they could lend you no more than twenty-five rubles, forty
at the most, but he had to get no less than 150. Of course there was the
last alternative, the limit of torment: to ask his mother-in-law. But that
would mean going downhill. Dmitriev could have forced himself to
take it, but Lena took such things very badly. She knew her mother better. All at once it came to Dmitriev—it was the same thought which had
vaguely come before and which now suddenly cut through—how was he
going to tell his mother about the exchange? After all, she knew perfectly well how Lena had felt about the idea and now for some reason
she had suggested moving in together. Why?

Just considering all this made Dmitriev sweat. He went out into the
hall where there was a telephone on a stand, and called Lena at work.
Usually it was not easy to get through to her. But he was lucky (a lucky
day!); Lena happened to be in the office and she picked up the phone.
Dmitriev hurriedly got out his doubts in one long confused sentence.
Lena was silent, then asked:

"That means what, that you don't want to tell her?"

"I don't know how. Couldn't I suggest it to her— you understand?"

After another silence Lena told him to call her again in five minutes
on another phone where she could speak more freely. He called. Now
Lena spoke loudly and energetically:

"Say it like this: say that you really want it, but I'm against it. But you
insisted. That is despite me, clear? Then it'll be natural and your mama
won't think anything of it. Put it all on me. Only don't overdo it—just
some hints...." Unexpectedly she began to talk in a changed, flattering
voice: "Excuse me please, just a minute, I'm leaving now! So everything's clear? Yes, Vitya, Vitya! Talk to somebody there in your office
who's accomplished an exchange successfully, you hear? Bye!"

What Lena said was, of course, correct and cunning, but anguish
gripped Dmitriev's heart. He was incapable of going back into the
room right away, and he wandered along the empty hall for a few minutes.

He didn't go find anyone or find anything out before lunch, but
after lunch he went up to the third floor to the economists. As soon as
he opened the door, Tanya saw him and came out. Not asking anything, she looked at him fearfully.

"No, nothing bad," he said. "Maybe even a bit better. Tan, do you
know, has anyone here made an exchange? Exchanged apartments?"

"I don't know. I think Zherekhov. Why?"

"I need some advice. We have to make an exchange, urgently, you understand?"

"You?"

"Yes."

"You want...," her face reddened, "to move in with Xenia Fyodorovna?"

"Yes, yes! It's very important. It'd take a long time to explain, but it's absolutely essential now."

Tanya lowered her head and was silent. There was a lot of gray in the hair which fell over her face. She was thirty-four, still a young woman, but in the last year she'd gotten to look a lot older. Maybe she was sick? She'd gotten very thin: the slender neck stuck out of the collar, in the thin face only the eyes—kind ones—shone out of the millet-colored freckled pallor in their habitual fright. This fright was over him, for him. Tanya would have been a better wife for him, probably. It had begun three years ago, had lasted one summer and had ended itself when Lena and Natashka came back from Odessa. No, it hadn't ended, it had dragged out in a thin thread, it broke for months, for half a year. He knew that if one were reasoning sensibly, she would have been a better wife for him, probably. But you know, sensibly, sensibly.... Tanya had a son, Alec, and a husband with the strange last name of Toft. He had never seen him. He knew the husband loved Tanya very much, had forgiven her everything, but after that summer three years ago, she could no longer live with him, and they separated. He was very sorry that it turned out that way, that the husband became unhappy, quit his job, left Moscow, and Tanya also became an unhappy person, but there was nothing to be done about it. Tanya wanted to leave IOGA, so that she wouldn't have to see Dmitriev every day, but getting away turned out to be very difficult. Then she gradually became reconciled to it all, and learned how to meet Dmitriev calmly and talk with him as an old friend.

Dmitriev suddenly realized what she was now thinking: this means—that's all, never.

"Well, what can I do?" he said. "You see, this would be a kind of a chance, a hope. It was my mother's dream to live with me."

"What are you talking about? She probably wasn't dreaming about this."

"I know."

"Oy, Vitya.... Well, have a talk with your Zherekhov. I'll call him now. Only he's a big mouth and liar, keep that in mind." Suddenly she asked: "Do you need any money?"

"Money? No."

"Vitya, take it. I know what being sick means. My aunt was sick for eight months. I set aside 200 rubles for a summer coat, but as you see, the summer's over and I didn't buy anything. So I can give it to you till spring with absolutely no trouble."

"No, I don't need money. I have some." He frowned. What else: borrow from Tanya! Suddenly he laughed. "Really, what a strange sort of day! One after another...."

"We'll go to my place after work, and I'll give it to you, all right?"

After a silence he said:

"I'm lying, I haven't got any money. But I don't want to take it from you."

"Fool!" She lightly slapped him on the cheek.

Dmitriev saw that she was glad. As they walked to the doors of the room Zherekhov was in she even took him by the hand.

"Leonid Grigorievich!" called Tanya. "Can I see you for a minute?"

Zherekhov, a small, affable old man, completely bald, with white, even false teeth, very kind and willingly began to recount how he'd made an exchange. Dmitriev didn't know Zherekhov very well, but he'd noticed that the latter was kindly and affable with everyone—probably because, finding himself at pitiful retirement age, the old man was fighting for his place and wanted to have the best relations with everyone. Because of this, he told the story at unbearable length and detail. Someone went abroad, someone was in a desperate situation. Someone had to pay. None of this was right. But then Zherekhov suddenly shouted, and his light-blue old man's eyes widened from the flood of benevolence:

"Yes. That's who you should see—Nevyadomsky! You know Alexei Kirillovich? From KB-3? It was the same story with him, he also made an exchange because..." Zherekhov lowered his voice, "the mother-in-law was hopelessly sick. She had an excellent room, almost twenty-five meters, somewhere in the city center. But Alexei Kirillovich lived at Usachevka. Everything had to be done very fast. And he succeeded, succeeded terrifically! He'll tell you. True, he had connections at the local Housing Commission. So in a word, like this: he succeeded in making the exchange, made repairs in the apartment—he was forced to do it by ZHEK[1]—he moved his mother-in-law, got the personal account, and the old lady died three days later. Can you imagine? The poor guy, he went through a lot that winter, I remember. Almost took to his bed. But now he's got an exceptional apartment, like a general's, deluxe.

Loggias, two balconies, lots of all kinds of secondary cubic capacity. He's even growing tomatoes on one balcony. You drop by, drop by, he'll tell you. Good luck!"

Zherekhov benevolently nodded, moving back, backed into the room with his seat. While he talked, Tanya stood beside Dmitriev and inconspicuously held onto the end of his little finger.

"Go downstairs at 6:00, and we'll go immediately," she said in a whisper.

"You understand I've got to go to Lora's in Pavlinovo. My mother's expecting me. She's at Lora's now."

He knew he was dealing a blow to certain hopes of Tanya's, but it was better to say it right away.

"Well, all right. Do what you have to." Everything immediately left an impression on her face: it darkened.

"No, and besides that...."

"I understand! You really think I do not understand! I won't hold you for a second. You'll get the money and then—be off."

Nodding, she walked quickly away from him down the hall. Not long ago, a year back, her tall figure was something exciting for Dmitriev. Especially at those times when she was walking away from him, and he looked after her. But now there was nothing left. It had all disappeared somewhere. Now she was just a tall, thin, very long-legged woman with hennaed hair in a bun on a slender neck. And still, every time he looked at her, he thought that she would have been the best wife for him.

Dmitriev returned to the office and sat over the papers for half an hour—his thoughts turned around the same thing: mother, Lora, Tanya, Lena, money, the exchange—and he saw that he'd have to leave work earlier, or else he'd get to Pavlinovo much too late. Tanya lived in an out-of-the-way place, a worse one you couldn't imagine—Nagatina. Dmitriev went to the little office of Varvara Alexeyevna, his superior, and said that if it was possible, he'd like to leave today at five. Varvara Alexeyevna agreed. Everyone in the office knew what was going on in Dmitriev's life and acted with understanding: every week, once or twice he could leave work early. Once even, it was such a sin, he ran to the Moskva department store under this pretext and bought a uniform for Natashka. Dmitriev went up to the third floor again and told Tanya to ask to leave at five. Then he went in to see Nevyadomsky, also on the third floor.

Dmitriev decided to go to Nevyadomsky after some hesitation. Relations between them were cool—through the fault of a friend of

Dmitriev's who, it's true, hadn't worked at IOGA for half a year. Nevyadomsky had had some kind of scandal with this friend at the local trade union committee. And they stopped speaking to each other. And when Nevyadomsky met Dmitriev in the company of this friend, he—at the same time—didn't say hello to Dmitriev either, and out of solidarity with his friend Dmitriev acted exactly the same way. However, when Dmitriev and Nevyadomsky met alone, they greeted each other totally correctly, although a little coolly, and even exchanged two or three phrases. All this was utter nonsense, and Dmitriev decided to ignore it and go. And if Nevyadomsky really has *connections*, will he share them?

Nevyadomsky, a lean dark-haired man with a blackish-reddish curly little beard, raised his eyebrows in surprise when Dmitriev, stopping by the office, asked him for "a brief audience." At a small table in the corner two were smashing away at chess, moving the figures about very quickly. Nevyadomsky was standing by them, watching. The favorite occupation of the "Kabetrishniki" [project researchers] was chess, they played blitzes, five-minute ones, but among the "Kabedvashniki" [proj-developers] ping-pong flourished. The battles took place during the lunch hour, but sometimes they borrowed from work time, especially towards the end of the day. Nevyadomsky, after saying: "Just a minute! I'll come!"—continued to observe the players. The latter were slamming the figures around the board with the speed of automatons, until one cried, "Oh damn!"—and with a blow of the hand tipped over his king. Nevyadomsky began to laugh maliciously and said:

"At that Balda said by way of reproach: if only you hadn't been so interested, priest, in the cheap price!"[2]

After that, he moved toward the door with the malicious smile still on his face, but, meeting Dmitriev with a glance, he wiped off his smile and again his brows rose in surprise. Dmitriev began clumsily to put forward his request, or more precisely, to hint at his request, cloaked in hurried and inconsequential mumblings. Nevyadomsky had to guess it: he was being requested to share his advice on how to behave in circumstances familiar to him. But Nevyadomsky didn't guess. His blackish-red curly beard rose higher, his eyes looked more and more coldly, and it seemed to Dmitriev, more haughtily.

"Excuse me, I don't exactly understand...."

"I'll explain right now. The problem is that the causes prompting you and me.... In a word, we're in the same situation."

"What have you got in mind?"

"What do I have in mind?" Dmitriev felt how his neck and cheeks were flooding with color. "This is what I've got in mind: I've got to make an exchange as quick as possible too. So I wanted to consult you about how it's done, generally? What do you start with?"

"What do you start with? What do you mean—what do you start with? With the exchange bureau, of course. You pay three rubles and make an announcement in the bulletin."

"But you understand, that if a person is seriously ill, very seriously, and every hour is dear...."

"But you can't start any other way. With the exchange bureau, I don't know any other routes," Nevyadomsky stuck a thumb into his nostril and began with concentration to extricate something from there. Obviously he was tensely trying to figure out whether it was worth it or not to let Dmitriev in on his connections. He decided: not worth it. "I didn't have any other ways." Suddenly Nevyadomsky chuckled. "You know, you've reminded me of the stupidest story! When I was a student, my father died. Two or three months went by...." While he related this, he continued to extract something from his nose with his thumb. "And a neighbor unexpectedly dropped by, an unknown man from another part of the building, and he says, 'My father died and I heard yours died not long ago too. So I've come to make your acquaintance and to ask you to share your experience.' What kind of experience? What? How? I, of course, courteously got rid of him."

"And I've got to take this too," thought Dmitriev, feeling numb. Turn around, leave, but he continued to stand there looking at the blackish-red beard. "There are tomatoes on the mother-in-law's grave. It's all the same. And this too. And there will be more of it."

"If you want it, I've got the number of one Adam Vikentievich, an agent. I could look for it."

Overcoming his numbness, Dmitriev turned and walked away down the hall. At five he and Tanya went out onto the square and there—rare occurrence!—an empty taxi turned up. Dmitriev whistled, they jumped in and drove off. The alleyway was filled with a crowd moving in one direction toward the subway. The factory shift had just ended. The taxi moved slowly. People glanced into the cab, someone knocked on the roof with their palms. When they passed the subway and escaped onto the avenue, Dmitriev began to talk about Nevyadomsky with malice.

Tanya took him by the hand.

"Why are you being so malicious? Don't! Stop it..."

He felt how her calm and joy poured into him. Tanya, smiling, said:

"We are all very different. We are people.... My cousin's little son died. There was incredible grief, of course, suffering, and along with it a kind of new passionate love for children, especially sick ones. She was sorry for them all, tried to help as much as she could. And I have an acquaintance whose son also died, of leukemia. That woman hated everyone so much, she wished everyone dead. She gets happy when she reads in the paper that someone's died...."

Tanya moved closer. She put her head on his shoulder and asked:

"Is it all right? Does it bother you?"

"It's all right," he said.

They traveled by way of the outskirts, through the new areas. Dmitriev told about Xenia Fyodorovna. Tanya asked about her with compassion—this was sincere, Dmitriev knew, she felt sympathy for this mother. And Xenia liked Tanya; they'd seen each other once or twice in summer, in Pavlinovo.... Tanya held his hand in hers, sometimes she softly tickled his palm with her finger. Tanya's caresses were always somehow schoolgirlish.

Without taking his hand away, he gave the details about his mother: what Zurin said, what Isidor Markovich said. Tanya began to laugh:

"Oh, what a rotten dame! She lends money and pesters with tendernesses, right?" She suddenly knocked against his cheek with her nose, snuggled. "Forgive me, Vitya.... I can't...."

He stroked her head. For a long time they rode in silence. They went past the Varshavka.

"Well, what's the matter?" he asked.

"Nothing. I can't...."

"What?..."

"I'm sorry for you, for your mother.... And for myself at the same time."

Dmitriev didn't know what to say. He simply stroked her head and nothing more. She began to sniffle, he felt dampness on his cheek. Then she moved away from him, turned and began to look out the window. Finally the embankment flashed by, they took the bus route past some factories, along a solitary, long stone fence. Near a beer stand there was a dense black crowd of men. Some of them, singly and in pairs, with mugs in their hands, stood at some distance. Dmitriev felt like his throat was dry—he wanted to have a drop of something, to get his spirits up. "I should ask," he thought, "Tanyushka used to have stuff around. Anything would do."

The new sixteen-story building stood on the edge of a field. The road went in a detour, around the field.

"Right here," said Tanya.

Dmitriev remembered quite well that it was here. The last time he'd been here was about a year ago.

"Will you have the car wait?" asked Tanya.

Of course he would have it wait. But his usual timidity—he saw that Tanya passionately didn't want that—made him answer:

"Yes, okay, let it go. I'll find one here."

"Of course, you will!" said Tanya.

They went up to the eleventh floor. Tanya lived alone with her son in a large three-room apartment. That poor devil Toft had constructed this ship in the coop building, and had just enough time to move into it when everything happened. At that time Alec was at camp, Toft was somewhere in Dagestan—he was a mining engineer—and Tanya lived alone in empty unfurnished rooms which smelled of paint. There were newspapers on the floors. In one room there stood a huge couch, and nothing more. And Dmitriev's love was inseparable from the smell of paint and fresh oak floors, as yet unpolished. Barefoot, he slapped over the newspapers into the kitchen and drank water from the tap. Tanya knew a lot of poetry and liked to recite it in a soft voice, almost whispering it. He was astonished at her memory. He himself didn't remember, if you please, even one poem by heart—just occasional quatrains. "You are still alive, my old one, and so am I, greetings to you by and by." But Tanya could whisper for hours. She had something like twenty notebooks, from her student days, where in the large clear handwriting of the A student was copied the poetry of Marina Tsvetaeva, Pasternak, Mandelstam, Blok. And so in moments of rest, or when there was nothing to talk about and it got sad, she would begin to whisper: "O Lord, how perfect are thy deeds, thought the sick man...." Or: "Take your palm from my breast, we are wires under current."

Sometimes when he got tired of the monotonous murmuring of her lips he would say: "All right my love, take a rest. Why is it that your Khizhnyak doesn't say hello to Alexeyevna Varvara?" After a pause she answered sadly: "I don't know." All of her resentments were momentary. Even when she could have taken offense for good reason. For some reason he was convinced that she would never fall out of love with him. That summer he lived in a state he had never experienced before: love for himself. An incredible state! One could have defined it as the condition of usual bliss, for its strength consisted in its constancy, in the fact that it lasted weeks, months, and continued to exist even when everything was already over.

But Dmitriev didn't think about why: why did he have this bliss? Why him exactly—a not very young, heavy man with an unhealthy color in his face, with the eternal smell of tobacco in his mouth? It seemed to him that there was nothing puzzling about it. That was how it should be. Generally, it seemed to him that he had just joined in that normal, truly human condition, which people should—and would in time—always be in. Tanya, the opposite, lived in constant fear and a kind of passionate bewilderment. Embracing, she would whisper, like she did the poetry: "Lord, for what? For what?"

She didn't ask for anything or about anything and he didn't promise anything. No, not once did he promise. Why should he promise if he definitely knew that no matter what she would never fall out of love with him. It simply came into his head that she would have been the best wife for him.

New furniture had appeared in the rooms—in one room there was a breakfront and a round polished table, in the other—a half-empty bookcase. But as before, the parquet hadn't been polished and it looked sort of dirty. Alec came out of the room, noticeably taller, a pale freckled creature of about eleven, with glasses on his thin little nose. He held his head slightly tilted back and to the side, perhaps because he wasn't well, or perhaps he could see through his glasses better that way. This set of the head and his small compressed mouth gave the boy an expression of superciliousness.

"Mom, I'm going to Andryusha's. We're going to trade stamps," he announced in a squeaky voice, and rushed through the hall to the door.

"Wait! Why didn't you say hello to Viktor Georgievich?"

"Hi," Alec threw over his shoulder, without looking.

Hurrying, he unlocked the lock and ran out, slamming the door.

"Be back no later than eight!" Tanya yelled to the closed door. "The young man doesn't shine in the manners department."

"He's probably forgotten me. I haven't been here for a long time, after all."

"And even if a stranger came? Doesn't one have to say hello?" Tanya went into the big room, opened the side door of the breakfront and said: "He didn't forget you."

She took a rolled newspaper from under a pile of clean linen, unrolled it and gave Dmitriev a bundle of money. He stuck it in his pocket.

"Well go," said Tanya. "You haven't got any time."

He suddenly pulled out a chair and sat down at the polished table.

"I'll sit a bit. I'm sort of tired." He took off his hat, touched his head with his palm. "My head aches."

"Do you want to eat? Could I get you anything?"

"Is there anything to drink?"

"No.... Wait!" Her eyes shone with happiness. "It seems to me that there's a bottle of cognac left someplace, which we didn't finish drinking. Remember, when you were here last time? I'll take a look right now!"

She ran into the kitchen and brought in the bottle a minute later. There were about a hundred grams left at the bottom.

"Now we'll have some hors d'oeuvres. One minute!"

"What do we need hors d'oeuvres for?"

"Just a second, just a second!" Again she rushed headlong into the kitchen.

Dmitriev got up and went to the balcony doors. There was a wonderful view from the eleventh floor of the stretching field, the river, and the village of Kolomensk, visible by the cupolas of its cathedral. Dmitriev thought of how he could move into this three-room apartment tomorrow, see the river and the village in the morning and evening, breathe in the field, go to work on the bus to Serpukhovka, from there on the subway, it wouldn't take so long. Tanya carried in sprats, two tomatoes, bread and butter on a crystal dish, and wine glasses. He poured half a glass for himself, and the rest for Tanya. She always drank very little, she got drunk quickly.

"What are we drinking to?" asked Tanya.

"To everything going well with you."

"Well, all right! No. Not to that. Everything will go well with me anyway. Let it be to everything going well for you. All right?"

"Okay." It was all the same to him. He'd already drunk up, and was chewing on a tomato. He grunted, "The tomatoes are from the grave of Nevyadomsky's mother-in-law, aren't they?"

"Because, Vitya," she said, "it's not likely that things are ever going to go well with you. But suppose, all of a sudden, they do? To that then."

He didn't think to ask what she had in mind. Superfluous conversations. After the cognac it got warm and he ate the tomato with pleasure and looked at Tanya, who was hunched over in reverie, leaning on the table with her elbows, and gazing at the corner of the room.

"Don't slouch!" he said, paternally slapping her lightly on the shoulder blades.

Tanya straightened up, continuing to gaze at the corner of the room. On her stupefied face, with cheeks flushed from the cognac, suffering was distinctly visible. For one moment he pitied her very sharply, but then he remembered that somewhere far and near, through all of

Moscow, on the shore of this same river, his mother was waiting for him, his mother who was experiencing the sufferings of death, but Tanya's sufferings belonged to life, so—what was there to pity her for? There is nothing in the world except life and death. And everything that is dependent on the first is happiness, and everything dependent on the second is the destruction of happiness. And there is nothing else in this world. Dmitriev got up with a jerk, with sudden haste, exactly as if someone strong had grabbed him and pulled him by the arms, and saying, "Bye! I've got to run!"—bolting with quick steps down the hall to the door. Tanya didn't have time to say anything to him. Maybe she didn't want to say anything to him.

Dmitriev went by bus to the subway—there was of course no taxi around at all—transferred twice and came out on the last station of the new line. A fine snow was drizzling down. Moscow was far away, its large buildings were white against the horizon, but here was a field torn up by foundation pits, pipes lay on the damp earth, and a line of people waiting for the trolley stood by a pillar on the highway. The sky was full of clouds, arranged in layers—on the top something motionless and dark-violet was thickening, lower light, crumbly clouds were moving, and lower still there flew on the wind a kind of white cloudy rag, like wisps of steam.

About forty years earlier, when Dmitriev's father, Georgy Alexeyevich, had built a house in the settlement of Red Partisan, this place, Pavlinovo, was considered a dacha-resort area. It was a resort, and until the revolution they came here by horse train from the point. In the 30s the boy Vitya, a mediocre student, but diligent bike-rider, fisherman, and player of "501," devourer of Sienkiewicz, and Gustav Emar, came here on summer days, on the squeaky old bus which left at hourly intervals from the cobblestoned Zvenigorodskaya Square. It was always stuffy in the bus, the windows didn't open, it smelled of sackcloth. Waste lands flashed by, orchards, little villages, an ice-house, a radar field, a school with a white brick fence, a church on a knoll, and suddenly the arc of the millpond opened and the heart of the boy Vitya tightened. The road from the bus stop went through pines, past unpainted fences black from rain, past dachas hidden by lilac bushes, sweetbriar, and elder, with their small-paned verandas showing through the green. You had to walk for a long time along this road, the tar ended, then there was the dusty high road, to the right there was a pine grove on a little hill with a spacious clearing—in the 1920s a plane crashed there and the grove had burned down—and to the left the fences continued to stretch out. Behind one of the fences, in no way camouflaged by young bushes, a log building of two stories and a basement jutted out, not at all similar to a resort house, but more to a trading post somewhere in the forests of Canada, or to a hacienda in the Argentine savannah.

The building had been built by a cooperative, with the resounding name of Red Partisan.³ Georgy Alexeyevich wasn't a Red partisan; his brother Vasily Alexeyevich, who was a Red partisan and an OGPU⁴ worker, and the owner of a two-seater sports Opel, had invited him into the co-op. The third brother, Nikolai Alexeyevich lived in a little dacha nearby. Also a Red partisan, he'd worked for Vneshtorg⁵ and had lived for months at a time in both Japan and China. From China he'd brought the game of mah-jongg—a mahogany box containing 144 stones (bamboo on one side, ivory on the other) placed on four little pull-out shelves. At first the grownups gambled for money at mah-jongg, then when the grownups got bored or couldn't take it anymore, the game passed into the possession of Nikolai Alexeyevich's children, and the whole crowd of the Pavlinovo children's commune. Nothing was left of those evenings with the phonograph music ("The weary sun tenderly said farewell to the sea"), with the loud conversation of the two deaf Red partisans who were always arguing about something on the second floor, the clack of the Chinese stones on Nikolai Alexeyevich's veranda. It's not just people who disappear in this world, it turns out, but whole nests, tribes with their environment, conversation, games and music. They disappear completely, so that it's impossible to find their traces. Although Lora was still left there in Pavlinovo. But besides Lora there was no one—not one single person. Of the brothers, the eldest, Georgy Alexeyevich, died first. Instantaneous death from a stroke—they called it apoplectic stroke then—occurred right on the street one sweltering day.

Dmitriev remembered his father poorly, in fragments. He remembered a dark mustache and beard, gold-rimmed glasses and a very thin, yellowish tussore shirt, soft to the touch, with flakes of tobacco, a fat belly under it, and constant chuckling at all people and things. Georgy Alexeyevich was a railway engineer, but his whole life he'd dreamed of leaving that job and taking up writing humorous stories. It seemed to him that this was his calling. He always went walking with a notebook in his pocket. Dmitriev recalled how quickly and easily his father composed funny stories—they went walking in the evening to the garden to water the cucumbers and saw how Marya Petrovna, the aunt of one of the Red partisans, was trying to knock down her nephew Petka's ball from a pine tree. First she threw a stick, the stick got stuck; then she began throwing her shoe, and the shoe got stuck too. While they were walking to the garden, his father told Dmitriev a hilarious fairy tale about how Marya Petrovna hurled her other shoe at the pine, then her blouse, belt, skirt; all this hung on the pine, and Marya Petrovna, naked, sat beneath, and then Uncle Matvei came running and started to throw his shoes and pants. A few days later his father came from town and brought with him a journal in which his story "The Ball" was printed. Georgy Alexeyevich made fun of his brothers, whom he considered none too bright, and as a joke called them "woodchoppers." He himself had graduated from the university, but his brothers hadn't even managed to finish high school: the civil war was raging, tossing one to the Caucasus, the other to the Far East. Sometimes talking with his mother he marvelled: "And how is it they send such woodchoppers abroad when they can't say two words in any other language?" He further reproached his brothers for greed, for the fat life, mocked their Chinese stones, their eternal fussing with the car on days off—he always added a "Zh" when referring to his brother's Opel.[6] And in Kozlov, aunts related to them went hungry, dying one after another; their nephews had no means of getting to Moscow. Only Georgy Alexeyevich helped as much as he could.

Sometimes the brothers would quarrel—for months at a time he didn't visit them, or they him. His mother considered that Maryanka and Raika were to blame for the quarrels and all the brothers' subsequent misfortunes, since they were contaminated by the petty-bourgeois mentality, but things didn't turn out so sweet for them later on either, the poor things.

Generally, his father had been the best one, more intelligent than his brothers, a rather good man. But unlucky. He died early, didn't have time for anything. What was preserved of his notebooks, in which there had been so much that was funny and wonderful? They had gone, just like all the rest. Raika was also gone, Nikolai Alexeyevich's wife, who'd been a beauty at one time, and the main fashion plate of the Red Partisan settlement. Gone too was the sandy slope on the river bank, where in the mornings, very early, there used to be excellent fishing. After eight o'clock the fish left here—the river passenger boat began to rumble between its moorage and the village, and the motorboats came out. You had to cross over to the other bank, there were quiet inlets there where fish hid, but sitting in the hot sun was unbearable—there was neither tree nor bush, just a naked meadow with stiff weeds.

Dmitriev jumped off the bus one stop before he should have. He wanted to walk to the place where his favorite slope had once been. He knew that now there was a concrete embankment there, but the fishermen still came anyway. New fishermen, from five-story buildings that were beyond the bridge. It was very convenient for them—they came by trolley.

He went down the stone steps—everything was done solidly, as in a real city park—at the bottom he walked along the concrete slabs which rose about six feet above the water level. You could walk along the river like that almost to the house itself. There was no crawling along the shore now. Every spring chunks of the bank crumbled down, sometimes along with the benches and pines.

The sky sparkled on the wet slabs, and not one fool was around. But no, there was somebody sitting there, off in the distance, and Dmitriev slowly walked up to him. The water seemed very clean, undirtied, but dark—autumn water. Dmitriev stopped behind the fisherman's back and began to watch the float. He watched for about five minutes, with increasing anxiety and a kind of sudden weakening of the spirit, thinking of how hard it was going to be to say it. Impossibly hard. With Lora too. What could he do? They would all understand, of course. However, it was possible his mother wouldn't—if one were to present the matter exactly as Lena had suggested, his mother was very unsophisticated—but Lora would understand it all right away. Lora was sharp, perspicacious, and didn't like Lena at all. If his mother, despite all of Lena's unfriendliness, had all the same made peace with her, had learned to pay no attention to this, forgive that, Lora's dislike had grown stronger over the years—on their mother's account. She once said: "I don't know what kind of person one would have to be to treat our mother without respect." True, friends loved Xenia Fyodorovna, her colleagues respected her, her apartment neighbors and Pavlinovo dacha neighbors esteemed her because she was benevolent, compliant, ready to come to your aid and sympathize. But Lora didn't understand.... Oh, she didn't understand, she didn't! Lora hadn't learned to look beyond what lay on the surface. Her thoughts never bent. They always stuck out and pricked like horsehair from a poorly sewn jacket. How could one not understand that you don't dislike people just because of their vices and you don't love them on account of their virtues!

It was all the truth, the real truth: his mother was constantly surrounded by people in whose fates she constantly *took part*. For months some elderly people she barely knew had been living in her room, friends of Georgy Alexeyevich's, and some old ladies who were even more decrepit, his grandfather's friends, and some casual acquaintances from vacation houses who wanted to get to the Moscow doctors, or provincial boys and girls, children of distant relatives who had come to Moscow to enter institutes. His mother tried to help all of them absolutely disinterestedly. But why should she help? All ties had been lost long ago, and she was worn out. But still—with shelter, advice, sympathy. She liked to help unselfishly. But to put it more exactly: she liked to help in such a way that God forbid any profit should come out of it. But the profit was this: in doing good deeds to be always conscious of being a good person. And Lena, sensing his mother's slightest weakness, said about her in moments of irritation: the hypocrite. And he would fly into a rage. He would yell: "Who's a hypocrite? My mother's a hypocrite? How dare you say that..." And—it would begin, get rolling.... Neither his mother nor Lora knew how he got violent on their account. Of course they guessed about a little of it, they'd been witnesses to some of it, but in full strength—with the whole battery of insults, Natashka's crying, the no talking for days on end, and at times even a little physical violence—this was unknown to them. They considered, Lora with especial firmness, that he'd quietly betrayed them. His sister one day said: "Vitka, how Lukyanized you've gotten." Lukyanov was the last name of Lena's family.

Dmitriev suddenly decided that he had to think through something important, definitive. He didn't have the strength to walk to the house, so he delayed it a minute.

He sat down not far from the fisherman, on a wooden box—also someone's fishing gear—which had lain there a long time, getting brown and damp all the way through. As soon as Dmitriev sat down, the box began to list slightly, and he had to lean very firmly on his legs to maintain balance. On the opposite bank, where there had been a meadow at one time, they were now making a huge beach, with cabanas, reclining chairs, and refreshment stands. The recliners were piled into two stacks, but for some reason two recliners still stood right by the water, making a spot of dim blue on the dark gray sand. Everything on that shore was dark gray, the color of cement. Beyond the beach a young grove of birches curled, planted some ten years before, and beyond the grove towered the mountains of housing in foggy white blocks, along which stood two especially tall towers. Everything on that shore had changed. Everything had "gotten Lukyanized." Every year something changed in its details, but when fourteen years passed, it turned out that everything got Lukyanized—finally and hopelessly. But perhaps that wasn't so bad? And if it happens to everything—even the shore, the river and the grass—does that mean maybe that it's natural and that's how it should be?

The first year Dmitriev and Lena had to live in Pavlinovo. Lora, then still without Felix, was living in Moscow with Xenia Fyodorovna, the dacha was empty and Dmitriev and Lena wanted to be alone. But they didn't succeed even so. The dacha apartment at Pavlinovo had been unoccupied for a long time. The roof leaked, the porch was rotting. The cesspool gave the most trouble—from time to time it overflowed, especially when it rained, and an unbearable stench spread throughout the entire area, blending with the smells of the lilac, linden and phlox. The inhabitants had come to terms with this blending of smells long ago, and it had become an inevitable characteristic of dacha life for them, and with it the thought that it was pointless to repair the cesspool, that it cost incredible money, which none of them had. The village had grown poor, the inhabitants were not what they had been— the former owners had died off, they'd all faded from sight, and their heirs, widows and children, lived a rather hard and not at all dacha-like life. Petka, for example, Marya Petrovna's nephew and the son of a Red professor,[7] worked as a simple truck driver at the lumber center. And Valerka, Vasily Alexeyevich's son, Dmitriev's cousin, got mixed up with trash and became a thief and landed somewhere in the camps. Some of the heirs, wearied by the dacha extortions and looking ahead—the city was coming—sold their shares, and totally strange people appeared in the village, who had no relation at all to Red partisans. And only the birches and lindens, planted forty years ago by Dmitriev's father, a passionate gardener, grew into a mighty forest, choked with foliage, and proudly gave notice to the passersby who looked through the fence that everything in the village was bubbling, flowering, thriving as it should.

And then suddenly Ivan Vasilievich Lukyanov, Lena's father, who came by to call on the youngsters and to be a guest for a day, said that Kalugin, the master plumber who had fixed the pipes in the settlement for thirty years, was a swindler and a no-good, and that he, along with the sewer man, who was invited regularly to come pump out the pool, was robbing the Red partisans and that it was possible to make the repair of the pool quickly and cheaply. Everyone was stunned. They collected the money. Ivan Vasilievich brought the workers, and in a week the repair was finished. The heirs of the Red partisans were very afraid that Kalugin, offended, would quit the settlement, leaving them at the mercy of fate, but Ivan Vasilievich managed it so that the old sot didn't get offended by anyone, but was even filled with respect for Ivan Vasilievich and began to call him "Vasilich."[8]

Lora, with her way of speaking her mind, remarked that this was probably because Kalugin had sensed a kindred spirit in Ivan Vasilievich. Where had he gotten the workers? Where had he gotten the bricks? The cement? Obviously underhanded. Through not exactly noble means. His mother was indignant: "How do you know? What right have you to so rudely slander someone without proof?"

"Well, I don't know, I don't know, Mama. Maybe I'm mistaken." Lora smiled mysteriously. "It was just a supposition. We'll see."

And Ivan Vasilievich really was a powerful man. His main strength was his connections, old acquaintances. In six months he had put in a phone at the Pavlinovo dacha. Ivan Vasilievich was a tanner by profession, he had begun with a master in the town of Kirsanov, but already by 1926, when they made him director of a factory—a crummy little factory requisitioned from a Nepman[9] in Marian Grove—he was moving along the administrative line. When Dmitriev first met him, Ivan Vasilievich was already quite old and heavy. He suffered from short breath, had had a stroke and all kinds of misfortunes, such as being fired, party penalties, reinstatement, appointment with a raise, the slanders and libels of various rats who aimed to ruin him, but as he himself admitted, "As far as those moments were concerned, I was saved by only one thing: I was on the alert."

The habit of constant distrust and unremitting vigilance had insinuated itself so much into his nature that Ivan Vasilievich displayed it about the slightest trifles. For example, he'd ask Dmitriev before going to bed at night: "Viktor, did you put the hook on the door?"—"Yes," Dmitriev would reply, and he'd listen as his father-in-law slipped down the hall to the door to check. (This was later, when they lived in the Lukyanov's apartment in the city.) Sometimes Dmitriev got so fed up that he'd yell: "Ivan Vasilievich, why are you asking, for God's sake?"—"Don't you get insulted, precious man, I do it automatically, with no evil intention." It was amusing that the same distrust for each and every one—first of all for the people living side by side—infected Vera Lazarevna too. Sometimes she'd telephone from somewhere and ask for Lena. Dmitriev would say that Lena wasn't home. In a little while there'd be another call, and Vera Lazarevna, changing her voice, would ask for Lena. And what comic scenes would occur sometimes in the evening when his mother and father-in-law would feed each other medicine! "What did you give me, Ivan?"—"I gave you what you asked for."—"But what, what exactly? Say it!"—"You asked for diabasol, it seems to me."—"You gave me diabasol?"—"Yes."—"Sure?"—"Why are you bringing up this question?"—"Tell you what: please bring me the container you got it out of—for some reason it seems to me that this isn't diabasol...."

There was a time when such conversations heard in passing soothed Dmitriev, as did his father-in-law's manner of expressing himself: "In this respect, Xenia Fyodorovna, I'll give you the following axiom." Or like this: "I was never my father's technical executor, and I demanded the analogical from Lena." They laughed silently about it. His mother called her new relative "the learned neighbor"—behind his back of course—and considered that he was not a bad man, in some ways nice even, although of course not at all of the intelligentsia, unfortunately. Both he and Vera Lazarevna were of a different breed—those "who know how to live." Well, it wasn't so bad to get related to people of a different breed. Inject fresh blood. Profit from someone else's abilities. Those who don't know how to live begin to oppress each other after living together—by their noble inability itself, which they are secretly proud of.

After all, could Dmitriev or Xenia Fyodorovna, or anyone else of the Dmitriev relatives, have organized and carried through the repair of the dacha as dashingly as Ivan Vasilievich? He'd lent the money for all that business, too. Dmitriev and Lena went away their first summer, to the south. When they returned in August the old little rooms were unrecognizable—the floors shone, the frames and the doors sparkled with white, the wallpapers in all of the rooms were expensive, with embossed patterns, green in one room, blue in another, brick-red in the third. True, the old furniture, which was wretched, and had been bought by Georgy Alexeyevich a long time ago, was still there. It hadn't been noticeable before, but now it struck the eye: what shabbiness! Some iron bedsprings on a sawhorse instead of a bed, tables and cupboards of painted plywood, a wicker trestle bed, another wicker object, impossibly dilapidated. Lena of course took all of the junk out of the large room with the green wallpaper where the young couple was installed, and bought a few very simple but new things: a mattress with legs, a student desk, two chairs, a lamp, some curtains, and brought in two rugs from the other rooms—old rugs, but very good ones, Bukharas, one for the wall, the other for the floor. Dmitriev was amazed: how wonderfully things had changed! Even his mother said: "See what taste Lena has! We lived here so long and not once did we think of hanging that rug on the wall. No, she's got very fine taste!"

Vera Lazarevna and Ivan Vasilievich settled into the middle room temporarily, the blue one, for August and September, to help Lenochka, who was already expecting a child. Xenia Fyodorovna lived in the small brick-red room and now and then Lora stayed over. It was then that Lora's tedious romance with Felix began, and she wasn't interested in the dacha. Their grandfather, Xenia Fyodorovna's father, was still alive, and he also was a guest sometimes—he slept in the connecting room on the trestle bed. Strange to remember it. Could it have really been like that: everyone sitting together on the veranda at the big table, drinking tea, Xenia Fyodorovna pouring, Vera Lazarevna cutting the pie? And she called Lora *Lorochka* at one time, and arranged for her to have her best dressmakers. It had been like that, for sure. It had been, it had been. Only it didn't stay in his memory, it rushed past, vanished, because he couldn't live for anything or see anyone but Lena. There was the south, sultriness, hot Batum, old lady Vlastopulo, from whom they rented a room next to the bazaar, an Abkhazian he'd fought with over Lena, on the embankment at night, the Abkhazian had tried to pass a note to Lena in a restaurant. They sat there with no money and only cucumbers to live on, they telegraphed to Moscow, Lena lay with no energy, naked and black on the sheet, and he ran to sell the camera. And then all of it continued on, although it was different, Moscow, he was already working—one wild summer flew with momentum—again Lena lay like a mulatto on the sheet, again there was bathing at night, races to the shore, a cooling meadow, conversations, discoveries, tirelessness, suppleness, fingers ashamed of nothing, lips always ready for love. And besides that her devilish powers of observation! Oho, how she could pick up the weak or the funny things. And everything pleased him, he was struck by everything, astonished, registered it.

He liked the facility with which she made friends and became intimate with people. This, as it happened, was exactly what he lacked. Especially remarkable was the way she succeeded in making *necessary* acquaintances. She'd hardly settled in Pavlinovo when she already knew all the neighbors, the police chief, the watchmen at the wharf, and was on familiar terms with the young directress of the sanatorium and the latter gave Lena permission to have dinner in the sanatorium dining room, which was considered the height of comfort in Pavlinovo, and a success almost unattainable by mere mortals. And how she scratched Downstairs Dusya, who lived in the semi-basement, when the latter appeared with her usual arrogance, to demand that they clean their own, the Dmitrievs', shed, which it was true Downstairs Dusya had used as her own for the past ten years! Downstairs Dusya flew from the porch as if the wind had knocked her down. Dmitriev was delighted, and whispered to his mother: "So, how do you like it? This isn't how it

was with us milksops, is it?" But all his secret delight quickly passed because he knew that there wasn't and couldn't be a woman more beautiful, intelligent, and energetic than Lena, therefore—why be delighted?
It was all natural, in the order of things. No one had such soft skin as
Lena. No one could read Agatha Christie so entertainingly, at the same
time translating from English into Russian. No one could love him like
Lena. And Dmitriev himself—that remote thin one with the absurd
curly forelock—lived stunned and stupefied, as during heat, when a
man can't think well, doesn't want to eat or drink, and just dozes off,
lying in bed half asleep in a room with draped windows.

But once in the evening, at the end of the summer, Lora said:
"Vitka, can we talk?" They stepped off the porch, down to the road,
and while they were in the square of light which fell from the veranda,
they walked in silence until they were in the shadow of the lindens.
Lora, laughing unsurely, said: "Vitya, I wanted to talk about Lena, all
right? It's nothing really, don't worry, just little things. You know I'm in
favor of her, I like her, but the main thing for me is that you love her."
This introduction offended him right away, because the *main thing* was
not at all that he loved her. She was wonderful by herself, unrelated to
him. And already on guard, he prepared to listen further.

"I'm just surprised by certain things. Our mother would never say it
herself, but I see it.... Vitka, you won't take offense?"—"No, no, what do
you mean! Go on."—"Well, this is really nonsense, trivial—that Lena
took all our best cups, for example, and that she puts the bucket by
Mama's door...." ("Lord!" he thought. "And Lorka's saying this!") "I
didn't notice it," he said aloud. "But I'll tell her."—"You don't have to!
And I shouldn't have pointed it out to you." Lora again laughed somehow abashedly. "That's all you needed, to be told every bit of nonsense!
But I scolded Mama. Why not simply say: 'Lenochka, we need the cups,
and please don't put the pail here, put it there.' I said that today, and I
don't think she got offended at all. Although it's very unpleasant to talk
about such trivial things, believe me. But something else jarred me—for
some reason she took Father's portrait from the middle room and put
it in the connecting room. Mama was very surprised. You should know
about this because it's not some domestic trifle, but something else. In
my opinion it's just tactlessness." Lora was silent and for a while they
walked, not saying anything. Dmitriev ran his open palm over the lilac
bushes, feeling how the little sharp twigs were pricking him. "Well, all
right!" he said finally. "As far as the portrait goes, I'll tell her. Only listen: what if you happened to come into a strange house, Lora?
Wouldn't you commit some involuntary tactlessnesses, slips?"—"It's

possible. But not that kind. Generally we shouldn't be silent, but should speak out—I think that's correct—and then everything'll turn out right."

He told Lena about the portrait, not that night but the next morning. Lena was amazed. She'd taken down the portrait only because she needed the nail for the wall clock, and there had been absolutely no other meaning in her action. It seemed odd to her that Xenia Fyodorovna didn't tell her about such a trivial matter herself, but sent Viktor as an ambassador, which gave the trivial matter exaggerated significance. He remarked that Xenia Fyodorovna hadn't talked to him about this at all. But who had said it? At this point he blurted out from stupidity—how much would be "blurted out" from stupidity later on!—that Lora had spoken. Lena, reddening, said that his sister had apparently taken upon herself the role of rebuking her: sometimes independently, sometimes through a third person.

When Dmitriev returned from town that day it was unusually quiet in the apartment. Lena didn't come out to meet him right away, but appeared a few minutes later and asked the unnecessary question: "Shall I warm your dinner?" Lora had gone to Moscow. His mother didn't come out of her room. Then Vera Lazarevna appeared, dressed in town clothes, powdered, with beads on her powerfully jutting chest, and said, smiling, that she and Ivan Vasilievich thanked them for the hospitality, and were waiting for him to say goodbye. Ivan Vasilievich would arrive soon with the car. Through the door, which was opened for a second, Dmitriev saw that his father's portrait was hanging in its former place. He wondered: why so suddenly? They had wanted to live there all of September. Yes, but some business had come up—with Ivan Vasilievich at work, and she had household chores, had to make jam, and in general—haven't your dear guests tired you out.... Xenia Fyodorovna came out to say goodbye to the relatives—she had a dispirited look—and invited them to come again. Vera Lazarevna didn't promise to, "I'm afraid we won't manage it, dear Xenia Fyodorovna. Really, there are so many concerns of all possible sorts. So many friends want to see us, they're also inviting us to their dachas...."

They left, and Dmitriev and Lena went to the dacha next door to play poker. Late that night, when Dmitriev returned, Xenia Fyodorovna called him into her room with the brick-red wallpaper, and said that she was in a rotten mood and that she couldn't get to sleep because of this business. He didn't understand: "What business?" —"Well, because they left."

Dmitriev had drunk two glasses of cognac at the neighbors', was slightly excited and wasn't thinking clearly. Waving his hand, he said with annoyance: "Oh, nonsense, mother! Is it worth talking about?"— "No, but Lora is uncontrolled. Why did she start all this? And you passed it on to Lena for some reason, she—to her mother, there was the stupidest conversation.... Complete absurdity!" "And because you don't go around moving portraits!" said Dmitriev, hardening his voice and shaking his finger with severity. Suddenly he felt himself to be in the role of family arbitrator, which was sort of pleasant even.—"Well they left, so fine. Lenka said absolutely nothing to me, she's a smart lady. So don't get upset and sleep quietly." He gave his mother a smack on the cheek and left.

But when he went to Lena and lay down beside her, she moved away to the wall, and asked why he'd stopped in at Xenia Fyodorovna's room. Sensing danger of some sort, he began to make excuses, said that he was tired of conversations and wanted something else entirely, but Lena, alternating between severity and caresses, got what she wanted to know out of him anyway. Then she said her parents were very proud people. Vera Lazarevna was especially proud and touchy. The problem was that she'd never been dependent on anyone in her whole life, therefore the slightest hint at dependency was taken badly by her. Dmitriev thought: "How is it she's not dependent, since she never worked and lives as a dependent of Ivan Vasilievich?"—but he didn't say it out loud, but just asked how they'd infringed on Vera Lazarevna's independence. It turned out that when Lena related the conversation about the portrait to Vera Lazarevna, the latter simply oohed: Lord, did they really think we'd had any pretensions to that room? Dmitriev didn't understand something here at all: "Have pretensions? Why have pretensions?" Besides that, he wanted something else. It ended with Lena making him promise that he'd call Vera Lazarevna from work the next day, and gently, delicately, not mentioning the portrait or insults, invite them to Pavlinovo. Of course, they wouldn't come, because they were very proud people. But he should call. To clear his conscience.

He called. They arrived the next day. Why had he remembered this ancient business? Later there was a lot that was worse, blacker. Well, probably because the first was engraved forever. He even remembered what dress Vera Lazarevna was wearing when she arrived the next day, and with a look of unshakable worth—proudly and vainly looking before her—ascended to the porch, carrying a boxed torte in her right hand.

Then there was the matter of his grandfather. The same autumn that Lena was expecting Natashka. Oh, grandfather! Dmitriev hadn't seen his grandfather for many years, but there had smoldered in his heart for an incalculably long time the splinter of childhood devotion. The old man was so alien to any kind of *Lukyanovableness*–he simply didn't comprehend a lot of things–that it was of course crazy to invite him to the dacha when those people were living there. But then no one understood that, or could foresee it. It was impossible not to invite their grandfather, he'd recently come back to Moscow, was very sick, and needed a rest. In a year he got a room in the southwest region of Moscow.

His grandfather said to Dmitriev, marveling: "Some worker came today to move the couch, and your marvelous Elena, and no less marvelous mother-in-law, used the familiar 'you' with him in a friendly way. What does it mean? Is it accepted now? To the father of a family, a man of forty?" Another time he started a funny and unbearably tiresome conversation with Dmitriev and Lena because they'd given the salesman in the electronics store–and made merry when they told about it–fifty rubles so he'd put aside a radio for them. And Dmitriev couldn't explain any of it to his grandfather. Lena, laughing, said: "Fyodor Nikolaich, you're a monster!" His grandfather wasn't a monster, he was just very old–seventy-nine–there were very few such old men left in Russia, and of jurists who'd graduated from Petersburg University still less, and of those who'd been involved in revolutionary activities, had been in prison, exiles, fled abroad, worked in Switzerland and Belgium, been acquainted with Vera Zasulich–there were no more than one or two in all. Perhaps his grandfather, in a sense, was a monster after all.

And what kind of conversations could he have with Ivan Vasilievich and Vera Lazarevna? No matter how they exerted themselves, both sides found nothing in common. Ivan Vasilievich and Vera Lazarevna were absolutely disinterested in his grandfather's past, and his grandfather understood so little of modern life that he couldn't report anything useful, and so they acted with indifference: just an old man. He shuffled along the veranda, smoked cheap, stinking cigarettes. Vera Lazarevna usually talked with his grandfather about his smoking.

His grandfather was small in height, dried up, with bluish-copper tanned skin on his face, and stiff hands, rough and disfigured by hard work. He always dressed neatly and wore a shirt and tie. He polished his boyish little shoes, size eight, to a shine and liked to take walks along the shore. There was one Sunday, the last hot one in September, when everyone got together for a walk–a strain had already appeared in their conversations, no one needed this excursion, but somehow it was agreed: they gathered at the same time and strolled along together.

There were loads of people around that day. They bumped against each other in the woods, on the shore, they sat all over the benches: some in sports clothes, some in pajamas, with children, dogs, guitars, and fifths on newspaper. And Dmitriev began to get ironical about the contemporary dacha residents: the deuce knows, he said, what kind of public this is. But before the war, he remembered, others with beards, in pince-nez, strolled here.... Vera Lazarevna unexpectedly supported him, saying that before the revolution Pavlinovo was also a marvelous resort area, she'd been a little girl here at her uncle's. There had been a restaurant with gypsies, called The Riverside, they'd burned it down. Generally solid people had lived here: stock market speculators, businessmen, lawyers, artists. Over there in the clearing, Chaliapin's dacha had stood.

Xenia Fyodorovna was interested: who was her uncle? To which Vera Lazarevna answered: "My papa was a simple worker, a furrier, but a very good, qualified furrier, they ordered expensive things from him...." "Mamochka!" laughed Lena. "They ask you about your uncle, and you tell about your father." The uncle, it turned out, had a leather goods shop: purses, suitcases, briefcases. On Kuznetsky, on the second floor, where there is a woman's dress shop now. During NEP there had been a leather goods store there, but no longer her uncle's, because uncle had disappeared in 1919, during the famine. No, he hadn't run away, hadn't died, he'd just disappeared somewhere. Ivan Vasilievich interrupted his spouse, remarking that these autobiographical facts weren't too interesting to anyone anyway.

And at that point, grandfather, till then silent, suddenly began to speak. "So, dear Vitya, just imagine, if your mother-in-law's uncle had lived to the time when the beards and pince-nez strolled here, what would he have said? Probably: what kind of public, he'd say, is in Pavlinovo now! Some riffraff in Tolstoi blouses and pince-nez.... Ah? Wouldn't he? And even earlier there used to be an estate there, the landowner ruined himself, sold his house, sold his land and fifty years later some heir would drop by here in passing, out of a sad interest, would look at the merchant's wife, the bureaucrat's wife, at the gentlemen in bowlers, at your uncle," grandfather bowed to Vera Lazarevna, "who rode up in a cab and thought: 'Foo, filth! Well, this bunch of people are just trash!' Ah?" he laughed. "Wouldn't he?"

Vera Lazarevna remarked with a certain astonishment: "I don't understand, why trash? Why talk like that?" Then grandfather explained:

contempt is stupidity. One doesn't have to be contemptuous of anyone. He said this for Dmitriev, and Dmitriev suddenly saw that his
grandfather was to some degree right.... In some way which touched
close to him, Dmitriev. Everyone grew thoughtful, then Xenia
Fyodorovna said no, that she couldn't agree with her father. If we
refuse to be contemptuous, we deprive ourselves of our last weapon.
Let this feeling be inside us, absolutely invisible from the outside, but it
should be there. Then Lena, giggling, said: "I agree completely with
Fyodor Nikolaich. How many people are conceited about who knows
what, myths, chimeras. It's so funny."—"Who exactly, and what are they
conceited about?" asked Dmitriev in a half-joking tone, although the direction of the conversation had begun to disturb him slightly. "Who
knows," said Lena, "you want to know everything, don't you?"—
"Conceit and quiet contempt are two different things," pronounced
Xenia Fyodorovna, smiling. "That depends on who's looking," answered Lena. "I hate honor in general. In my opinion there's nothing
more repulsive."—"You take a tone—as if I were proving that honor is
something beautiful. I don't love honor either."—"Especially when
there's no basis for it. Built on empty space...."

And so from this, from an innocent altercation, developed the conversation which concluded with Lena's heart attack that night, the call
for the ambulance, cries from Vera Lazarevna about egotism and cruel-
heartedness, with their hurried departure by taxi the next morning,
and then Xenia Fyodorovna's departure and the silence which came
over the dacha when two were left: Dmitriev and the old man. They
walked by the lake, talked for a long time. Dmitriev wanted to have a
conversation about Lena with his grandfather—her departure worried
him—to curse her for her nonsensicality, her parents for idiocy, and
maybe damn himself, or somehow pick at the wound; but his grandfather didn't utter a word either about Lena or her parents. He talked
about death, and how he wasn't afraid of it. He'd carried out what he'd
been appointed to do in this life, and that was all. "My God, I wonder
how she is doing there? What if something serious happens suddenly,
to her heart?"

His grandfather talked about how the past and his whole endlessly
long life didn't interest him at all. There was nothing stupider than
looking for ideals in the past. He only looked ahead with interest, but
unfortunately saw little.

"Should I call or not?" thought Dmitriev. "Anyway, no matter what
her condition is, that doesn't give her the right...."

He called in the evening.

His grandfather died three years later.

Dmitriev came to the crematorium straight from work, and looked stupid with his thick yellow briefcase in which there were several cans of Saira,[10] bought by chance on the street. Lena loved Saira. When they entered the crematorium's premises from the street, Dmitriev quickly went to the right and put his briefcase on the floor in a corner, behind a column, so no one would see it. And repeated mentally, "Don't forget the briefcase." During the funeral ceremony he remembered about the briefcase several times, looked at the column, and at the same time thought that his grandfather's death had turned out to be not as awful an experience as he had supposed it would. He was very sorry for his mother. She was supported under her arms by Aunt Zhenya on one side and by Lora on the other, and her face, white from tears, was new somehow: simultaneously very old and childish.

Lena came too, sniffled, wiped her eyes with a handkerchief, and when the moment of farewell came she suddenly began to sob in a loud low voice, seized Dmitriev's arm and began to whisper that his grandfather had been a good man, the best of all the Dmitriev relatives, and how she loved him. That was news. But Lena sobbed so sincerely; real tears were in her eyes, and Dmitriev believed. Her parents also appeared at the last minute, in black coats with black umbrellas; Vera Lazarevna even had a black veil on her hat and they managed to throw a bouquet of flowers into the coffin, as it was lowered into the cellar. Then Vera Lazarevna said in amazement: "How many people there were!" That's why they came, out of old people's curiosity: to see whether there were a lot there to see him off. To Dmitriev's amazement a lot came. And the main thing was that there had come creeping from somewhere, in no small number, people who had seemed to disappear; but no, those strange old men were still alive, and old lady smokers with angry dry eyes, and friends of his grandfather, a few of whom Dmitriev remembered from childhood. One hunchbacked old lady with a myopic ancient face came, who his mother said had been a desperate revolutionary, a terrorist, and had thrown a bomb at someone. This hunchbacked lady gave the speech over the casket. In the courtyard, when everyone came out and stood in bunches, not dispersing, Lora came up and asked if Lena and he were going to Aunt Zhenya's, where the friends and relatives were gathering. Until that moment, Dmitriev had thought that they were definitely going to Aunt Zhenya's, but now he wavered: there was the possibility of choice in Lora's question itself. That meant that both Lora and his mother supposed that he, if he so desired, could not go, that is, that it wasn't necessary for him to go because—suddenly he understood it—in their eyes he no longer existed as a part of the Dmitriev family, but as a different thing, connected with Lena, and maybe even with those in the black coats with the black umbrellas; and they had to ask him like an outsider.

"Are you going to Aunt Zhenya's?" The question was casually asked, but how much it signified! Among other things: "If you were alone, we wouldn't have asked. We always want to see you, you know. But when we have grief, why have strange people around? If it's possible, it'd be better to do without them. If it's possible, but—whatever you want...." Dmitriev said that most likely they would not go to Aunt Zhenya's. "Why? You go!" said Lena. "I don't feel so well, but you go. Of course, go!" No, he wouldn't go, Lena had a bad headache. Lora nodded understandingly, and even smiled at Lena with sympathy and asked whether she should give her some aspirin. "Yes!" said Dmitriev. "I forgot my briefcase!" He went back to the crematorium's premises, where a new deceased was already lying in a coffin on a pedestal, around which a small group of people were huddling, and on tiptoe he walked behind the column. After getting his briefcase he stopped, to be alone for a minute. The feeling of irrevocability, of being *cut off,* which comes at funerals—one thing had irrevocably gone, cut off forever, and now continues the other, but not that, something new, in other combinations—was the most tormenting pain, even stronger than the sadness about his grandfather. His grandfather had been old after all, he was due to die, but along with him disappeared something not directly connected with him, existing separately: threads of some kind among Dmitriev and his mother and sister. And this disappearance was revealed so implacably and immediately, a few moments after they came out of the heavy floral smell into the air. Lora calmly agreed to his not going to Aunt Zhenya's, and he came to terms with her calmness easily. And only his mother, turning halfway around, made a weak farewell gesture with her hand, and he suddenly felt that he'd added a pain to her, so he rushed to catch up—rushed internally for a moment—but it was already too late, irrevocable, it had been cut off; Lena pulled him to the taxi to go home.

Along with his mother, Lora, Felix, Aunt Zhenya and other relatives, there was also Lyovka Bubrik. Maybe he'd been there earlier, but Dmitriev noticed him only when they came outside. Lyovka was hatless, dark, tousled, and his glasses were blindingly bright. He didn't come up to Dmitriev, but nodded from a distance. Lena asked in a whisper: "Why's Bubrik here?" Dmitriev, stifling a feeling of unpleasant surprise, said: "Well, so? He's related somehow. Second cousin twice re-moved."

This was the first time Dmitriev had seen Lyovka Bubrik for several months after that tedious incident with the institute. And he immedi-ately remembered that his deceased grandfather had censured him on account of Lyovka. There had been a conversation in which his grand-father had said: "Xenia and I expected you to become something else. Of course nothing terrible happened. You're not a bad man. But not wonderful."

He'd known Lyovka since childhood, they'd gone to school at the same institute. Not friends "you couldn't separate with water," but friends connected by the ties of home and family. Lyovka's father, Dr. Bubrik, who'd taken care of Dmitriev even in infancy, was the brother of Aunt Zhenya's husband, who died during the war. So Lyovka was an unrelated nephew of Aunt Zhenya's. Right after the institute Lyovka went to Bashkiria and worked there for three years in industrial survey-ing, while at the same time Dmitriev, who was older, and had gotten his diploma a year earlier, stayed to work in Moscow at the gas factory, in the laboratory. They'd offered him various enticing odysseys, but it had been difficult to accept them. His mother wanted him very much to go to Turkmenia, to Dargan-Tepe, because it wasn't far from Lora's native Kunia-Urgench—some 600 kilometers, a trifle!—and the brother and sis-ter could have met over a cup of kok-chai tea and have been homesick together. Natashka was born weak, she was sick, Lena was sick too, she had no milk so they found the wet nurse, Frosya, the school cleaning lady who lived in the barracks near Tarakanovka, Dmitriev went there in the evenings for the bottles. Sure, Dargan-Tepe! Yes, and there was to be no Dargan-Tepe. There were dreams in the morning, in the si-lence when he awoke with the unexpected cheerfulness and thought: "It would be nice if...." And it all rose up before him, so transparent, clearcut, as if he'd gone up a mountain on a clear day and looked down from it. "Vitya," said Lena (or "Vitenka," if it was a period of serenity and love),"why are you fooling yourself? You can't go away anywhere from us. I don't know whether you love us, but you can't, you can't! It's over! You're late. It should have been earlier...." And embracing him, she looked into his eyes with the dark blue caressing eyes of a witch. He was silent because these were his own thoughts, which he was afraid of. Yes, yes, he was too late, the train had left. Four years had gone by since he'd finished the institute, then five, seven, ten went by. Natashka became a schoolgirl. The English Special School on Utiny Lane, the ob-ject of lust, envy, the measure of parental love and *putting yourself out to*

get it. Another school district, almost unthinkable. And no one but
Lena would've had the strength. For she gnawed on her desires like a
bulldog. Such a nice-looking lady-bulldog with short straw-colored hair,
and an always pleasantly tanned, slightly dark face. She didn't let up
until her wishes—right in her teeth—turned into flesh. A great trait!
Wonderful, amazingly decisive in life. The trait of real men.

   "No expeditions. Not for longer than a week"—that was her wish. A
poor simplehearted wish with dents in it from iron teeth. Lena's other
wish, which occupied her during the course of several years, was: to get
into IICI. Oh, IICI, unattainable, beyond the clouds, like Everest!
Conversations about IICI, telephone calls in connection with IICI, tearful despair, flashes of hope.

   "Papa, did you talk with Grigory Grigorievich about IICI?"—
"Lenochka, they called you from IICI!"—"From where?"—"From
IICI!"—"Oh, my God, from the personnel section or just Zoika?" Two
friends, ideally situated in this life, worked in IICI—the Institute of
International Coordination of Information. Finally she succeeded. IICI
became flesh and crunched in her teeth like a well-cooked chicken
wing. Convenient, it was piece work, beautifully located—a minute's
walk from GUM[11]—and her own boss was one of the friends she had
studied with at the institute. Her friend gave Lena as much to translate
as she asked for. Later on, they had a fight, but for about three years everything was "okay." During their lunch break they ran to GUM to see
if they'd put out some blouses. On Thursdays they showed foreign
films in the original language. But unfortunately Lena couldn't get
Dmitriev's dissertation done for him. At that time Dmitriev was getting
130 at the laboratory, but an acquaintance of his from the institute,
from the same class—a little gray guy, but a big worker, clever Mitri,
who'd denied himself everything and didn't even get married ahead of
time—received twice that because he'd sat through his dissertation on
his lead rear. Lena wanted Dmitriev to become a Ph.D. terribly.
Everyone wanted it. Lena helped him with English, his mother approved, Natashka spoke in a whisper at night, and his mother-in-law
grew quiet, but after half a year he gave up. Probably because of that:
the train had left. He didn't have the energy, every night he came home
with a headache, and with one desire—to tumble into bed. And he did
tumble in if there wasn't anything worthwhile on television—football,
or an old comedy. And after giving up, he began to hate all that dissertation junk, he said it was better to receive the honest 130 rubles than
to torture himself and overtax his health and humble himself before
the necessary people. And now Lena looked at it the same way and con-

temptuously referred to the Ph.D.'s of their acquaintance as smart op-
erators and sly foxes. At this time, as never more opportunely—but perhaps inopportunely—Lyovka Bubrik showed up with his request about
the Institute of Oil and Gas Apparatus, abbreviated IOGA.

Lyovka couldn't find work for a long time after he returned from
Bashkiria. Then he found IOGA. But he had to find a way to get in.
Neither he nor anyone else would've gotten into IOGA if Ivan
Vasilievich hadn't called Prusakov. Then he went to see Prusakov himself in an official car. Prusakov was holding the job for someone else,
but Ivan Vasilievich pressed and Prusakov agreed. In the end it wasn't
Lyovka's father-in-law who went, but Dmitriev's! True, on Lyovka's behalf. That was true. Because Lena had asked her father, she was sorry
for Lyovka and his wife, that fat hen Innochka. Then Innochka made a
big mess when they were all guests at mutual friends', and cried:
"You're an awful person!" But Lena had been ready for all of this and
held on staunchly and coolly. Their friends said that Lena held on mag-
nificently. She took everything on herself and said that Dmitriev hadn't
wanted it, but she'd insisted. "I'm guilty, only me, don't blame Vitka!
You'd have wanted us to live on 130 and Vitka to kill three hours on
the road?"

Of course, that's how it was. The thought first came to her when
Ivan Vasilievich came and told what kind of job it was. And Dmitriev really didn't want to do it. He didn't sleep for three nights, he wavered
and worried but gradually that which it was impossible to think of,
which was not the thing to do, turned into something inconsequential,
diminutive, well-packed like a pill you had to—it was necessary even, for
your health—swallow, despite the nastiness it contained inside. There is
no one who doesn't notice the nastiness after all. But everyone swallows the pills. "I respect Lev," said Lena, "and I even love him, but for
some reason I love my husband more. And if Papa, an old man who
can't bear to be obliged, got ready and went....."

They should have told them right away, but they didn't have the
nerve—they dragged it out, kept quiet. They found out from someone
else. And how they cut them off: they didn't come, they didn't call. The
devil knows, maybe they were right, but it isn't done that way either:
you come, you talk nicely, you find out why and how. And when they
met at friends', Bubrik turned up his nose, but Innochka yelled like a
fishwife. So the hell with it, forget it. And it was only after about four or
five years—it was Xenia Fyodorovna's birthday, winter, the end of
February—that the whole story was stirred up again. His mother and
grandfather had pestered Dmitriev about it before, but not very spite-

fully, because they correctly considered that Lena had started every-thing. And what could you expect from Lena? You had to reconcile yourself to Lena as with bad weather. But then, on his mother's birth-day....

It was as clear as if it were now. They go up the stairs, stop at the door. Natashka holds the presents, a box of candy and a book in English, Thackeray's *Vanity Fair,* and Lena is leaning with her shoulder against the door and with closed eyes whispers as if to herself, but of course to Dmitriev: "Oh, my God, my God, my God. God...." Look, she says, what ordeals I go through for your sake. And he begins to seethe as usual. Lena doesn't like to go to her mother-in-law's. Each year she has to force herself more. What was there to do? Well, she doesn't like to, she can't, can't stand it. Everything irritates her. No matter how nicely they fed them, no matter how kindly they conversed, it was use-less: like heating the outdoors. Dmitriev talks tenderly to his daughter, purposely, hugging her: "So, little monkey, are you happy that we've come to grandma's?"—"Uh-hunh!"—"You like to come here?"—"I like to!" But Lena, smiling, adds: "I like to, say, but I've got to go to bed early. And little papa, say, don't stay too long so that we've got to drag you from the table by force. Say, we should get up and go at 9:30."

Everything would have been avoided then if it hadn't been for that fool Marina, his cousin. As soon as he glimpsed her red physiognomy at the table over the pies and wafers, he immediately understood: it's going to be bad. Lena was much smarter than she was, but in some ways they were similar. And whenever they met at family gatherings, some sort of cockfight always started between them. Sometimes they fought out in the open, other times they pricked slyly, so that you wouldn't notice it from the sidelines. Like water polo players, who hit each other with their legs under water, which the spectators don't see. At night Dmitriev would suddenly be stunned: "Why did your cousin taunt me all evening?"—"What do you mean, taunt?"—"Didn't you hear it?"—"What exactly?"—"Well, even what she was saying about women of the East? About their behinds and legs?"—"But after all, you're obvi-ously not a woman of the East, are you?"—"Oh! What point is there in talking to you...."

And then in February—he remembered every last word for some rea-son—it all started with the most innocent underwater bumps. He re-membered it because it was the last time Lena was ever a guest at his mother's. Since that time, never. It had been five years, and not once. Xenia Fyodorovna would come to visit her niece, but Lena never went to her. "How are you, Marina? Everything the same with you?"—"Of course! And you? Still working at the same place?" These phrases, said with a smile and within the boundaries of the rules, in actuality meant: "So, Marina, as before, no one's bit? I'm sure no one's bit, and never will bite, my dear old maid."—"But that doesn't upset me because I live the creative life. Not what you do. After all, you work, but I create, I live by creation." At the time Marina was working as an editor in a publishing house. Now somewhere in television. "Have you published anything good lately?"—"We've published a few things. What kind of fabric is that you've got? Did you get it at GUM?" Here were the resilient underwater kicks: "What creative work are you babbling about? Have you personally edited even one good book, put it out?"—"Yes, of course. But there's no sense in talking about it with you, it couldn't interest you. Mass production's what interests you." There were some arguments about poetry, about worldwide philistinism. Marina liked this subject a lot and didn't let a chance slip to trample on philistinism. Oh, the philistines! When she was boiling on account of those who didn't recognize Picasso or the sculptor Erzu, something curled up in her mouth and even seemed to sparkle.

Everything hateful that for Marina was connected to the word "philistinism" was contained for Lena in the word "phoniness." And she declared that "All that's phoniness." Marina was amazed: "Phoniness?"—"Yes, yes, phony."—"Loving Picasso is phony?"—"Of course, because those who say they love Picasso usually don't understand him, and that's phoniness."—"My God! Hold me back!" laughed Marina. "It's phony to love Picasso! Oy-oy-oy!" Both of their faces were burning, their eyes blazed with an unjoking brilliance. Picasso! Van Gogh! Sublimation! Acceleration! Paul Jackson! What Paul Jackson? It doesn't matter, because it's phony! Phony? Phony, phony. No, you explain then: what do you call phony? Well, everything that's done not from the heart, but with an ulterior motive, with the desire to show oneself in the best light. "Aha! That means you are being phony when you visit Aunt Xenia on her birthday and you bring her candy?"

Lena, after glancing at Viktor with a smile in which there was almost triumph (I predicted it, but you insisted, so take it, enjoy it!), said that her relations with Xenia Fyodorovna weren't the best but she'd come to wish her well not out of phoniness, but because Vitya had requested it. Something along those lines. Then there was a gap. The guests said goodbye. His mother stumbled along. Aunt Zhenya began to talk about Lyovka Bubrik, why—no one knew. She always wanted to do things right, but it always came out the opposite. His mother said: a disgraceful story, and she couldn't believe for a long time that Vitya could behave like that. "Ah, you consider me guilty for everything? And your Viktor had nothing to do with it?"—"I'm not justifying Viktor."—"But still—me?!"—Lena's cheeks were covered with a stormy flush and Xenia Fyodorovna's face showed granite features.

"Yes, sure, I'm capable of everything. Your Viktor's a good boy, I corrupted him." Aunt Zhenya spoke, shaking her benevolent gray head: "Dear Lena, you yourself explained it that way to Lyovochka, I remember it very well."—"What I explained doesn't matter! I was worried about my husband. And you don't have, you don't have...."—"Stop yelling!"—"And you're a traitor! I don't want to talk with you." Grabbing Natashka, she walked away from the table. "Why do you always keep quiet when I'm being insulted?" And—down the stairs, out into the frost, forever. He ran downstairs and slipped on a frozen puddle. Lena and Natashka were stupidly bounding away from him to the bus, the door closed, and he didn't know where else to go, what would be. He couldn't go anywhere. When his home was destroyed he couldn't go anywhere, to anyone. No, she had gone to his mother's one more time after that February—there had been no way out of it, Ivan Vasilievich was laid up with a stroke and his mother-in-law was spending her days and nights with him; but Dmitriev and Lena were hot for a trip to Golden Sands—and there was no one to leave Natashka with. In Bulgaria they took walks in sweaters, and loved each other very strongly. In the daytime the room got very hot even though they opened the curtain, the shower water was warm. And they had never loved each other so strongly.

Dmitriev stood in front of the house and looked at the single lighted window—the kitchen. The second floor and the left side of the building were dark. At this time of the year no one lived around here. Lora was doing something in the kitchen. Dmitriev saw her head lowered over the table, the black hair with the gray streaks, which shone under the electric bulb, the tanned forehead—the yearly five months in Central Asia had made her almost an Uzbek. From the darkness of the garden he viewed Lora just as if on a luminous screen, as a strange woman—he saw her lack of youth, the diseases earned through years of life in the tents, saw the rough anguish of her heart, now gripped by one anxiety.

What was she doing there? Ironing or something? He felt that he couldn't say anything to her. At any rate today, now. The hell with all that! Nobody needed it, it wouldn't save anyone, it would just bring sufferings and new pain.

Because there is nothing dearer than a kindred soul.

When he went up the steps of the porch his heart was thumping. Lora was cutting the newspaper on the table into long strips with the scissors. Felix came in with a basin which contained paste. Dmitriev began to help them. First they sealed the window in the kitchen, then they moved to the middle room. His mother had gone to sleep at six o'clock, but she would probably wake up soon. At about four thirty it had gotten bad, the pains had started, Lora had been very frightened and wanted to call an ambulance, but his mother said it was useless, that she should call Isidor Markovich, or the doctor from the hospital. She took papavirin and the pains went away. What was the matter? Their mother was very depressed. Such a sudden worsening. The first since the hospital. She says it's just exactly like it was in May: pains exactly as strong and in the same place.

They conversed in an undertone.

"I called you at four!"

"Yes, and everything was all right. But an hour later...."

Felix, humming something, was stuffing an old nylon stocking into a crack between the folds of the frames with a kitchen knife; Lora spread strips of newspapers with paste and Dmitriev pasted them. Then they sat down to tea. They listened for sounds from their mother's room the whole time. Lora's eyes were pitiful, she answered irrelevantly, and when Felix went out of the room she whispered quickly:

"I'm begging you: he's going to start about Kunya-Urgench, so say you're definitely against it.... That you can't."

Felix came back with a black packet in which there were photographs. Still humming, he began to show them. They were color pictures of the Kunya-Urgench excavations: crocks, camels, bearded men, Lora in trousers, a quilted jacket, Felix squatting, with some old men, also squatting. Felix said that they had to leave at the end of November. At the very latest—the beginning of December. They had to be there by the fifteenth, sharp. Lora said he'd be there, be there, just not to get worried. She'd let him go. Of course he must go, eighteen people were waiting. Collecting the photos and sticking them into the black packet— his fingers trembled slightly—Felix said that Lora, unfortunately, had to go too. Because eighteen people were waiting for her as well.

"We agreed: first you go...."

"How can you imagine that?"

The glasses were bouncing on Felix's big nose, and he raised them up with a special sort of movement of his cheeks and brows.

"And how do you imagine everything?"

"But there's Vitya, I believe, her son...."

"Well, that's enough! Vitya, Vitya. It doesn't matter about Vitya....
We can't talk about this today."

Felix stuck the packet into the pocket of his bike jacket, headed for
the door into the other room, but stopped at the doorway.

"And when do you plan to discuss it? We have to send a telegram to
Mamedov."

Lora waved her hand again, more energetically, and Felix disappeared, closing the door. Lora said that Felix was very good, loved
Mama, Mama loved him, but sometimes he was dense. Sometimes it
seems pathological to Lora. There are things it's impossible to explain
to him, and then one simply had to say categorically: such and such,
you say, and nothing else! And then he's resigned himself. He can't
argue. Dmitriev should have said that he can't stay with Mama, and
then he'd stop being so tiresome. And how could Dmitriev stay, really?
Take Mama to his place? Move to Profsoyuznaya? Lena would never
agree to either of these choices. It was important to Felix to go to
Kunya of course, to her as well, all very true, but what could they do?

In Xenia Fyodorovna's room it was still quiet as before. Felix took
the coal bucket and stamped across the veranda and down the stairs to
the shed. He made a clatter with the shovel, getting the coal. Dmitriev
said that he could of course try to exchange the two rooms for a two-
room apartment—which he'd tried to do before—so as to live with his
mother, but that was a whole story. Not so simple. Although there was
at the moment such a possibility right now.

He didn't want to say it, but it somehow said itself, comfortably and
appropriately. Lora looked at Dmitriev slightly surprised. Then she
asked:

"Is this idea Lena's or something?"

"No, mine. My old idea."

"Only don't report *your idea* to Felix, all right?" said Lora. "Because
he'll grab it. And Mama doesn't need this at all. When she's in such bad
shape, to go through something else. . . . I know: everything'll be fine at
first, noble, and then the irritation will start. No, it's an awful idea. A
nightmare. Brr, I can imagine!" And Lora convulsed her shoulders with
an expression of momentary fear and aversion. "No, I'll be with Mama,
I won't go anywhere, and Felix will manage somehow."

Felix returned with the bucket of coal. You could hear how quiet he
was being so as not to awaken Xenia Fyodorovna, scrabbling with his
hands in the bucket, taking out the coal pieces and with care putting
the pieces on an iron leaf in front of the stove. A slight clanging of the
iron damper. Lora grinned, wanting to say something, but she re-

mained silent.

"What is it?" asked Dmitriev.

"No, nothing. I often wondered, by the way: why don't you get yourself a co-op apartment? It's not so expensive. The relatives would help. They love their granddaughter so much...." Her face was smiling, but there was spite in her eyes. This was the old familiar Lora face from years ago. They'd often fought in childhood, and Lora, enraged, was capable of hitting with anything that came to hand—a fork, a teapot.

"What are you talking about in there?" asked Felix from the kitchen. He had sensed something in Lora's voice.

"I'm saying: why don't Vitya and Lena build a co-op apartment? A little one, two rooms. Right?" "We don't need any apartment at all," said Dmitriev in a choked voice. "We don't need it, you understand? In any case *I* don't need it. I, me! I don't need a damn thing, absolutely not a damn thing. Other than our mother to be well. She's always wanted to live with me anyway, you know that, and if it could help her now...."

Lora covered her face with her palms. Only her lips remained visible: they were worrying, compressing. Dmitriev thought in despair: "Idiot! Why am I saying this? I really don't need anything...." He wanted to throw himself at his sister, embrace her. But he continued to sit there, chained to the chair. Felix, standing in the doorway, with a distracted look, looked now at his wife, now at his wife's brother. He walked like a master among these rooms—an unfamiliar squab in a bike jacket with slant pockets, something jackdawish, round, alien, in squeaky house slippers with inner soles—among the rooms in which Dmitriev's childhood had passed. He looked upon the crying sister in bewilderment, as upon disorder in the house, like a buffet door left open for some reason. Dmitriev muttered:

"Felix, get out for a minute!"

The man in the bike jacket got out. Dmitriev went up to Lora and with awkwardness tapped her on the shoulder:

"Come on, stop."

She shook her head, she didn't have the strength to raise it....

"As you wish, as you wish.... If she wants it—all right...."

In precisely a minute Felix's voice was behind the door: "Can I come in, friends?"

He came in with an envelope.

"Today, see here, came a message from Ashirik Mamedov. The poor guy's asking if he should buy sleeping bags on our share. This is at Chardzhu, at the base of the Guber. He's got the money, but we have to answer fast: to have him get them or not. By telegraph."

He hummed and squeaked his inner soles, standing near Lora's chair with the envelope in his hand. They heard a sound from Xenia Fyodorovna's room. Dmitriev rushed to the door on tiptoe; he immediately saw his mother's face was different.

"Well, you see this ugliness?" said Xenia Fyodorovna in a weak voice, trying to get up.

A book that had been lying on the blanket slipped to the floor. Dmitriev bent over: it was the same *Doctor Faustus,* with the bookmark after a hundred pages.

"I talked to you this morning!" said Dmitriev in a kind of fervent reproach, as if this fact were extremely important for his mother's condition and the whole course of the illness.

"How is it now, Mama?" asked Lora. "Here's the medicine. And put in the thermometer."

Xenia Fyodorovna sat a moment on the bed, not moving, with an expression of deep concentration—she penetrated into herself with all her feelings. Then she said:

"But now it's as if"—she carefully extended her hand and took the cup of water from Lora. She bent a little forward.—"It's as if there's nothing there. Foo, such nonsense!" She smiled and made a sign to Dmitriev so that he'd sit on the chair next to the bed. "Still, it's an awful filthy thing, this ulcerous disease. I'm indignant, I want to write a protest. To demand the complaint book. Only from whom? From the Lord God or something?"

"Are you comfortable lying like that?" asked Lora. "Move over a little closer here. Now hold the thermometer, and then I'll bring tea. Give me the hot water bottle."

Lora went out. Dmitriev sat down on the chair.

"Yes, Vitya! It's good that you came," said Xenia Fyodorovna. "Lora and I were arguing today. About that chocolate bar. See the drawing from your childhood? Over there on the windowsill. Lorochka found it in the green cupboard. I think you drew it in the summer of '39 or '40, but Lorochka says it was after the war. When that one was living there, what was his name? Well? Such an unpleasant guy, with the eastern name. I forget, tell me yourself."

Dmitriev didn't remember. He also didn't remember the drawing. Everything connected with his art work was cut out forever. But his mother cherished these memories, and for that reason he said: yes, '39 or '40. After the war the ornamental fence was no longer in existence because they'd burned it. Xenia Fyodorovna asked about Dmitriev's business trip, and he said that as it happened, today it had been decided that he wasn't going.

Xenia Fyodorovna stopped smiling.

"I hope it wasn't because of my illness?"

"No, they just put it off. What does your illness have to do with it?"

"Vitya, I don't want even the most minor of your affairs to be upset. Because business before everything. For what? All old ladies are sick, that's their profession. We lie around a bit, groan a bit, get up on our legs, but you lose precious time and wreck your job. No, that's not the way. For example, what's tormenting me now..." —she lowered her voice—"is Lorochka. She lies to me without compunction, says that it's not necessary to go this year; Felix hems and haws, answers evasively. And I know what's going on with them! Why do they do that? Am I really a helpless old lady that can't be left alone? Nothing of the sort! Of course there may be relapses like today, even strong pain, I'll admit, because the process works slowly, but in principle I'm getting better. And I'll get better alone beautifully. Aunt Pasha will come. You're near, there's a telephone—Lord, what problems are there? There is Marinka, of course, there is Valeriya Kuzminichna, who gladly...."—she became silent because Lora came into the room with the tea.

"Mama, don't get excited," said Lora. "Let Vitka talk and you listen. Why are you so excited?"

"Certain people make me indignant when they don't tell the truth."

"Ah! Well. Give me the thermometer....." Lora took the thermometer. "Normal. Vitka, don't make Mother get excited, you hear? Or I'll chase you out. And come have supper in ten minutes."

When Lora left, Xenia Fyodorovna began to whisper about the same thing again: how to fix it so that old people could be sick quietly, and then nothing would get disturbed with the children. As always, his mother spoke half-jokingly, half-seriously. Dmitriev began to get a little annoyed. Why talk about it so much? These were pointless conversations. You couldn't change anything anyway. Then Dmitriev was called to the phone. Lena was asking if he was coming home, or if he was going to spend the night at Pavlinovo. It was already after eleven. Dmitriev said he'd stay there. Lena instructed him to give warm greetings to Xenia Fyodorovna, and asked if he'd taken the key. He answered "Good night"—and hung up the receiver.

This applied only to him. He alone could decide: to ask for the key or not to. About an hour and a half before bedtime, he seized a minute when Xenia Fyodorovna was alone and said:

"There's still one other possibility: we could make an exchange, settle with you all in one apartment—then Lora would also be independent...."

"Make an exchange with you?"

"No, not with me, but with someone else, so you could live with me."

"Ach, that? Well, of course I understand. I wanted to live with you and Natashenka very much. Xenia Fyodorovna became silent. "But now—no."

"Why?"

"I don't know. I haven't had the desire to for a long time."

He was silent, stunned.

Xenia Fyodorovna looked at him calmly, and closed her eyes. It looked as if she were going to sleep. Then she said:

"You made an exchange, Vitya. The exchange has taken place...." Again silence fell. With eyes closed, she whispered some gibberish: "It was a long time ago. And it always happens, every day, so don't be surprised, Vitya. And don't be angry. Just like that, unnoticeably...."

After sitting there a while he got up and left on tiptoe.

Dmitriev went to be in the room in which he'd lived with Lena at one time, that first summer. As before, the carpet hung there on the wall, nailed up by Lena. But the beautiful green wallpaper with the embossed pattern had noticeably faded and grown worn. Falling asleep, Dmitriev thought about his old watercolor: a bit of garden, a fence, the porch of the dacha and the dog Nelda on the porch. The dog had looked like a sheep. How could Lora have forgotten that after the war there was no Nelda? After the war he'd drawn like mad. Was never separated from his sketch pad. The pen-and-ink things came out especially well. If only he hadn't failed the exam, and hadn't thrown himself in his misery into the first thing that came along, no matter what—chemical, oil, the food industry.... Then he began to think about Golishmanovo. He saw the room in the barracks where he'd lived last year for a month and a half. And he thought of how Tanya would have been the best wife for him. Once in the middle of the night he awoke and heard Felix and Lora talking in undertones.

In the morning Dmitriev left early while Xenia Fyodorovna was still sleeping. He gave Lora the hundred rubles. Lora said it was most welcome. They had breakfast in a hurry and he ran to the trolley. It was a dark dawn. The night rain ran off the trees in the garden. At the stop there were two men standing slightly apart, and a big German shepherd sitting on the ground. Who he belonged to was unclear. The empty trolley stopped, they all got in, and after everyone else the shepherd unexpectedly jumped in. The dog was big-bellied, it jumped heavily and sat down on the floor near the ticket dispenser. Two people, frightened, went up ahead, but Dmitriev stayed there in indecision. The shepherd looked out the window. It needed something in the trolley. Dmitriev thought that the driver perhaps might take it far away and it would get lost. After all, no one would understand what it was doing and why it was on the trolley. At the next stop, when people were dashing from the door, Dmitriev got out and called: "Come out, come out!"—and the dog jumped down obediently and sat on the ground. And Dmitriev managed to jump back on. Through the glass of the departing trolley he saw the dog, who was looking at him.

Xenia Fyodorovna called Dmitriev at work two days later and said that she agreed to move in together, but that all she asked was that it be fast.

The whole drag started. The Markusheviches, of course, passed it up, many others did too, and then there appeared an expert on the sport of biking and everything was accomplished with him in the middle of April. Xenia Fyodorovna wasn't so bad. They even had a housewarming, relatives came, the only ones that weren't there were Lora and Felix, who hadn't returned yet from their Kunya, where, as usual, they were sticking around until the big summer heat started. But their troubles didn't end there: they still had to transfer both personal accounts to the name of Dmitriev, which turned out to be no less burdensome than the exchange. First the executive committee refused because the claim hadn't been correctly composed and some papers were lacking. The old geezer, Spiridon Samoilovich, the agent, who'd always boasted that the jurist of the regional housing section was his close acquaintance, turned out to be a plain liar. The jurist didn't even say hello to him when they ran into each other face to face. But this jurist was the major screw in the matter, because the claimants aren't summoned to the meeting, and the decision is only carried out on the basis of the jurist's conclusions and the presented documents. At the end of July, Xenia Fyodorovna took a sharp turn for the worse, and they took her to the same hospital which she'd been in almost a year before. Lena managed to get a second hearing of the claim. This time the jurist was inclined properly and all the documents were in order: (a) the document affirming family relations, i.e., witness about Dmitriev's birth; (b) a copy of the orders given out at one time for the right to occupy floor space; (c) extracts from the building records; (d) copies of the financial personal accounts given to ZHEK in which the OZHK[12] requested that the executive committee satisfy the request that the personal accounts be united. Well, this time the decision was favorable.

After Xenia Fyodorovna's death, Dmitriev had a high blood pressure crisis, and he spent three weeks in the hospital strictly confined to his bed.

What could I say to Dmitriev when we once met at mutual friends' and he related all this to me? He didn't look too well. He'd somehow gotten older all at once, had turned gray. Not yet an old man, but already middle-aged, with the flabby cheeks of an old uncle. I can remember him still a boy at the Pavlinovo dachas. Then he'd been a fat boy. We called him Vituchni. He's three years younger than I and in those days I was closer to Lora than to him. Not long ago they took away the Dmitriev dacha as well as all the surrounding dachas, and built the Stormy Petrel Stadium, and Lora and her Felix moved to Zyuzino, into a nine-story building.

1969

Translated by Ellendea Proffer

THE LONG GOODBYE

I

In those days, about eighteen years ago, the spot where the butcher shop now stands was covered with lilac bushes. There was a yellow country fence (the area was in fact full of dachas, and the residents here felt as if they were living in the countryside), and behind this wooden fence the lilac bushes clustered. Unable to confine themselves to the limits of the fence, the luxuriant branches overflowed into the street in a burst of riotous growth. However much passersby might grab hold of them, pinch them, pull them or break them, the branches still managed to preserve their full, rounded contours and every spring would astonish this dusty, narrow street with their blossoms and fragrance. When the lilacs were in full bloom and one saw them from a distance, their blossoms clustering one upon another in patches of white and mauve, they reminded one of an old city at twilight—a southern, seaport city, where the streets are cut into the cliffs and the houses are stuck one on top of another; a city with monasteries and winding stone steps, where old ladies sit in the shade, selling small boxes encrusted with seashells.

But of course this was all a long time ago. Today in the spot where the lilacs stood, there is an eight-story apartment building with a butcher shop on the ground level. At that time, in the days of the lilac bushes, the people who lived in the small house behind the yellow wooden fence had to travel a long way for meat—by streetcar to Vagankovsky Market. Today they would be able to buy their meat much more conveniently. But today, unfortunately, they no longer live there.

Things were pretty miserable when the company first arrived in Saratov. They were lodged in a bad hotel, the heat didn't let up, and no one came to the theater. Everything seemed to go wrong: the actors began getting sick, and Sergei Leonidovich, who couldn't stand either hot weather or bad hotels, took off for Moscow, leaving Smurny in charge. Smurny had joined the theater two years ago and right away had started giving Lyalya the eye. She had rejected his advances without hesitation since it was rumored that he was scheming against Sergei Leonidovich, trying to take his place. This struck Lyalya as despicable and mean, and she couldn't stand mean people. True, she didn't know exactly how he was scheming against Sergei Leonidovich or to what lengths he would be willing to go, but people said that something underhanded was going on, and with some special instinct which she had learned to rely on, Lyalya believed the rumors. Smurny was extremely polite. He had a fair complexion, languid, caressing eyes, and the provincial manner of throwing back the hair from his forehead with a proud, sharp movement of his head. In this connection, Sergei Leonidovich once gave a humorous imitation of a scene he had observed by accident. Smurny had proceeded through the empty lounge at his usual brisk, energetic pace, suddenly stopped and examined himself in the mirror, and then threw back his head with such an air of haughty satisfaction that Sergei Leonidovich was, as he himself admitted, quite taken aback. Sergei Leonidovich's imitations were always killing. He didn't have to say a thing—the personality was rendered in seconds, just by his facial expressions and gestures.

Smurny, of course, was not about to forget that Lyalya had rejected him and soon began getting even with her by giving her a hard time professionally, holding her back in any way he could. At the same time, however, he continued to put out feelers, to see if she might still come around. He had directed two plays on his own when Sergei Leonidovich was sick, and both had been flops. One had dragged on for half a season, the other even less. But this was beside the point. The point was that he hadn't given Lyalya a part in either of them. One of the roles had been perfect for her and everyone in the theater knew it. Nonetheless he somehow managed not to give the part to her. Instead he gave it to one of the promising graduates of their theatrical studio. The whole thing was perfectly obvious, and even Lyalya's girlfriends began saying to her, "Why are you being so stubborn? The man's pride is hurt, give in to him just for the hell of it. After all, you've nothing to lose." But it was as if something had jammed inside of Lyalya. She couldn't even bring herself to sit next to him in the cafeteria, much less "give in" to him.

Something like this had happened once before in her life. The war was just over, Lyalya was eighteen, and a happy group had gathered at

Allochka Schlaefer's place on Putnikovsky Lane. Some of the guests had just come back from the front, some from the hospital, and others had recently been evacuated from such faraway places as Kamyshlov and Namangan. Everything was starting up anew: hopes, songs, the youthful urge to live life to its fullest, feelings of love and sympathy for everyone who had returned, long evening strolls through Moscow, and lingering farewells in doorways. Then suddenly there appeared in their midst one young man who was thirty years old, with prematurely gray hair and light eyes as clear as crystal. He didn't ask, he didn't beg, because everyone came to him without his having to ask. He said that he was organizing a theater studio called *The Blue Ark*. Lyalya was dying to get into this studio because she had already decided that life without the theater would have no meaning for her. The studio venture fell through, of course, but she and her friends had believed in it for a long time. At this time Yasha and Lazik were the men in her life. She was torn between them since she felt sorry for both of them. Yasha had come into her life first, in 1943, when he had just been released from the hospital. The rest of his family had perished somewhere outside of Minsk. He was twelve years older than she, an outstanding mathematician, but as awkward and helpless as a child. Lazik was a poet and walked with a limp, having lost one leg at the Leningrad front. He wrote songs and sang beautifully, accompanying himself on the guitar. But the young man with the gray brush-cut and clear eyes was a completely different story: her whole future depended on him. Lyalya didn't know how to behave in his presence. Then came that particular Saturday when some twenty young people had crowded into Allochka's enormous, empty apartment (her parents were off fulfilling some important state function in newly occupied Germany), and all of a sudden he had led her into the hallway and said in a commanding voice that they should go to his place right now so that he could give her the book that he'd promised her a long time ago. Lyalya was unable to utter a single word and began to tremble. And she trembled imperceptibly in the streetcar, all the way to his place, and even had to clench her teeth to prevent them from chattering. It wasn't that she was afraid of anything, she wasn't trembling from fear. What kept pounding through her head was her dream of *The Blue Ark*. Up till now he had never spoken to Lyalya about anything. He had not, it seemed, even noticed her. Nor had there ever been any talk about a book. As soon as they entered his apartment and before the light had been turned on or Lyalya had even taken off her coat, he grabbed her by the shoulders and almost knocked her over as his mouth sought hers in the dark. He kissed her so roughly and possessively that she was stirred to anger and began pushing him away. He wouldn't let go and kept dragging her farther inside. As they struggled in the dark, she punched him in the face, apparently quite hard, because he cried out in pain. At this point she managed to escape.

For two whole days she stayed upstairs in her attic room, telling her parents that she was sick, when in fact she was crying because her life was over, because dreams don't come true, and because people can't be trusted. On the third day she left the house, walked to the Sokol subway station, and bought some ice cream. Ice cream was something new, a prewar delight which was just beginning to reappear, though at high, free-market prices. But this meant that rationing would soon be ended, that former joys were close at hand, and new ones not far off. And now, just from eating this ice cream, she regained her inner calm. As was usually the case, it had come unexpectedly, and from the most trifling of causes. Suddenly she no longer regretted the fact that *The Blue Ark* had fallen through, that she had punched an older man in the face, or that she would never go to Allochka Schlaefer's place again. And remembering and reflecting on what had happened, she discovered something new about herself. It occurred to her that the most frightening and unbearable thing in this world is dependence. When you're dependent, that's the end, a blind alley, something you can't get around. After all, when she was riding on the streetcar, trying with all her might to suppress her trembling, she already knew what was going to happen and why she was going there. She had to make a decision. And right then and there, on the streetcar, she realized: no! She had made a lot of mistakes in her short life, but they had all been mistakes of feeling rather than of calculation. She accidentally ran into this man three years later at the home of one of Grisha's friends, and both he and she pretended that they had never met before.

And Smurny too, who had the same crystal-clear eyes as this first man, appealed to many, especially to younger women, of whom there is always a surplus after a long war. Smurny's influence in the theater grew with every passing month, all the more so since Sergei Leonidovich wasn't well and was often absent for long periods at a time. It was common knowledge that Smurny had separated from his wife, very nobly leaving her their big apartment and taking with him only a pair of underwear and a typewriter (query: what did he need with the typewriter?). It was also known that he lived alone in a modest, one-room apartment near Krasnye Vorota. He was thirty-eight—an ideal age for a man—and it was clear to everyone that before very long he would have everything he wanted, all of life's blessings. Lyalya, in the meantime, languished in second-rate roles and seemed to be stuck there. After her initial rebuffs Smurny had soon stopped looking in her direction, and when he took over for Sergei Leonidovich in Saratov, he put her in the worst room on the ground floor, together with the makeup woman.

In Saratov they were performing a play staged by Sergei Leonidovich that spring, in which Lyalya had only a walk-on role—two appearances onstage and some twenty-five words. It was a boring production, not through any fault of Sergei Leonidovich, but because of the play itself—some sort of dull fare about forest conservation. They had staged it because of its theme. The newspapers praised it, but theater attendance had been poor. The Saratov papers were especially enthusiastic about the play because its author—a new and relatively unknown playwright—was a native son. Actually, the playwright lived in Moscow, but he had spent his childhood and youth in Saratov. And now that the company was here on tour, he had returned to his native city and was staying with his mother and his mentally retarded young daughter. And on a hot July day—a Monday, when there were no performances—he had invited all the actors connected with the play to come to his home for supper.

The day got off to a bad start. That morning Smurny ran into Lyalya in the hotel corridor and without even saying good morning—which seemed strange, since he was normally very polite—he asked her to come to his hotel room for a talk.

"Just for five minutes!" he said, thrusting the open fingers of one hand somewhat foolishly before Lyalya's face.

Smurny's room—the best in the hotel—was classified as "family deluxe." It had curtains of raspberry-colored velour, and a cloth of the same material covered the oval table in the center of the room, on which there stood a carafe of water. There was an alcove, also draped with raspberry-colored velour, and in its depths something loomed large and white. At the moment, the room stank of cigarette butts and inexpensive eau de cologne. Lyalya took a seat by the oval table as Smurny disappeared into the alcove, only to reappear seconds later with a piece of paper in his hand.

"Take a look at this. It arrived yesterday from Moscow. It was forwarded from the Ministry to our Moscow address, and they forwarded it to me here."

Lyalya saw several sheets of paper covered with writing and was horrified to recognize a familiar hand. It was a letter from her mother!

Here it was, the very worst—the thing Lyalya had always been most afraid of: her mother out to get justice. Good Lord, how many times had she told her, beseeched her, gotten down on her knees and begged her not to interfere, not to write any letters of complaint.

But letter writing was her mother's favorite occupation. At one time she used to write to the principal of Lyalya's school, demanding that her letters be discussed at the parents' council meeting. She had also written letters to the District Office of Education. Then, later on, when Lyalya wasn't accepted into drama school, she had written to the Ministry. Even at home, when she was angry at someone, she would use letters as a means of clarification. And quite often Lyalya would wake up to find two or three sheets of paper lying on her table. Sometimes there would be even more—a whole school notebook covered with large, run-together sentences without any punctuation: "Lyudmila you should know that when you borrow something from someone you should return it without waiting to be asked that's very inconsiderate you took my black fur shawl...."

Stifling a groan, Lyalya took the handwritten sheets obviously torn from her father's big ledger and began quickly reading through them, skipping every other line. She didn't have the strength to read slowly, pausing over every word. "As the mother of a young actress, I am writing to... Even in her school dramatics club, which was directed by a distinguished actor... She's already been a member of the theater for six years... Is it possible that our young actors and actresses are supposed to ... How long is this tyranny of directors going to..."

"Well, what can I say, Herman Vladimirovich?" Lyalya threw down the sheets of paper and gave a despairing glance at Smurny who was leaning over the table and looking down at her with a stiff smile on his face. "This was written by my mother. You must realize that I can't be responsible for what she does—especially since she's a sick woman."

"A sick woman? You'd never guess it from her letter. It's quite coherent, and she makes serious accusations, though of course they're unsubstantiated and only so much slander. But the letter is cleverly written and she makes certain insinuations between the lines. A sick person wouldn't be capable of that."

"What do you mean, between the lines?"

"Well, right here!" he said, pointing with his finger. "Here's a juicy spot."

Lyalya read the line which she had skipped in her first reading: "...she did not respond to his advances, and so he took his revenge. In both of the plays which he directed, she was not..." Oh-oh! Why did she have to bring that up? My God, why, why that? And now Lyalya couldn't bring herself to look up at Smurny. As the seconds passed, she moved her lips, pretending that she was having trouble deciphering her mother's handwriting.

Smurny waited patiently, then finally said, "Well? I'd like to hear what..."

"Well, what can I say?"

Lyalya looked up at him. He wasn't smiling. His eyes were leaden and stern, and his lips were pursed.

"What can you say? You can tell me the meaning of all this rambling! What revenge? What's this nonsense all about?"

"I don't know, Herman Vladimirovich, I really don't...."

And suddenly, unable to restrain herself, she burst out laughing. It was all such pathetic nonsense. Did she really have to spell it out for him? And that face of his—crimson and trembling with rage. Granted, her mother had behaved foolishly, but what she had written was the truth, after all. He knew that it was the truth, and yet there he was, gazing at her with dull eyes and demanding—my God, what was it he wanted from her?—that she, Lyalya, should feel shame for her mother, that she should die of shame, so that he in some small way would be compensated for the unpleasantness he had experienced, receiving such a letter forwarded from the Ministry.

But now it no longer mattered what she did, so why should she feel shame for her mother? Why be ashamed of an unhappy woman who tormented herself and was unable to sleep at night because of her daughter's problems, a woman who tried as best she could to.... Yes, and after all, the point was—the real point was that she had written the truth! Everything she had written was true, from start to finish.

And now, completely calm, Lyalya began to explain all this to Smurny. Her mother was, of course, no diplomat, she had acted foolishly—and for this she would get a good scolding—but she was right in some of the things she said. Right in what? What are you talking about? Well, about that, about that. You know perfectly well what I'm talking about! You seem to be terribly sure of yourself! It's just that I have nothing to lose. No, my dear, you have plenty to lose. You don't frighten me, Herman Vladimirovich. Even a job with the Moscow Variety Theater or on the radio would be better than working here, under your wing. Don't think it's going to be so easy to find a job, especially for someone like you without any professional degree. Don't worry, I'll always be able to earn my 650 a month,[1] and even more. Well, fine, I'm not really interested in your personal plans. But as for

this concoction of your mother's, we're going to send this on to Sergei
Leonidovich today and see how he swallows it. The higher-ups demand
an answer. Well, it's all the same to me, do as you please. Well then, the
matter is settled. Goodbye. All the best. And by the way, Herman
Vladimirovich, you really should air out your room. There's some sort
of bad smell here.

Lyalya ran from Smurny's room out onto the street. She wandered
around the square for a while, mechanically getting into line for something or other. Then she returned to the hotel, went to her room, and
lay down. Her heart was pounding, and all of the just and nasty things
that she had left unsaid came rushing to mind. And why should
Milyutina, who was completely new in the theater?...—and so forth and
so on. But she wasn't going to harbor any ill will against Zhenka
Milyutina—poor thing, with a child to bring up all on her own. But what
a beast that Smurny was: "without any professional degree!" This was
the second time he had shoved that in her face. One could have a degree and still be a fool. There were plenty of examples of that around!
One is born an actor, it's not something that can be taught, idiot! She
had been accepted into the company at the personal request of Sergei
Leonidovich, and he certainly knew a lot more than someone like
Smurny. But that wasn't what bothered her. What bothered her was the
shame she felt for her mother. No, not for her mother but for herself.
She felt unbearable shame for herself. That much he had succeeded in
doing: he had made her burn with shame. And to tell the truth, that
was what she felt like doing now. She would simply stretch out, grit her
teeth, close her eyes, and lie there motionless, burning with shame. Oh,
to disintegrate and disappear. For her, life in the theater would become a nightmare. Sergei Leonidovich would bawl her out, and the actors would laugh and make nasty jokes at her expense when they found
out, which they were sure to do, Smurny would see to that. And eventually she would leave the company. But that was impossible, she didn't
have anywhere to go. If only Grisha had made some progress with his
career, she might be able to risk it.... But as things were now—how
could she? Where was she going to earn her 650 a month? And as always after she had received a slap in the face (she had received a good
many such slaps in her life, and each year they became more painful),
after the hurt and silent despair, after the hasty and confused consider-
ations as to what to do next and how to protest, suddenly she would be
overtaken by doubts. And these doubts were the worst of all—the thing
that nearly killed her. What if they're right? What if I really have no talent? And they all see it, they all realize it. Sergei Leonidovich takes pity

on me because of our old friendship, but Smurny has no reason to."

Depressed by such frightening thoughts, Lyalya lay for a long time without moving in the empty room. The makeup woman had gone off somewhere, so there was no one with whom to share her thoughts. Suddenly a cry from the corridor delivered her from her gloomy paralysis: "Telepneva, you have a phone call!" It was Monday. And her mother always called on Mondays when there were no performances.

It was a good connection and her mother's voice was as clear as a bell: "Lyalya, darling! How are you? What's new?"

The telephone was in the hotel lobby, and there were all sorts of people milling about. Pasha Kornilovich and Makeyev crossed the lobby with shopping bags in their hands, probably headed for the outdoor market. As he passed by, Pasha slapped Lyalya's behind, ruffling her skirt in the process. That wretch, he was always slapping her! And now, despite the fact that she was upset and already deep in conversation, Lyalya put her hand over the receiver and shouted, "Come back here and straighten it, come back and straighten it this minute!"

Pasha obediently ran back and straightened her skirt. She didn't want her admirers to lose interest, not now.

Here in public she obviously couldn't tell her mother what was seething inside her, so she asked instead about her father's health. Her mother reported that he was feeling well and was continuing to make efforts to save his garden, though there was no progress as yet. Grisha was staying on Bashilov Street and a few days ago had brought them some vegetables at her request. The potatoes, of course, had been a mistake. They were small and expensive—right now young potatoes cost 3.5 rubles a kilogram everywhere—and he had made a foolish purchase. He'd set off early in the day and had paid 4 rubles for them.

This talk about potatoes put Lyalya slightly on edge, for there was a hint here of her mother's usual dissatisfaction with her son-in-law. And now with a certain irritation she interrupted her mother, saying that the price of potatoes didn't interest her; what did interest her was Grisha's work—had he received an answer from the film studio? Her mother seemed to be waiting for just such a question, since she now replied in an aggressively complaining tone, "You ought to know by now that your Grisha never tells us anything about his work!"

Normally Lyalya wouldn't have paid any attention to such a remark, considering it merely normal. But on this occasion, when she could barely keep from screaming at her mother, she simply could not keep quiet and replied in an equally aggressive tone, "But you could at least express an interest, couldn't you? You know how important this is for us."

"I don't like to interfere in other people's business."

"Oh yes, you do!" Lyalya burst out. "You do so!"

And no longer able to restrain herself, she blurted it all out: how she had asked her a hundred times not to do this, had begged her, reasoned with her, and now to have it happen here—how stubborn and mean did she have to be? Now there'd be a scandal. Well, okay, there was no point in discussing it, what was done couldn't be undone, but things had turned out very badly.

Her mother, not understanding, sputtered at the other end of the line, "What is it? Speak more clearly!"

"I'm talking about your verses!"

"What verses?"

"The ones you like to jot down and send off in every direction!"

"Good heavens, why that was... when was that? Four months ago."

The conversation was pointless, and Lyalya said in a weak voice, "Well okay, Mother, goodbye." And she hung up the receiver.

The elderly actress Almazova was on her way to the boiler for some hot water for tea. But she had loitered in the lobby with her ears pricked up, and when Lyalya hung up the receiver, she was briefly aware of the old woman's avid glance. Either she had overheard Lyalya's conversation and guessed what it was all about, or else Smurny had already begun to spread rumors. In any case, that evening when they were visiting the playwright, one of the other actresses whispered anxiously in Lyalya's ear, "Is it true what they're saying about your having written some sort of complaint against our directors?"

Lyalya's mood was such that it would have been better not to have gone to this supper at all. She had hesitated, but then had decided that anything was better than staying alone in her room. That would be just too depressing. And it was a free meal, after all. She'd be able to drink a little wine and improve her mood. But in this large room where they were packed together like sardines, she found it distressing to see Smurny's smug face before her at the head of the table. It was irritating to watch him throw back the hair from his eyes—his eyes now carefully avoiding hers—and to listen to the silly toasts, jokes, and mutual eggings on. Equally revolting was the way in which the actors—especially Pashka Kornilovich and Makeyev in their usual vulgar fashion, and Smurny too, though somewhat more subtly—teased the poor author, actually ridiculing him. The author didn't understand their jokes, or at least not all of them, and would make feeble attempts to joke back. His elderly mother, who was intimidated by the group, would either sigh or mumble words of thanks. The guests kept roaring with laughter at their own jokes, all of which seemed to turn on the subject of food.

"Hey, Pash, the cabbage pie's gone bad, don't you think?"

"No, I don't your excellency. But the mushrooms, I dare say, are not quite right."

"What do you mean, not quite right? Why didn't you speak up sooner? I've already tossed down two platefuls of them!"

"A mushroom in the stomach is not a permanent guest, your excellency. An autopsy will show that...."

Such was the style of their repartee, which the actors obviously found amusing. And laughing themselves to tears, they sat there drinking, munching, and gulping. Suddenly someone jumped up and exclaimed fervently, "Dear Nikolai Demyanovich! Thank you for every line that you've written! Thank you for your very existence!"

They applauded and shouted "hurrah." Poor Smolyanov sat there embarrassed, his face drained of color, just as it had been that spring, at the time of the play's premiere. Not knowing whether to thank them or to respond with a joke, he merely smiled and nodded mutely.

"Nikolai Demyanovich!" shouted Makeyev. "You've completely talked our heads off! You don't give anybody else a chance to open his mouth!"

Once again they roared with laughter and Smolyanov nodded and smiled.

Lyalya found all of this very distasteful. She didn't like it when people made jokes at others' expense. Well, so what if it was a weak play and he was no Shakespeare? Perhaps he was a good man. He had invited them with an open heart and he had squandered some 3,000 rubles on them. And they had all come, after all, they hadn't declined. Smurny had come too, even though Lyalya herself had once heard him abusing Smolyanov in the director's office, calling his play sycophantic. (Lyalya hadn't known the meaning of the word *sycophantic* and had had to check on it afterwards.) And Bob Mironovich was here, hovering around the meat pies and vodka, even though he had openly spoken out against Smolyanov's play at meetings of the theater council, had quarreled with the executive director over the matter, and had tried to persuade Sergei Leonidovich to reject the play. All of them, all of the secret critics and scoffers were here. They had all come running for free drinks and a free meal. Ah, the unfortunate lot of the actor! Eat, drink, and be merry. My God, what a revolting spectacle! One felt sorry for them, poor things, and at the same time one couldn't help laughing at them. They were like children. They played, made lots of noise, amused themselves over trifles, and at the same time they could be cruel and destructive—just like children.

And now, not wanting to be outdone by the others, the pathetic little actor Ivan Vasilievich Yeroshkin suddenly stood up and added, "Dear author, allow me to raise my glass and express the hope that you will honor us many, many times in the future with your splendid... (pause) cabbage pies!" This was followed by shouts of "hurrah" and "bravo." Unable to look at the author's tormented face any longer, Lyalya went into the next room and began to help Smolyanov's mother, Yevdokia Nilovna, prepare the table for tea and dessert.

The poor old lady was wearing herself out. Lyalya had been drawn to her the moment she saw her, because she was like her grandmother—just as bustling and eager to please. Her grandmother had died two years ago in Izmailov, where she had continued to live in grandfather's old house.

"Oh, don't put out the pies," Lyalya whispered to the old lady. "The cookies will be enough!"

"I shouldn't put them out?" the old lady asked apprehensively.

"Oh, don't worry about the guests. They'll get along without them." She felt sorry for all the trouble Yevdokia Nilovna was going to. In only half an hour they had polished off two dishes of meat pilaf and an enormous plate of meat pies.

A little later Lyalya made her way up the creaking staircase to the second floor. The old lady was taking her up to meet Smolyanov's retarded young daughter. And now Lyalya was surprised once again. At home in Moscow she had just such a small attic room, in which she had spent her childhood and youth and where she now lived with Grisha. Smolyanov's daughter was thirteen years old. She was plump and well developed, with a full bosom like that of a grown girl, but her face was sheeplike and she gazed at them with an empty, mindless look. It was obvious that Yevdokia Nilovna loved her Galochka. She immediately spoke to her in a soft, gentle voice and began straightening her socks, fastening the buckle on her shoe. All the while the young girl continued to rock back and forth in her rocking chair as she played with a rubber ball fastened to a piece of elastic. After straightening her granddaughter's clothes, Yevdokia Nilovna gave her a piece of pie on a plate and a cup of tea. Galochka didn't want the tea and pushed it away with her hand, but she ate the pie. She refused to let go of her ball as she ate, and kept bouncing it on the floor.

"And I was wondering who that was, banging upstairs," said Lyalya.

"Bouncedy-bounce," said the old lady affectionately. "That's our

Galochka going bouncedy-bouncedy-bounce...." Then she whispered in Lyalya's ear, "She keeps bouncing like this all day long. It's sad, terribly sad...."

Downstairs in the front room they had begun to sing. Someone was starting to do a Russian dance, and the others were making a lot of noise as they moved the furniture. Lyalya felt a sudden, strong desire to go home, to see her father and Grisha! To go out into the garden. And now she remembered that at home they would sometimes sing and dance like this. Some of her Moscow relatives would get together—Uncle Kolya, Aunt Zhenya with the children and Uncle Misha. At other times her father's relatives would descend on them from the Urals. Someone would strike up a song, and later on, when Lyalya tired of it all, she would run upstairs to her room and start reading a book. And downstairs the noise and dancing would continue.

The little girl kept throwing her ball, not looking at Lyalya and apparently not noticing her presence at all. The old lady informed her in a whisper that Galochka was the daughter of Nikolai Demyanovich's first wife, who had died. She had grieved terribly over her daughter, whereas Marta, his second wife, was a self-centered woman who didn't even want to meet Galochka or to see her, Yevdokia Nilovna. She had no intention of coming here for a visit, nor did she ever write to them. She even forbade Nikolai Demyanovich to visit them. Send them money, she would say, and nothing more. And what did he send? To tell the truth, it wasn't a very large sum—400 rubles a month. And it was only when he and Marta had been quarreling that he would come and visit them—every once in a great while. Mama, he would say, she's not at all the right woman for me, she's unstable and unpredictable, but I do love her, and she helps me in my work.

Lyalya listened to the old lady, sympathized with her, and as she looked at the dull, sheeplike face of the girl, it occurred to her: "There's some sort of misfortune in everyone's life. He's a playwright, after all, a successful one...." And the very thought that everyone had some such misfortune and that there were even worse ones than this, made her own troubles seem lighter and more bearable.

An hour later Smurny put in a call for their special bus and the guests began making preparations to leave. Ivan Vasilievich Yeroshkin, who had succeeded in behaving outrageously, had to be dragged out by the heels, and it was midnight when they finally departed. Lyalya felt sorry for the old lady, however, and stayed behind to help with the dishes. The bus driver promised to return for her in half an hour, but for some reason he never showed up.

Clad in a T-shirt and pajama bottoms, Smolyanov hummed as he passed from room to room, dragging furniture along the floor, putting it back in place, and bringing the dirty dishes out to the kitchen. Every now and then he would approach the sideboard and take a nip of vodka. Lyalya thought that he must be about ready to collapse, but he kept going, gazing at her with kindly blue eyes through his round-framed spectacles and smiling deferentially, like a waiter. He was obviously happy that the guests had left and that it was all over with.

Lyalya kept hoping that he would drop in his tracks and begin to snore, as one expects of a man who has had too much to drink and as had always been the case with her father and with Uncle Misha and Uncle Kolya. And with Grisha too, who would sometimes fall asleep and start snoring at the table, even when they had guests. But apparently the playwright was made of stronger stuff. He had an athlete's broad back, and tattooed above the elbow of his left arm was a mermaid and two names. When Lyalya caught sight of the mermaid, she began to feel uneasy. It occurred to her that right here and now in the middle of the night, in this house where there was no one but an old woman and a retarded child, this playwright might turn out to be no playwright at all, but merely a normal male who in his drunken state might try something. But Smolyanov apparently wasn't thinking of trying anything.

Nor did he even seem to realize that a young woman was spending the night in his house—for, after all, where was she to go at 2 a.m.? Suddenly he took her hand, pecked at it with moist lips—just as he had done onstage back then, on the day of the premiere—and mumbled in a low, tearful voice, "Forgive me, my dear... don't be angry with me, okay?"

"I'm not at all angry with you, Nikolai Demyanovich," said Lyalya, though at the same time carefully removing her hand just to be on the safe side.

"I'm nobody important, nobody worth mentioning—I know my own worth," muttered Smolyanov. "I'm nobody like your... but damn it all, what sort of man am I?... But all of them are nobodies too.... Only, please don't be mad at me, okay? My dear, kind..." and once again he tried to peck at her hand.

Lyalya began to feel nervous and called out loudly, "Yevdokia Nilovna!"

Smolyanov slumped over the table and suddenly began to cry. Then he took off his glasses and began wiping his eyes with the palm of his hand.

Since she had no place to go, Lyalya lay down on the sofa, covering herself with her coat. But she was upset and felt so terribly awkward about the whole situation that she couldn't fall asleep. Somehow she felt herself guilty for all of this—for Pashka and all the others who had played the fool. Why on earth did they have to insult this man? Such a strong, broad-shouldered, broad-chested man, not at all old, though he did already have a bald spot.... And why was he crying, why should he be unhappy? After all, he must be wealthy. No, wealth doesn't make you happy. Something else was needed for happiness, something essential. And at this thought a vague feeling of happiness, a feeling of her own good fortune, came over Lyalya. For it seemed to her that she possessed that mysterious something which was necessary for happiness. She couldn't quite explain what it was, but she knew for certain that she had it. And the reason she knew this was that when other people were unhappy, she always felt sorry and wanted to make things easier for them—to share something with them. And the fact that she always felt this desire to share with others meant, of course, that she had something to share. Sometimes she thought that this desire arose from the fact that she had no children. But probing deeper, she realized that having children would not lessen her desire to share with others this essential something that was necessary for happiness. For her own children would merely be an extension of herself.

And growing all the more anxious, Lyalya asked the playwright if he wouldn't like her to make some strong coffee. He said he would, and Lyalya went out to the kitchen, emerging a few minutes later with a cup for each of them. After the coffee—by now it was two-thirty—neither of them felt like sleeping. Smolyanov had sobered up and began telling her about his life—how difficult it was and how difficult he found it to write. He had no friends—people didn't trust him, and things hadn't worked out in his personal life. He had come to Moscow four years ago, having worked in the provinces until then. He had been a newspaper reporter at the front during the war, and before that, in the thirties, an Arctic explorer, spending his winters in Dikson. He had served as a border guard and as a police detective, and had also worked in various physical education departments, having previously trained as a boxer. At the Kalach railroad station he had once shot and killed a bandit with his own hand. And now this was already his third play—the other two had been performed in the provinces—but he was lacking in education; he'd had to do everything on his own, by sheer grit. And that past winter he'd had such a tough time getting *Distant Forests* accepted in Moscow that his strength had almost given out. They'd wanted to throttle him—they'd already prepared the noose—but things hadn't worked out according to their expectations. He knew now what vile people there were in this world—and in her beloved theater too, oh yes! And suddenly he burst out laughing: so, you don't want anything to do with my cabbage pies, eh? Well, never mind, my friends. Someday you'll beg for them, someday you'll come crawling on your knees for them. Dear Nikolai Demyanovich, please give us one of your cabbage pies! Lyalya listened with avid interest and was suddenly struck by the thought: he's probably right, that's probably just what will happen. In the meantime they were throwing his lack of education in his face, using this against him. She could just picture them all coming after him, bearing down on him with a noose and he, this rugged specimen, letting them have it with a right hook.

It was growing light and the roosters had already begun to crow. Smolyanov and Lyalya went out into the yard and descended along a path through some underbrush where they caught the fusty scent of nettles. Then they passed by an old cemetery whose crosses drooped at various angles, and finally came out onto a bluff above the Volga. Here they sat down on a log.

"My entire youth is bound up with this dear old log," said Smolyanov. "And why didn't they use it for firewood during the war.... Of course, there weren't any men around...."

Lyalya was hunched up and shivering from the cold, and he put his arm around her. The river was covered with whitecaps, and only at its outer edges did one see dark expanses of water. Hulking next to the shore was the black form of a barge, and on the shore itself were some other black forms—probably skiffs. Down on the sand, in the midst of these dark shapes, someone had lighted a campfire. Smolyanov told her that this was a gathering place for various criminal types and that the area was unsafe. And if they were to venture down there right now, somebody might knife them—just like that, for no good reason. He told her something about this gang and reminisced about some of the bandits he had known. He was interesting to listen to, and Lyalya didn't feel the slightest bit afraid—only cold.

As they made their way back, his arm still around her, he suddenly stopped and awkwardly pressed her to him, trying to keep her warm. And thus they stood. It was, in fact, incredibly cold—hard to believe that it could be so hot during the day. He began to warm her by rubbing his palms up and down her back and sides, and as he did so, he kept muttering to himself and humming. He stroked her slowly and firmly, ever more firmly, and the longer this lasted and the more she felt his strength, the more for some strange reason she felt sorry for him.

After returning to the house, they drank some vodka in order to warm up, and then went upstairs. They stole into a small, dark room where the blinds were still lowered and which smelled of dogs and male life. Here they continued to converse in a whisper so as not to wake up his daughter, who was sleeping in the next room.

As he went on in a hurt voice, muttering incomprehensibly, threatening someone, Lyalya could not help but feel ashamed of her fellow actors. And feeling that she had to make excuses for them and at the same time wanting to comfort him—after all, they had insulted him for no good reason, simply for being nice to them—she did her best to make him understand. There was no need to get angry with them. They were naive and goodhearted, terribly goodhearted. And what splendid friends and colleagues they were, ready to share their last crumb with you. It was just that they sometimes said dumb, stupid things, just to be witty. So forget about them. She, Lyalya, always forgave them because—well, because they had a hard life. Just try to get by on 700 rubles a month. And Ivan Vasilievich—Yeroshkin—had a family of five. He had to love the theater a great deal—for its own sake, not for money. And even she, Lyalya, had enemies—people who were out to get her, trying to hold her back—but still they couldn't spoil her enthusiasm for the theater. And for the sake of this enthusiasm and perhaps even for the happiness which she felt in the theater—however fleeting this happiness might be—she had to be patient and to forgive because... well, why should one do otherwise?... And by now he was comforted, and he nodded, "Yes, yes, I understand you...."

And then came Lyalya's ultimate demonstration of kindness and pity. Much later that morning, as she pried open her eyes and had trouble remembering where she was, she heard a knocking sound. And it suddenly came to her: it was Smolyanov's retarded daughter, bouncing her ball in the next room.

II

A month and a half later Lyalya returned to Moscow from the Crimea, where she had gone on vacation after the tour. On almost her first day back she ran into Smolyanov, who told her that he was working on a new play. He had submitted the first act to Sergei Leonidovich, and the latter had apparently approved it.

Lyalya knew that she always looked her best after the Crimea. Almost everyone looks more attractive after a summer vacation, but with Lyalya this was especially the case. As her close friend Mashka would declare, she looked *disgustingly* attractive—and this because she would lie fearlessly in the sun until her skin turned black, her light hair faded to the color of straw, and her blue eyes shone all the more brightly in her tanned face. And she would spend hours in the water, swimming as tirelessly and as far out as the best of them. Then in the evenings there would be volleyball and tennis. And although she wasn't necessarily a first-class player, still she played as hard as she could, just for the pure joy of running, jumping, laughing, and exerting herself to the point of exhaustion. And she never permitted herself any summer affairs—that wasn't for her, and no good ever came of them anyway. As a result, when she returned, she was always full of energy and full of longing for her husband, her girlfriends, the theater, and simply for her own, familiar street running past the church and the vegetable store.

Smolyanov gave Lyalya a long, lingering look and smiled. In his smile there was something joyful, masculine, and uninhibited—something which Lyalya always loved to feel, since this feeling meant that all was well and everything was just as it should be. At such moments of inner rejoicing even her voice would change. And it was with this changed voice that she greeted Smolyanov, offering him her hand and noticing how her voice took on a slightly affected, sing-song quality: "Well, Nikolai Demyanovich, so you've got something for us. That's great, really wonderful!"

As she said this, she was amazed to think that there had been a night when she had felt so terribly sorry for this man with his dull face—good Lord, whatever for? There was something doughy and sodden about Smolyanov's face.

He was mumbling incomprehensibly, in his usual fashion, and rubbing her hand. Lyalya said lightly, "Nikolai Demyanovich, I'll see you soon! So long for now!" And with this she was off. But a second later she stopped, and glancing back, she said, "I'm very glad you're back here at the theater with us again!"

A few days later it was as if every trace of the Crimea had vanished. Or perhaps it was simply that Moscow had overwhelmed her with its rain, chill, and feverish tempo—not to mention her father's illness, Sergei Leonidovich's anger, her worries about the new fall production, and her endless running from one store to another in search of some rubber-soled shoes for the wet weather.

As Lyalya had expected, she was given no part at all in the theater's fall production. But in December Smolyanov submitted his new play *Ignat Timofeyevich* and started coming frequently to the theater—first for readings, then for discussions, then for revisions, and finally for casting the roles. Initially Lyalya was promised nothing, then she was given a small, insignificant role, and finally a good one—as one of the heroines. She hadn't asked for anything; rather it was the playwright himself who thought to bring the matter up with Sergei Leonidovich. Smurny protested at a meeting of the theater council, but Nikolai Demyanovich said firmly, "This is the way it's going to be!"—and Smurny shut up.

Although the role of Yevdokia, Ignat Timofeyevich's wife and the principal of the seven-year village elementary school, was not a particularly enviable one—it was terribly overdone, with all sorts of jealousy, sufferings, and didactic conversations—still, Lyalya hoped to impress everyone, to show what she could do by "turning a carp into a suckling pig," as Sergei Leonidovich would say. She put heart and soul into the part and revealed such nuances and depth of character in her heroine that the author himself was astounded.

"Well, well! It never occurred to me that..."

Whatever such know-it-alls as Bob Mironovich, Nika Gerasimov, or even her own Grisha might say about Smolyanov—some out of snobbishness, others, sad to say, out of envy at his success—nonetheless, his name began to be mentioned more and more frequently and favorably in the newspapers. *Distant Forests* was already playing in forty theaters, and there was in fact something solid and appealing in this provincial playwright, some sort of clumsy ability to win over his audience and to get to the heart of the matter, to make his point, with swift, bear-like strides.

By now Smolyanov was coming to the theater every day to sit in on rehearsals. Sometimes he and Lyalya would slip off from the others after rehearsal and go to a restaurant together, usually to the tenth-floor dining room of the Hotel Moscow, where he knew the head-waiter. From there they would drive to the empty apartment of one of Smolyanov's friends who had gone off to China and left Smolyanov his key. On one occasion they drove to the outskirts of town and visited a shoe store where the manager was a friend of Smolyanov's. Here they managed to buy the rubber-soled shoes which Lyalya had been hunting for ever since fall. All she had to do was open her mouth, and suddenly there they were, just what she wanted! Lyalya was amazed. Why, here he was, a relative newcomer to Moscow and already he knew all the ins

and outs of the city and had a flock of acquaintances. And it wasn't that
he was terribly sociable, he was even somewhat morose—not at all one
of your lively, outgoing types. So he must have some special talent.
There are such people: in their own quiet way they succeed in everything they do. Their business affairs go well, they're never short of
money, and women—foolish creatures— seem to be attracted to them
like bees to honey. It's a talent—the most precious talent of all!—to be
able to set up one's life, to furnish it, so to speak, as one would furnish
an apartment. If only Grisha had even a little of this talent.

And so it was that what in Saratov had been a chance occurrence, a
compassionate gesture, an early morning chimera—had it really happened at all?—became now, toward the end of the winter, a normal part
of her life, something which it seemed she simply could not do without.

In March, when the play was about to have its premiere, Lyalya noticed that Smurny had begun to smile at her and would be the first to
nod a respectful greeting from a distance. And by now all the unpleasantness of winter—the cold and the slush—had been forgotten, and it
seemed to her that it had been warm and sunny all along and, more to
the point, that it would always be this way. In the depths of her heart
she had long feared, had even resigned herself to the fact, that she
would never have the chance to make good. But now, suddenly something was happening that she had been dreaming of for years, almost
without hope. Sergei Leonidovich had begun working with her alone,
and the makeup woman—hypocrite that she was—had started address-
ing her respectfully as Lyudmila Petrovna. There was even one occasion when the executive director's car was sent to pick her up and take
her to the radio station where she along with the executive director and
Sergei Leonidovich were to discuss their work on the new play. All
these and other equally happy circumstances occurred at the end of the
winter of 1952, when Lyalya had just turned twenty-five. She got used
to these changes very quickly, perhaps even instantaneously, and it
seemed that things would stay this way and perhaps be even better in
the future.

What had brought about this sudden change in her life remained for
Lyalya a mystery, nor did she give it much thought. Perhaps the winds
in the sky had shifted direction. Perhaps hurricanes had spent themselves thousands of miles away. Her deceased grandmother used to
love to quote the saying: "Everything comes at its appointed hour."
And now Lyalya's hour had come—and why not? She had waited so patiently and persistently. Her mother, of course, thought that this
change for the better had come about thanks to her own recent letter

of complaint. Perhaps this was true. Or perhaps it was Nikolai Demyanovich's influence. Or more likely, it was Sergei Leonidovich himself.
Ever since the time of her drama school entrance exams, which she had
failed, he had always been nice to her, almost too nice. Then he had
gotten used to her, even tired of her, and now it was as if he had suddenly taken a fresh look and had been astonished: "My dear colleagues,
what on earth are we doing to Lyudmila Telepneva?" As she learned
later, he had once said of her, "Well, she's got appeal, a great deal of
appeal, but does she have anything more than that?" Yes, but after all,
if one appeals to people, that's already half the battle. You don't find
this sort of appeal just lying around on the street. "The ability to appeal
to others is a God-given talent," Xenofont Fyodorovich, the set de-
signer who had conveyed Sergei Leonidovich's words to her, used to
say. "You have to cherish and foster it, and not turn up your nose at it."
Xenofont Fyodorovich was a wonderful person, and Lyalya had loved
him like a father. He had died, poor thing, of a heart attack. He had
drunk a lot.

But all the same, it was her grandmother who was wiser than anyone
else: "Everything comes at its appointed hour."

The curtain came down, and the actors rushed offstage. But Lyalya
didn't manage to catch up with the others, and when the curtain went
up again, she was caught in a loud wave of applause. Finding herself
alone on stage, she couldn't make up her mind whether to take a bow
on her own or to wait for the others. Someone grabbed her by the
hand, and squeezing her fingers painfully, dragged her to the foot-
lights. She bowed and saw out of the corner of her eye that it was
Makeyev. Smiling at the audience, he whispered spitefully, "Well, go on
and bow! They're applauding you!"

Then it happened again. Pushing and crowding one another the actors hurried offstage, but Lyalya for some reason was left behind, and
the wave of applause caught her alone. Someone threw a bouquet.
Then the actors stopped bowing, and then forming an uneven line,
they too began applauding. Everyone turned toward the right wing of
the stage, where Sergei Leonidovich was emerging with that pale,
weary, and somewhat jaded expression which he usually wore by the
end of rehearsals. Looking at Sergei Leonidovich, Lyalya was barely
able to hold back her tears. She wanted to embrace him and tell him
what a wonderful person he was. Suddenly he took her by the hand
and led her forward. They stood alone before the auditorium, which by
now was half empty. Those who remained roared their approval as they

surged and pressed toward the stage with even more enthusiasm than before.

"Thank you, Sergei Leonidovich," said Lyalya, "thank you...."

"Face the audience, the audience!" he mumbled without looking at her.

Then Nikolai Demyanovich appeared onstage in a handsome, light-colored suit, sporting a white handkerchief in his pocket. He was wearing a new pair of glasses with thick, black, American-type frames, and these glasses changed his appearance completely. Somehow he seemed a changed man. No longer did he bend low, making his bows like a waiter; his face was no longer covered with a deathly pallor, nor did it glisten with sweat. He held himself erect and bowed in proper fashion, merely lowering his head as if he were nodding in agreement with someone, "Yes, yes." After bowing to the audience, he walked up to Sergei Leonidovich, embraced him and kissed him. Lyalya noticed how Sergei Leonidovich flushed crimson as he spontaneously embraced Nikolai Demyanovich and said something in his ear. After this, Nikolai Demyanovich walked up to Lyalya, kissed her hand, and whispered, "Tonight we're going to have to celebrate."

Before Lyalya had a chance to reply, he had walked off and begun shaking hands with the actors and kissing the hands of the actresses. When the applause finally died down and faded away, they all descended the narrow staircase to the dressing rooms. Everyone was talking at once, laughing loudly and congratulating one another. Sergei Leonidovich continued to hold Lyalya's arm.

"Seven curtain calls! Seven!" shouted Lemberg, the stage manager. She was standing at the bottom of the stairs, indicating the number seven with the outstretched fingers of her hands. "It's a success, Sergei Leonidovich!"

"Yes, well, we'll see," the director nodded. "But I must say, Ada Maximovna, you were in an awful hurry with that curtain. You overdid it, just as they would in the provinces."

"But you asked me to yourself, Sergei Leonidovich!"

"You have to use your common sense. When you see that the play's a success, there's no need to hurry with the curtain. They'll clap without that. Just use your common sense. Well, never mind, it's not important. Congratulations, you've done a good job." And smiling wearily, he shook Lemberg's hand. "Oh, make a note that the clouds should be removed from the third act. They don't accomplish anything and just look messy."

Sergei Leonidovich walked on, and Lemberg embraced Lyalya from behind, taking her by the shoulders and kissing her on the cheek. "Congratulations, Lyalya dear! Oh, sorry, I've smeared your cheek. Well, never mind, you'll be taking your makeup off anyway. Everything was marvelous, wonderful—there's only one little spot in the last act. When Makeyev is approaching the porch and you turn..."

Lemberg rattled on excitedly, moving her large, painted mouth, but Lyalya took in very little of what she was saying.

"Thanks, Adochka, thanks a lot," she nodded and smiled, almost in a trance. Then she too kissed Lemberg on the cheek. As she did so, it suddenly struck her that only a month ago—or even yesterday!—she would not have dared to address her familiarly as Adochka, much less to kiss her. And now this had happened so simply and naturally, and Lemberg herself seemed to be glad that Lyalya had kissed her. Everything around her continued to change, and Lyalya could feel that she herself was changing. That was how it should be. There was nothing strange about it, nor any reason to be surprised. Everything that surrounded her and was connected with her was changing, changing inexorably with each passing second, and people seemed to sense this, just as birds sense a change in the weather.

After removing her makeup and changing her clothes, Lyalya went into the backstage room where Sergei Leonidovich stood surrounded by a group of actors. He was commenting on a particular scene, demonstrating how it should be played and where the mistake lay. And from the humorous, animated way in which he was acting out the scene, it was obvious that he was in an excellent mood. Not only was he savoring the success of the evening's premiere, but someone must have already forecast the play's bright future. The actors sensed this and roared with delight as they watched his demonstration. Smurny was there too, with a feigned expression of joy frozen on his smiling face. As Lyalya approached, he turned and said, "Tremendous, really tremendous, Lyudmila Petrovna! My sincere congratulations!"

From the expression of his eyes it was clear that his congratulations were anything but sincere. Nor was Zhenka Milyutina sincere when she kissed Lyalya and said that it was high time for the younger actresses to unite and put an end to the old women's reign of terror. Earlier, when things had been going well for Zhenka and it was Lyalya who was out of favor, she had not made any such proposals. But none of this bothered Lyalya at the moment. She wanted to forget about the bad times—to be kind and generous. And now, reading in Smurny's eyes a deeply concealed, animal-like terror, she even felt something akin to sympathy for her former enemy. And she replied cheerfully, "Thank you, Herman

Vladimirovich, thank you!"

At this point Nikolai Demyanovich entered the room and announced something about a banquet at the Grand Hotel, presumably on Monday. Lyalya wasn't listening very carefully; she was more concerned with what was going to happen next. Grisha was waiting downstairs and she would have to introduce him to Nikolai Demyanovich. Nikolai Demyanovich now approached her and said softly but calmly, as if there were no one else around, "I'll wait for you downstairs, outside the executive director's office. I'll have two friends with me."

And with this he disappeared.

Lyalya returned to her dressing room, packed her things in her small suitcase, gathered up her flowers. Before leaving the room, however, she sat down for a moment in front of the mirror. She felt uneasy, her present happiness clouded by feelings of apprehension at the horribly awkward situation that was about to develop. Grisha hadn't been at all eager to attend the premiere, nor did he like coming to the theater in general. He was painfully proud, and people offended him here. But she had persuaded him to. Her mother, who wasn't able to leave Lyalya's father, had also tried to persuade him, though in her own fashion: "Go ahead, you go! Someone has to be there to meet Lyalya and escort her home."

Her relatives were attending in droves—Uncle Kolya with all of his family, her mother's youngest sister Veronika, and Aunt Zhenya and Uncle Misha with Lyalya's two cousins, Mayka and Borka. Mayka was an ardent theater fan and would be sure to be there. Valentina Abramovna, Uncle Misha's sister, also wanted to come, and Aunt Toma planned to make a special trip in from Alexandrov. Her mother had gotten them all so worked up that Lyalya had even quarreled with her. Was it really necessary to organize this Telepnev march on the theater?! Actually, it would be more accurate to call it a Fomichev march, since all of them were her mother's relatives. And if anyone from her father's side were to come, it would only be Slavik, Uncle Fedya's son.

In any case, they had all been told in no uncertain terms that there was to be no waiting around in the lobby to greet her, no bouquets, no hurrahs or family demonstrations. At the end of the third act—collect your coats, boots, and off you go! I'll see you at home, at 32 Chetvyortaya Pochtovaya Street. Only Borka, an avid photographer, was to be permitted to take one or two pictures of her in the lobby when it was all over. And only Grisha was to meet her and escort her home. But Grisha, as Lyalya knew full well, was the one person who had come here without any enthusiasm and probably without even any bouquet. Well, never mind that; it wasn't really important. One could forgive his morose state of mind. At times she felt terribly sorry for him and would lie in bed at night, racking her brains, wondering what was to be done and how she could help him. And right now it seemed to her that if she hadn't dragged him to the theater tonight, he would have been even more depressed, sitting at home in his beloved library. Everything would have been all right if Nikolai Demyanovich hadn't suggested that they go out somewhere after the performance. Apparently he was alone, without his wife. They must have quarreled again. What a horrible woman—to pick a fight with him on this particular day! She managed to spoil all his special occasions. Oh, how nice it would be to go somewhere—to the Aragvi, for instance—and have a good meal and something to drink, a nice, dry red wine. At the very thought Lyalya could feel a gnawing in her stomach and the taste of *sat - sivi* on her tongue. But Grisha... Yet what if the three of them were to go out together? And really—what would be so strange about that?

Lyalya looked at herself in the mirror. Her face was pale except for a slight rosy hue at her temples, and the light-colored German lipstick she was wearing gave her lips a moist and somehow very fresh, girlish luster. Everyone said that Lyalya had a beautiful mouth, and she knew it for a fact. And now she looked at her mouth with satisfaction. She was taking her time. Let the other actors disperse; there was no need to hurry. It would be easier to meet Nikolai Demyanovich in an almost completely empty lobby and then introduce him to Grisha somewhere by the cloakroom in the front lobby. And let her relatives disappear. Mayka was especially dangerous with her untimely comments, as was Uncle Kolya's wife Lipa, Olimpiada Afanasievna, the universally acknowledged fool in the family. And of course there was no way of avoiding a certain awkwardness between Grisha and Nikolai Demyanovich. Perhaps Grisha already sensed something, though most likely he didn't—he was so caught up in his own misfortunes. There had, of course, been that awkward incident with the shirt she had bought as a birthday present for Nikolai Demyanovich. She had kept the shirt in their bureau and Grisha had accidentally discovered it. He had been surprised and had asked about it. The neck was forty-five centimeters and obviously too big for him; he wore a forty-one. So she had had to lie, saying that she had picked out the shirt as a collective gift for one of their colleagues, a nice man named Tamarkin, who was a cellist in the theater orchestra. She was ashamed of herself, but what else could she do? If she had told him the truth, she would have dealt a monstrous blow to his pride. This would have been inhumanly cruel, especially now, in his present state of mind. And besides, "the truth" in this case would not really have been the truth, but only a partial truth. For what had gone on between Lyalya and Smolyanov could not be called a love affair in the usual sense of the word, nor could it be called by any other precise term. Lyalya didn't know what to call it. She hadn't asked or expected anything of him, nor had there been any of the inflamed passion, the burning desire to see him and know what he was doing every day, every hour, which she had experienced in the past with others. Weeks could go by without her seeing Smolyanov and she would not suffer from the fact that he didn't call her at the theater or come looking for her. But when she did see him, it always felt good. And she always felt sorry for him for one reason or another. She knew that he needed sympathy, for he could not expect any from his egotistical wife, his retarded daughter, or even from his old mother in far-off Saratov. Much less could he expect any sympathy from his theatrical friends or the theater-going public. In fact, he used to tell Lyalya, "You're the only one who even half understands me."

To leave Grisha for him! Perhaps he would even have liked her to, but the question had never come up and Lyalya would never have agreed to it—she would have felt even worse about leaving Grisha. And the fact that they weren't even officially married was quite beside the point. Her whole life—her school days, her youth, the war and its famines, her hopes, and her unborn children—all were bound up with Grisha! And to leave him now, just when things were beginning to look up for her....

Lyalya's throat suddenly constricted as she pictured what would happen to Grisha if she were to abandon him. No, never! Right now it was raining—she could hear the water gushing down the iron drainpipe—and Grisha was undoubtedly out on the street somewhere. He wouldn't think of waiting for her inside the theater or even under the theater marquee, but would be standing somewhere off at a distance, huddled against a wall. That was the way he was. He was full of complexes and overly sensitive about everything. And now Lyalya began to hurry, snatching up her small suitcase, the flowers, and turning out the light as she hastily left the room.

As she proceeded quickly down the corridor, almost at a run, she overheard the fragment of a conversation:

"Did you notice how she detached herself from the rest of us and remained onstage by herself? Just like some provincial prima donna."

"Good Lord, what do you expect? In this theater that's the only way you can win any recognition...."

For a second she was tempted to go back and see who it was. But never mind. She would have to put up with that sort of thing now—it was starting already. But that was inevitable and just as it should be. The lights had been turned down in the lobby, and the audience had almost completely dispersed. Thank God there were no familiar faces. Suddenly there was a blinding flash from the left—it was Borka who had jumped forward and clicked his camera at almost point blank range. Lyalya hadn't even glanced in his direction. At the other end of the lobby Nikolai Demyanovich was talking with two strange men, and right beside him stood the theater's executive director, Roman Vasilievich, and the business manager, Bravin. Lyalya walked past them, nodding modestly as she wished them all the best. The men replied casually and gaily. They seemed to be a bit high already from the cognac they had drunk. The executive director flashed a smile with his gold-filled teeth and the business manager shouted, "Lyudochka, be so kind as to join us for tea! To celebrate the premiere!" Nikolai Demyanovich said to her, "Lyudmila Petrovna, can I give you a lift? I have a car at my disposal."

Rebrov, of course, had missed the performance. To attend one of Smolyanov's plays—that was asking too much! Since eleven o'clock that morning he had been ensconced in Scholars Reading Room No. 3 of the Lenin Library, reading about Ivan Gavrilovich Pryzhov. The day before he had ordered everything he could find in the card catalog: *The Russian Archives* for the year 1866, *A History of the Tavern* and *Beggars in Holy Rus*, articles in *The Voice, The Moscow Gazette,* and *The Saint Petersburg Gazette,* Altman's book, a collection of articles and letters from the year 1834, *Bygone Years,* and a great deal more. It was splendid reading material for several days. As for why he needed Pryzhov, Rebrov himself didn't know. Why *did* he need him?! This habit of sitting in the library and devouring old books, newspapers, and journals had become so irresistible that it was like a passion for cards or drugs. Rebrov had stumbled onto Pryzhov at the time he had been researching Nechaev.[2] Actually he had first come upon his name a year ago when he had been reading some old journals right here in Scholars Reading Room No. 3. There was no point at all to this reading; it was simply a narcotic which he couldn't do without. If fact, there were days when he didn't even bother to eat, but would simply visit the smokers' lounge. Yet what he needed to do was to get something down on paper, to write some sort of sketch from which he could work out a film scenario. For Rebrov simply could not get Ivan Gavrilovich

Pryzhov off his mind. And this despite the fact that he was a completely useless character long forgotten by everyone, an unsuccessful rebel, a historian, a drunkard and a parasite, and at the same time a man of great nobility of character, a chronicler of Russian everyday life and customs, who had lived 100 years ago. Could it be that all this preoccupation with Pryzhov was merely a reflection of his own insatiable curiosity or worse, of his own laziness? This was a question which Rebrov had asked himself often.

By six that evening he had managed to fill up some twenty pages of a notebook—my God, what on earth for?!—with various facts and ideas drawn from Ivan Gavrilovich's life and writings. Then, as spots were already dancing before his eyes, he left the library and set off to have supper in the cafe of the Hotel National. Here he settled in his favorite seat by the window and ordered a schnitzel and a helping of dry mashed potatoes which they knew how to prepare properly only here at the National. All evening he nursed his cold schnitzel along with several cups of coffee. He also had two glasses of brandy, to which he was treated by acquaintances who stopped by his table to talk. Rebrov himself was broke. That morning, in fact, he'd had to borrow a ten-ruble note from Lyalya.

Everything followed a set pattern in the National: people shared tables, got acquainted, and left; others came bearing messages, reporting on the events of the day, cracking jokes; some tried to intimidate, others got indignant, some lent money and made deals, others got drunk and created a scene. After six o'clock people began arriving from the races, telling about their winnings and any new swindles that had been unearthed. At nine, as always, the artist Rysev appeared, a man who was rumored to be an informer and whom you had to be careful with. Between nine and ten, actors began showing up—those who didn't have to appear onstage during the last acts. "They say it's a real flop at the Maly...." "Was Myshchikov really fired?" "Listen, do you know this one? A rabbi comes to a prostitute and..." "For that little item you'd have to go to Riga!" "Hey, look at that pretty girl sitting with our friend!" "What's going on: Lyalya has a premiere, and he's carousing here? Why aren't you there, in the director's box, scoundrel?"

Not wanting to start any explanations, Rebrov gave a lazy, contemptuous wave of his hand. His contempt was directed both at the content of the question and at the individual who had asked it. Was one supposed to give an accounting to every sot in the tavern? And the words *scoundrel* and *Lyalya* jarred on him—that excessive familiarity which one always found among actors. He was still under the spell of Ivan

Gavrilovich, and talking with these drunkards, he thought of him. The tavern syndrome, it seemed, had remained unchanged over the years: the same yearning for company and for forgetfulness. It was no accident that Pryzhov had burned the last two volumes of his *A History of the Tavern*, fearing that the government would increase its surveillance and begin harassing these miserable establishments. No one at the National, of course, had any idea of what was passing through Rebrov's mind.

At about ten o'clock, when Rebrov was just getting ready to leave (it didn't take more than fifteen minutes by trolley bus to get to the theater), Shakhov appeared. He was on the run as usual and asked Rebrov hastily how his work was going. His manner was businesslike, like that of some inspector, and as he asked the question, he cast an eagle-eyed glance over the neighboring tables, not wanting to waste a moment. Rebrov replied that there was nothing new to report and added à la Pryzhov, "I'm dying, but one leg is still kicking."

"Well then, I'll tell you what, dear fellow," said Shakhov, now catching sight of someone in the far corner of the room, "you call me in about five days, or I'll call you. Maybe we can come up with something. We'll do a bit of kicking together...."

Out on the street it was cold and raining hard. People were already leaving the theater, but only a few at a time—those who were dashing off before the play was over. Not wishing to run into any actors or any of the familiar pests who usually attended on opening night, Rebrov did not come and stand under the marquee.

Above all, he wished to avoid running into any of Lyalya's relatives. It wasn't that he disliked these people, most of whom were from Irina Ignatievna's side of the family, but he tried to keep his distance from them. Perhaps some of them were fine people, perfectly decent, but in each one of them he seemed to detect something of his mother-in-law. He pressed against the side of the building in order to protect himself from the rain and at the same time to keep an eye on those who were emerging. And why—for heaven's sake why!—couldn't he have stood by the entrance, greeted acquaintances with a smile, shaken hands with Lyalya's relatives, and jokingly responded to their greetings? "What have we here—a nervous husband?" "Well, what can you do? *C'est la vie!*" Or even better, why couldn't he have waited with a bouquet of flowers in the downstairs lobby, rushed forward to greet her in front of everyone, and hugged and kissed her to the approving murmur of the crowd?

But all of this was completely impossible. The thing which Rebrov feared most in this world was to make a fool of himself. This trait, characteristic of those who are proud and reserved by nature, created a lot of difficulties in his life. These difficulties had begun a long time ago, as far back as grade school. He and Lyalya had been in the same class and he had always liked her. He had felt some sort of painful, mute attraction to her, though he didn't know why—whether it was her braids, her voice, her early developing feminine figure or the boldness with which she had sung the role of Nelly in their school performance of *Till Eulenspiegel.* He couldn't tell her his feelings; he couldn't even bear to look in her direction. And as a result, he suffered. Once he had run out into the schoolyard with some of his friends after class and Lyalya had asked him whether he was on his way home. Instead of shouting back, "Sure, let's go!"—he had almost choked and muttered, "Well, no, I'm staying here...." If only the other kids hadn't been around! But they were keeping an eagle-eye on both of them, and Lyalya walked off. She didn't ask him again, and thus it continued for a whole year—the two of them sometimes walking off in the same direction, but never together.

Then, when they were both in the ninth grade, there was an evening movie in the dark auditorium in some club on Tverskaya-Yamskaya Street. On the screen people were dashing about on horseback, and foes of the Revolution were being rounded up and shot. But Rebrov and Lyalya, who were sitting in the last row, didn't understand a thing that was going on. His left hand and Lyalya's right had joined together in the dark and were caressing and fondling each other, squeezing until it hurt. All this went on for an hour and a half. Neither of them said a word and their faces remained focused on the screen. When the lights were turned on, they got up and headed for the door, still not looking at each other nor saying a single word. When they were out on the street, Lyalya suddenly burst out laughing and said that he was very funny. Wounded to the quick, he mumbled, "You're funny too!"

Yes, yes, it was his old fear of making a fool of himself. But there were to be worse moments than this. Simply to say "I love you" struck him as ridiculously absurd, a breach of good form, and as a result he maintained a dumb silence which was even more absurd. Actually, it was she who first suggested that they get married—in the winter of '47. By this time their relationship had long been consummated. But he still couldn't bring himself to ask her, for what if she should suddenly refuse? What was he to do then—hurl himself in the path of an oncoming train? And there had always been other men in her life: the one with the limp; the one who had helped her to get into the theater; then some Yasha or other and a certain Valery, a childhood friend and the son of one of his mother-in-law's best friends. His mother-in-law had long dreamed of Lyalya's marrying this Valery and even now she apparently still clung to this wild hope.

Yet Grisha had always loved her the whole thirteen years they had known each other. Not a single day had gone by that he hadn't thought about her. Whenever she went off on tour or on vacation to the South—she liked to go on vacation by herself, and that was already the established rule—he didn't know what to do with himself. He would wander about, numb with longing and unable either to work or to go out and have a good time. His friends would introduce him to girls in an attempt to distract him, but it was precisely when Lyalya was traveling and the ideal time was presumably at hand that he lost all interest in such distractions. Now if she had been in Moscow and everything were as it should be, then he would have had nothing against it. Though even in such cases it was more a question of talk than of action. "Wouldn't it be nice to—break loose, right here and now...," he would say to a friend over a cup of coffee, glancing at some sallow-complexioned young coed in the library cafeteria. But, good Lord, in all of those years there had been only two or three times when he had actually "broken loose." Was that any "big deal" for a young man? It was really nothing at all. Contributing to his fidelity was a superstition or, more accurately, a sort of secret terror which he did not admit even to himself: that if he allowed something to happen, then she too would allow something to happen. And the suspicion that this something had already happened tormented him more than anything else in his life. For she was terribly openhearted and thought nothing of kissing a man or responding casually to his advances. This did not mean, of course, that she would go all the way, but she would go *part* of the way without a moment's hesitation.

And it was not a question in this case of that familiarity one usually associates with actors or of environment, but simply of her own character—of that damned kindness of hers. There had been an incident a long time ago, before the war—that is, just before the German invasion in June of '41. After one of their school exams the two of them had gone swimming at Shchukinsky Beach. Before the war there hadn't been any beach there, but only a very high and steep sandy bluff. It was the very beginning of summer, and of course the water had been cold. They had taken two or three dips and were lying on the sand when suddenly three young fellows appeared from nowhere and began flirting with Lyalya. At the same time they began to heckle Rebrov and eventually drew him into a fight. As always in such situations he put up with the heckling for a long time, grew increasingly tense, and then, as if exploding, furiously went at them with his fists. They started hammering away at him too and would probably have beaten him to a pulp if Lyalya hadn't rushed up to defend him, shouting, "Stop it! What are you doing? What do you want from us?!" And then suddenly adding, "Well, if you want me to, I'll kiss each one of you." And in fact, she did kiss all three of them, one after another. And as they stood there, too stunned to protest, she took Rebrov by the hand and led him away. She took him home with her on the streetcar. Her parents were horrified at what had happened and bathed his wounds with some sort of ointment. Then they fed him and had him spend the night on the veranda of their small house. Lyalya came to him in the middle of the night, but nothing happened except for the caresses which were an impetuous manifestation of her pity. Nor did Rebrov feel any need to prove his manhood—he had proved it with every inch of his proud, battered body. There was only one thought which tormented him, making it difficult to fall asleep. And the next morning, as the birds were singing and the sunlight filtered through the leaves, this same thought woke him with its sharp, nagging aches: how could she have kissed them, all three of them, and so easily? And later, when he asked her about it: good Lord, she had simply wanted to save him. And she had saved him, she had! But what if in order to save him she had had to do something worse? With all three of them? After a moment's pause she answered firmly: if she had to, in order to save him, she could have done it. He groaned and fell back on the couch, biting his lip until it bled. What made him feel such despair was not the fact that she could have done it, but the fact that she had responded so easily, so firmly, without hesitation.

Three years later, after being tossed around by the war—after serving at the front, after being wounded and evacuated to a Siberian hospital—he had actually run into Lyalya at somebody's house near Sretensky Gate. He saw her sitting next to the lame poet whose claim to fame was that he wrote songs for the blind and the disabled. He was a frail, pitiful creature, an alcoholic, and Rebrov was told that Lyalya looked after this Lazik—such was the lame man's name—like a nurse and was terribly devoted to him. And when the poet was discarded—with difficulty, to be sure—and had been crossed off her list with thick, black indelible ink, still for Rebrov this was not the end of it. For in his own mind he saw peering through this thick, black ink not only Lazik but also the three young fellows on the shore and some other scoundrel who had tried to rape Lyalya, as well as many unknown figures whose existence he could not be sure of, but could merely guess at. And he was unable to rid his mind of any of these figures for good.

Different periods brought different anxieties. Later on there was Makeyev, then Sergei Leonidovich himself, about whom she always spoke with a certain breathlessness, as if he were some sort of divine being. More recently he had been troubled by the new director Smurny, even though Lyalya hated him—which should, of course, have put his mind at ease. But with Lyalya's softheartedness Rebrov knew that the strongest hatred could easily transform itself into feelings of pity or even sympathy, so he would have to keep his eyes and ears open. Nor was it easy to put up with Valery and his mother, whom his mother-in-law was always inviting over for dinner. Sometimes there were playwrights who provoked his suspicions, especially such successful ones as Fedka Arnoldov, with his dark eyes and jet-black hair which were quite to Lyalya's taste. Smolyanov might also represent a certain danger. But it was a certain actor named Kornilovich who irritated him more than anyone else. Under the guise of camaraderie this Pashka was terribly familiar with Lyalya, and even in Rebrov's presence he would tell her dirty jokes, address her by the familiar form, put his arm around her, and take her hand. And for this reason Rebrov did not like to be around Lyalya's actor friends. And what was he supposed to talk to them about? Not only did he find them boring, but he also felt tense in their company and was continually having to suppress his jealousy, which in turn led to all sorts of nasty and degrading behavior on his part. And herein lay his problem, for however tormented he felt, he did not want anyone to know his true feelings. He would rather die from a fit of grief than rush off to the city where she was on tour or to the resort town where she had flown off on vacation with her girlfriend. Nor did he ever call her when she was out of town. Rather it was her mother who would call and afterwards report to him everything Lyalya had said. And as he greedily took in her every word, he would assume a calmly subdued and even absentminded expression which his mother-in-law secretly resented. For she assumed that if he didn't feel very excited at hearing about Lyalya, this meant he didn't love her very much. And this only helped to confirm what she suspected already. But whenever Lyalya returned—oh, happiest of days!—from the very first minutes, as they were leaving the railroad station or the airport, he would try as subtly as possible to ferret out any changes which might have occurred during her absence, and even the slightest change in her habits, voice, health, or attitude toward him would be subjected to his intense scrutiny. The very first night upon her return she would secretly be put to the test, and heaven forbid that her lovemaking reveal any new experience. Lyalya, of course, never had any inkling of Rebrov's suspicions. And it was probably because of these suspicions that he did not find it easy to come here to the theater, to smile and converse with these people. When the company had come back from Saratov the previous summer and Rebrov had gone to the railroad station to meet her, Kornilovich had spoken up in an intentionally loud, jesting voice, "Well, Lyalechka, shall we confess everything to Grisha? Shall we? Let's tell him!" The actors had roared with laughter and Grisha had done his best to smile, but inside he felt torn apart: who could be sure, perhaps something had actually gone on between them?

There was another reason why he didn't like to come to the theater. People humiliated Lyalya there and he wasn't able to defend her, for they humiliated him as well. He had submitted two plays to the theater—one a young people's play about the construction of a university, the other a sort of fable for children about the Korean war—and both had been rejected. True, Rebrov's own attitude toward these plays was ambivalent. On the one hand, he didn't take them very seriously. He saw their weak points, their obvious contrivance, but wasn't very upset by it because in his own mind these plays were something secondary and unimportant. On the other hand, however, they were very important—more important than anything else from the financial point of view—for his future depended on them. And quite apart from that, it was insulting to have them rejected. Were they really so bad, or indeed any worse than anyone else's plays—any worse, for instance, than the sort of nonsense turned out by Smolyanov?

By now the audience was streaming out of the theater in droves. The rain was coming down harder, and those who passed by were talking about taxis or the subway or about how they had to stop off at the bakery. No one spoke of the performance. "Well, naturally! Just as one would expect," thought Rebrov without the slightest bit of surprise. He had never met Smolyanov, had never seen or read his plays, but for some reason he was convinced that he was a scheming nonentity and that his plays were absolute nonsense.

All of a sudden he noticed the theater's chief literary consultant Boris Mironovich Marevin, or Bob, as he was called in the theater. This Marevin had held on to Rebrov's plays for four months, the swine, and only recently had sent a message through Lyalya that they weren't suitable. He couldn't even find time to invite him to his office to discuss them. Nor did he write him an official letter of rejection. Well, why stand on ceremony? You're one of our own people, Lyalechka's husband, not really an author. But when Berg or Fedka Arnoldov submitted one of their plays, he probably devoured it in one night and called them up the next morning at the crack of dawn: "Listen, you should be shot for depriving me of my sleep, I simply couldn't tear myself away from it...."

Out here on the street he looked completely different from that intimidating Marevin before whom authors trembled when ushered into his office with its inkstand of green marble decorated with bronze. And especially in the rain he seemed rather pitiful—a homely, ill-proportioned little man in a beret, with a briefcase at his side, and wearing a coat which was no better than Rebrov's. As he came running out into the rain, his body bent and thin, little legs twitching like a mosquito's, he glanced from side to side, and catching sight of Rebrov, he bowed. Rebrov responded with a haughty nod. At this point a strong, wet gust of wind hit Marevin full force and swept him toward the wall of the building. Having been brought involuntarily to Rebrov's side, he had to greet him and say a few words.

"Are you waiting for Lyalya? This was a big day for her. My congratulations to you too..."

Not wishing to discuss Lyalya with him, Rebrov asked, "Well, and what about the play—was it a tremendous success? Did the audience applaud madly?"

"Are you crazy?!" whispered Marevin. "It's the usual sort of crap. Well, all the best...."

And with that he was off, running along with little hopping steps. Suddenly it occurred to Rebrov that one could write an excellent play about Ivan Gavrilovich. His life had all the necessary ingredients—drama, death, picturesque shabbiness, a woman's devotion, and all the torments of an impoverished literary man who was willing to sell his manuscripts for a glass of vodka. But how would one handle the murder? For of course he hadn't wanted to kill Ivanov; he had refused, pleaded, said that he was old and blind, but the others had said, "We'll take you to him." And apparently all they had to do was fill him up with vodka. And therein lies the whole horror of his situation. Dostoevsky created a brilliant caricature of the incident in *The Possessed*, but if one were to tell his story simply, just as it was... But why should one? And who would want to hear it?

Makeyev emerged from the theater entrance in an elegant coat with a fur collar. He was wrapped up to his nose in a white scarf, his hands were in his pockets, and someone behind him was carrying his small suitcase. Makeyev's young female admirers had been waiting under the

marquee and now started squealing in unison, "Makeyev's a darling—
rah! rah! rah!" Then a large crowd came pushing through the door. In
the center of this group was Lyalya with an enormous bouquet of flowers which she held cradled in one arm like a baby. Some woman kissed
Lyalya on the cheek, and shouting and waving their hats in farewell, the
group quickly dispersed. Rebrov moved out from the wall into the rain
and took a few steps toward the entrance. But Lyalya was still talking
with someone, and recognizing Smolyanov, Rebrov stiffened and
stopped dead in his tracks, telling himself that he wouldn't take another step in Lyalya's direction. Let her come up to him. Talking all the
while, Lyalya and Smolyanov gradually came closer. Lyalya had caught
sight of him, but was so engrossed in her conversation that she hadn't
nodded or smiled in his direction, nor made any sort of gesture that
would indicate that she had seen him at all. Apparently they hadn't
even noticed the rain. "Damn it all, why does she have to drag him
along?" thought Rebrov, beginning to feel upset. Lyalya and
Smolyanov came up to him, stopping a few feet away. And without
even looking at him, Lyalya handed him her bouquet.

"What's this for?" asked Rebrov, taking the bouquet. "Is this supposed to be a present or something?"

"Grisha, please hold it," said Lyalya, now looking at him for the first
time. She had a slightly dazed expression on her face, and her eyes
were sparkling. "Oh, sorry, Grishenka! You two don't know each other.
This is Nikolai Demyanovich Smolyanov. And this is Grigory Fyodorovich Rebrov. Grisha, Nikolai Demyanovich is suggesting that we go
somewhere to celebrate...."

Smolyanov touched his hat and shook Rebrov's hand. He had a sur-
prisingly strong handshake.

"My congratulations to you on this—er, special occasion..." mumbled
Rebrov, sensing something nasty and hypocritical in his own voice. But
then he immediately found justification for his words: after all, the
poor fellow could hardly be blamed for the fact that he had no talent;
and it was a premiere for him.

Smolyanov apparently hadn't caught what he said, since he didn't
thank him or bow even slightly in response to his congratulations.
Instead he began babbling some nonsense of his own:

"It's a strange thing, Grigory Fyodorovich. I wasn't acting or running around; I was sitting in a box seat and watching. And yet, you
know, my back aches as if I'd been carrying potato sacks. Watching
one's own play is really hard work! I'd even recommend that they give
playwrights milk free of charge, just as they do workers in high-risk oc-
cupations...."

At this point two men approached, and Smolyanov introduced them. One of them was from the central theater administration, and the other a friend of Smolyanov's from Saratov, who was now working in Moscow. This individual said goodbye, but the man from the theater administration offered them a lift in his Pobeda. Just as they were getting into the car, five or six of Lyalya's relatives suddenly appeared from out of nowhere.

Led by her loud and foolish Aunt Lipa, the whole kit and caboodle pounced on Lyalya, overwhelming her with kisses, flowers, and shrieks. A light bulb flashed, indicating that someone had managed to capture this moment of confusion on film. Finally Lyalya broke loose and escaped into the back seat of the car. Rebrov, whom, thank God, no one had noticed, climbed in behind her, and Smolyanov squeezed in last, slamming the door behind him. The car was so crammed full of flowers that they could barely move. For some reason or other Lyalya was laughing hysterically. Where were they headed? It was decided that they would try the new Hotel Sovetskaya on Leningrad Boulevard. The restaurant was supposed to have gypsy singers.

III

Before the Revolution the little house in which the Telepnevs lived had been the dacha of some minor factory or government official who had not had the stamina to settle in a real suburban dacha—one of those riverfront properties in Kuskovo or on Lociny Island. Because he had to come into Moscow every day to work, the main factor in his choice of a dacha had apparently been its proximity to the city. The Revolution had swept out all of the dacha owners, both the wealthy and those of modest means, and had populated their living rooms, porches and small, second-floor bedrooms with former soldiers and peasants— all working class people who had come streaming into the capital to escape the famines in their own regions. Thus it was that in 1922 the demobilized Red soldier Pyotr Telepnev settled here in this little house, which at that time was still located beyond the city limits. Originally from a lower class family in the city of Yekaterinburg, he was a master boiler maker by trade and a gardener by avocation. He completed his secondary education in a factory school, working first as a foreman and later on advancing to the position of shift engineer in a large new factory which had sprung up not far from his home, on the old Khodynskoe Field.

But more than his factory, more than his precious boilers, and perhaps more than his wife and his daughter, Pyotr Telepnev loved his garden, which he had cultivated over three decades. His dahlias were particularly magnificent and were known all over Moscow. Other flower growers called them "Telepnev dahlias," or sometimes simply "Telepnevs," since everyone knew which flowers were being discussed. And he had other flowers in his garden: tulips, asters, chrysanthemums, gillyflowers, and some splendid irises for which he was also famous. Finally there were lilacs—eighteen bushes of them—which grew luxuriantly along the entire length of the fence. For some reason, however, Pyotr Alexandrovich was less jealous and protective of his lilacs than of his many other flowers. He would transplant them from one place to anther, allow others to cut off branches, and would himself give them away right and left—all the more so since he had relatives all over Moscow.

During the war the garden had almost perished. He could hardly worry about flowers when his family was half starving and barely managing to stay alive; when his daughter had neither dresses nor shoes and even in the month of May had to run around in felt winter boots; and when his wife was suffering from an ulcer and had to be hospitalized for weeks at a time. Yet somehow they managed to live through it all and to save the garden as well. It was Pyotr Alexandrovich who saved it—by hours stolen during the day and during the night from the normal routine of his life and by his faith that someday, when the world came to its senses, people would ask, "What is it that seems to be missing? Wasn't there something that used to stand in the middle of the table?" And in fact, people did start asking for flowers once again, and Lorkh potatoes'and early radishes gradually began to go out of style. That is, although they had not yielded their position in people's vegetable gardens, they no longer functioned as powerful landlords, so to speak, but were more like temporary residents whom one puts up with out of necessity, because of their good income and because one has little hope of getting rid of them in the immediate future. But just at this point a new danger suddenly loomed on the horizon. Two years after the war was over they began lining all of the nearby streets with new buildings of stone and concrete. And now Pyotr Alexandrovich's lilacs and forty-eight varieties of *Dahlia variabilis* were threatened with the evil of demolition. It didn't matter about the house—it was only a pile of wood anyway, and they'd be given an even better apartment to take its place—but as for the garden, it seemed doomed to destruction.

Pyotr Alexandrovich set to work, drawing up various papers and documents. He collected signatures from important people who had at one time or another been the recipients of his lilacs, and he wrote petitions to the district soviet, the district housing administration, the Moscow soviet, the Moscow housing administration, and to the city's chief architect—and all with the same request: that this garden, which was one of a kind and would be bequeathed to the State after his death, be preserved in its entirety; and that its owner, Pyotr Alexandrovich, be given an apartment in the nearest apartment building so that he could continue to care for the garden and carry on his observations, which were of universally acknowledged scientific significance.

This had been going on for three years. Pyotr Alexandrovich kept writing, calling, hanging around reception rooms, knocking on every door. But still the concrete came closer. The whole street had been built up from the church to the Tarakanovka, and already this dirty little stream was strewn with rubble. The soil was already there with which to fill it in, the small park right next to it had been dug up, and the trolley bus was operating once again. Lyalya had already appeared in three plays but was still dissatisfied and wanted to quit; she and her poor, unlucky Grigory had separated a number of times and managed to get back together again; and their only child, a daughter named Varenka, had been born and had died immediately from meningitis. But still the fate of the garden remained undecided.

The district engineer told him, "Your house is in block eight. Right now we're winding up with the two blocks beyond the Tarakanovka, then it'll be your turn. If the Moscow soviet hasn't come to a decision by that time, you can expect a tractor at your doorstep."

To add to his troubles, two of Pyotr Alexandrovich's neighbors who lived in wooden houses just like his own began scribbling letters of petition and gathering signatures. But they, by contrast, were trying to speed up the demolition process and abused Pyotr Alexandrovich in every way they could. The policeman Kurtov gave him a particularly hard time. They had once gotten along well, had drunk vodka and gone fishing together, and their daughters, Lyalka and Margaritka, had been classmates and friends. But now, as a result of all this hullabaloo they did nothing but quarrel.

Pyotr Alexandrovich's face had dulled and his shoulders had become stooped from all this agitation and running around. One September day he had gone out into the garden to cut some white and yellow *Dahlia imperialis* which he planned to present to retired Colonel Dudarev who had just turned sixty. The dahlias were exceptionally beautiful that fall—good enough to put on exhibit in Geneva—and the *imperialis* were some fourteen feet high. But now it suddenly occurred to him that next year at this time neither he nor the *imperialis* would be here. Instead there would be a foundation pit with lime spattered all over the place and female laborers carting bricks in wheelbarrows. And at this very instant something pierced his heart like a sharp instrument and knocked him to the ground. He lay there on a bed of irises, fully conscious but terrified; the pain kept boring into him and he couldn't move a muscle. He called out in a weak voice, "Irina! Irina!" Irina Ignatievna didn't hear him, but Kandidka, smart dog, started barking by the fence, and a little later his wife came out and found him. For the next two months Pyotr Alexandrovich remained at home in bed, and for the first twenty days he was ordered to lie flat on his back without moving his head or shifting from side to side. Gradually he got better, was able to be up on his feet again, and in January he was sent to a sanatorium for six weeks. He returned home seemingly recovered, but only outwardly so. He looked well enough, but was not really his old self.

Such was Pyotr Alexandrovich's not very satisfactory condition at the time of Lyalya's premiere and great public triumph. Naturally he was happy for his daughter and especially for his wife, who had blossomed and even managed to forget about her ulcer, so proud was she of her daughter's success. Nevertheless, Pyotr Alexandrovich continued to be tormented by thoughts of his garden.

In the meantime he had had several new ideas. What if a letter were to come from the theater—from the whole collective? People's actor so-and-so; honored actress such-and-such. And get the artistic director involved too.... "Having learned of the barbarous destruction of this haven of horticultural development that is about to take place in the Leningrad District...." Lyalya had promised to speak to the theater's business manager, Comrade Bravin. He was, she said, a very knowledgeable and helpful individual whom people were always turning to with their problems. He would write letters for them, go to court, and help them in their efforts to obtain divorces and larger apartments. But somehow Lyalya never managed to speak to him. She needed to be alone with him in order to explain everything in detail, but in the theater everyone was always in a hurry or crowding around and there simply wasn't a quiet moment. But she had promised that the matter would be taken care of. "Perhaps," she said, "I should invite him home for a glass of vodka. That he wouldn't refuse."

Pyotr Alexandrovich's second idea was to have some sort of satirical sketch appear in the newspapers. For this he would have to lean on Grigory. He did, after all, know a lot of newspaper people and was himself good at writing. Pyotr Alexandrovich had a talk with him, and Grigory promised to help, but as usual you had to remind him at least ten times before he'd even begin to move. And it wasn't so easy to remind him, you had to choose just the right moment. He was often in a bad mood, secretly annoyed with Irina Ignatievna or quarreling with Lyalya. And sometimes, for no discernible reason, he would even be annoyed with Pyotr Alexandrovich himself. At other times, Lyalya would warn him, "Go easy on Grisha today, he's having a hard time working. He's very upset." But then, when did he ever have an *easy* time working? For the last few years he's had nothing but hard times and bad moods.

The right moment to remind and prod him would, in Pyotr Alexandrovich's opinion, be on Monday, when he and Lyalya returned from the banquet—if, of course, it was not after midnight. Pyotr Alexandrovich had observed that when Grigory drank, which was not very often (he didn't have the money to buy liquor himself, and nowadays people didn't very often buy drinks for you), he became talkative and outgoing and wasn't even stingy. In general, Pyotr Alexandrovich considered his son-in-law a stingy person—not so much with money as with other things. Whenever you asked him for some small thing, like a razor blade, a shaving brush, or a scarf to put on when you ran out on an errand, he would give it to you only after a while and with seeming reluctance. And when you asked for a book, Zhukovsky, say, or Anatole France, from his personal library on Bashilov Street—his library was quite extensive and very carefully chosen—he would promise, "Okay, Pyotr Alexandrovich, I'll bring it tomorrow." And then, when tomorrow rolled around, "Oh, I forgot! The next time I'm there, I'll definitely pick it up." He had shilly-shallied for two months with Zhukovsky and finally told him that he had made a point of looking for it just the day before, but hadn't been able to find it; it must have disappeared somewhere. He was stingy—what more could one say? On the other hand, of course, his life hadn't been easy. He'd been struggling for so many years now, and with nothing to show for it. No one would take his plays, nor his film scenarios either. And he wrote pretty well, splendidly in fact. He had a lot of talent—as much as the others at any rate. He had let him read his novella about the Siberian uprising—tremendous! It was written in a clean, crisp style and was well researched. Apparently he didn't have the right connections. In the literary field you couldn't get anywhere without them. You could beat your brains out for a hundred years, and all for nothing, you wouldn't get anywhere....

Pyotr Alexandrovich fell asleep before Grigory and Lyalya got home that evening, and had an oppressive dream. A tractor was slowly advancing into his garden, cracking and breaking down the wooden fence and trampling the flower beds, first the dahlias, then the pale-rose phlox in full autumn bloom, and finally the irises and the gillyflowers—everything trampled to bits. And now Mitka Kurtov, who was sitting behind the wheel of the tractor, shouted spitefully, "That's enough! We've won!" Pyotr Alexandrovich woke up with a stabbing pain in his heart. He called out to Irina, but in vain. There was a lot of noise, and people were talking in the next room. He could hear Lyalya's loud, happy laughter. It was half past one.

Suddenly Irina Ignatievna came running in and asked in alarm, "Father! Are you awake?"

"Where were you, old woman? It's going on two, time for decent people to be..." he mumbled angrily, still under the spell of his nightmare. Then his voice trailed off, "How long is this celebrating going to keep up?... Give me my heart medicine and something to wash it down with." When he felt this terrible pressure in his chest and was overcome by the frightening feeling that death might be close at hand, everything else seemed silly and unimportant: his wife's joy, Lyalya's successes and failures—everything, absolutely everything. And only one thing mattered—his garden. "Tell Grigory I want to see him."

"Petrasha, they have a guest out there, they're drinking tea," whispered Irina Ignatievna, bending close to her husband's face and for some reason smiling foolishly in the dark. "The playwright's here, the one whose play Lyalya's in...."

"So what! What the hell do I care about him. Go get Grigory right away. Tell him it's urgent!"

A little while later Grigory came in, pushing the door wide open and swaying somewhat as he cautiously sat down on the chair next to the couch. A strong smell of wine permeated the room.

"Grisha, what I want to discuss with you...." began Pyotr Alexandrovich, trying to adopt a strictly businesslike tone. He explained that they couldn't afford to lose a single day, a single hour. As far as the newspaper sketch was concerned, he must start in right away, the next morning. He should write it up, make phone calls wherever necessary, and deliver it in person. It was a crying shame, sabotage of the highest order, and anyone who heard about it would find it hard to believe that this sort of thing could still happen in the thirty-fifth year of Soviet rule.

Grigory sat with lowered head, his elbows resting on his knees, and nodded despondently, "Yes... yes... yes...." Then suddenly he raised his head and asked, "But Pyotr Sanych, why haven't you congratulated me?"

"What should I congratulate you for?"

"For the premiere of my common-law wife Lyudmila Petrovna Telepnova."

"Well, why not? Of course. My congratulations!"

"You certainly should congratulate me," he said, shaking an admonishing finger. "Everyone's been congratulating me, and I've been thanking them right back. Why, just now in the Sovetskaya everyone was shaking my hand and saying, 'We congratulate you, dear man.' Or else they'd say, 'We sincerely congratulate you, dear man.' And I would thank them right back. Thanks, thank you very much. One has to thank people! Mankind is perishing from a lack of gratitude—gratitude in the highest sense of the word, gratitude with a capital "G"...."

Standing in the doorway behind her son-in-law's back, Irina Ignatievna was making signs to her husband: kick him out, he's drunk—can't you see? From her jerky movements and foolish smile—in the middle of the night she'd taken it into her head, the idiot, to serve them tea—he could see that she was pretty far gone herself.

"Well, okay, you can go now...," he said in a weak voice. "We'll talk tomorrow. My congratulations."

"Thank you, thank you. I'm genuinely touched by your words...," whispered Grigory, shuffling his feet and bowing low, like some court jester. He always whispered this way and played the buffoon when he got drunk.

Irina Ignatievna turned out the hall light. Half a minute later Grigory turned it on again, pushed his way back into the room, and whispered, "By the way, the playwright's going to spend the night here—since it's so late. He says he's been quarreling with his wife and doesn't want to go home."

"Well then, let him stay here," said Pyotr Alexandrovich. "We've got enough room. Is that Comrade Smolyanov?"

"Yes. Comrade Smolyanov. And I must say he's a most enigmatic figure. Certain facts and the most trivial observations lead me to believe that..." he leaned over and whispered, "he hasn't even read Dostoevsky!"

"Really?" exclaimed Pyotr Alexandrovich, pretending to be shocked.

"Really, he hasn't. I swear he hasn't! Tss-tss-tss." Grisha giggled, waving his arms above the supine Pyotr Alexandrovich. "And I don't think he really knows his Tolstoi either.... By the way, in *The Possessed* Dostoevsky expresses the idea that to be happy, a man needs equal portions of good fortune and bad. That's very profound, Pyotr Sanych! You see, Ivan Gavrilovich Pryzhov.... Didn't I tell you about him? Well, never mind. He was a retired collegiate assessor.⁶ There's a whole story connected with him. But never mind that. The point is that this Pryzhov had an incredibly rough life—one misfortune after another— and yet despite all this, Pyotr Sanych, he was happy. How could he be happy, you wonder. Well, his wife, you see, Olga Grigorievna Martos... a really selfless woman.... Well, she wore herself out with him in Moscow—he never had a penny, was a continual failure and a terrible drunkard, an incurable one—and then, later on, she followed him to Siberia.... Yes, such is the mess he made of his life." Swaying slightly, Grigory wiped his tear-stained cheeks with the palm of his hand. He remained standing there for a whole minute without saying a word. Then he tiptoed out of the room.

The next day Lyalya brought the playwright, Comrade Smolyanov, in to meet her father. While Pyotr Alexandrovich and Nikolai Demyanovich were talking, Lyalya and her mother prepared breakfast. With them was Aunt Toma, who had made a special trip in from Alexandrov on Saturday to attend Lyalya's premiere. Grigory, in the meantime, had run out to get a bottle of vodka—for the morning after—at the nearest store, which happened to be right next to the church (they referred to it as the "church store") and a mere run through the park.

The playwright proved to be a nice, good-natured fellow, though at the moment he was suffering from a terrible hangover and couldn't wait for the vodka to arrive. It turned out that he was a great fishing enthusiast, and near his home outside of Saratov he kept a motorboat and tackle. Every summer he would flee from the unbearable noise and commotion of Moscow and take refuge there for a month or six weeks. Sometimes, he said, they caught sturgeon weighing up to forty pounds. His father, who way back when, in the year one, had been a fish merchant and had owned two Astrakhan longboats, used to tell how in his day they would catch sturgeon weighing close to 200 pounds. Gradually the conversation was brought around to the subject of gardens, and Pyotr Alexandrovich poured out to the playwright all his accumulated pain and anguish. Nikolai Demyanovich promised to help. He would discuss the matter with someone; and if, he added, there had been a telephone here in the apartment, he would have called up right away and straightened the matter out.

Pyotr Alexandrovich was overjoyed. He summoned his wife and demanded that their guest be taken outside and given a tour of the garden. His heart began to pound: could the playwright really be going to help him? He was, after all, an important man. If he wanted to, he could do it! Having ordered his wife to bring the folders with all his papers, he laid them out on the blanket—all his notes, letters, telegrams, and petitions.

"And, here's Struzhaninov, a doctor of sciences.... He's a prominent man too, and here he writes, 'Having been outraged to learn that....'"

At this point Grigory returned with the bottle of vodka and they sat down to breakfast. But just as Lyalechka was about to take up her guitar, there was a sudden knocking at the window and three people entered: their neighbor, Kurtov, who was dressed in his police uniform— that of a first lieutenant; another neighbor, Bespalov, who was retired; and Auntie Rosa Khalidova, the school janitress. Irina Ignatievna had once been on excellent terms with Auntie Rosa. She used to come in and do their laundry, run errands at the market, and sometimes even help Pyotr Alexandrovich sell his flowers. Irina Ignatievna had felt sorry for her and would occasionally give her something extra for the children—she had four of them and her husband had been killed during the war. But during the past year, as luck would have it, she and Irina Ignatievna had had a falling out.

Once again the commotion began. Auntie Rosa jabbered away in her thin voice, not making any sense whatsoever, and the retired Bespalov grumbled and shook his fists. Lyalya tried to reason with them and put an end to this scandalous outburst—how embarrassing in front of a guest!—but this only spurred them on, and they began waving some sort of document from the district architect. Pyotr Alexandrovich knew this man—a worthless sort, who would sign anything you put in front of him.

He lay back on the couch and didn't say a word. He was listening to the pounding of his heart. There was no feeling in his hands, and he began to feel faint as waves of numbness spread slowly through his whole body.

Irina Ignatievna suddenly cried out, "What are you doing, you scoundrels! There's a sick man lying here—can't you see? Swine!"

"Why shout and call people names?" thought Pyotr Alexandrovich almost indifferently. "That sort of thing isn't necessary, it doesn't do any good...."

Mitka Kurtov was droning something about the district social security office. "His pension will be taken away... they've been profiteering on their flowers...."

"You're a fool, Mitka," uttered Pyotr Alexandrovich so softly that probably no one heard him.

Nikolai Demyanovich suddenly grew crimson, his cheeks began to quiver, and his fist came crashing down on the table: "All of you are to get out of this room immediately! Out, out, out! Right away, this minute! And as for your behavior, Comrade First Lieutenant," he said, thrusting a finger at the stupefied Kurtov, "I'm going to have a talk with Ivan Grigorievich about you! What's your precinct? Are you in the Leningrad District?"

They were herded out of the room, but the noise could still be heard through the wall. Irina Ignatievna sat down next to the couch, covered her face, and burst into tears: "What a horrible day, Lyalechka, those scoundrels.... Petrasha, but what if they—oh, the hell with them! Your life is more important."

Pyotr Alexandrovich didn't say a word. He was listening to the inner workings of his body, and he didn't like the sound of things. His whole insides had become tremulous and fragile, and he didn't want to talk or move, because whatever it was that was pressing down on him might bring an end to this temporary fragility. And in fact, it was happening already—the pain was beginning. The playwright came back into the room and said, "We'll bring them to their senses! And don't be upset, they were just talking nonsense!" Out in the yard Grisha was shouting in a high-pitched voice. The pain, which was fierce enough without that, grew worse with each passing second. He was hardly able to utter the words, "Maybe you should call the doctor...."

IV

That summer was Leningrad—the first time Lyalya had ever been there. With Nikolai Demyanovich she went on outings and spent evenings at the Astoria Hotel, where there was a real jazz band—from somewhere in China—and dancing, with anyone you felt like, until the place closed down. Her heart was torn with pity for both the man she was with and the one she had left behind. Nikolai Demyanovich was hard to get along with, he drank heavily and sometimes the doctor had to be called in the middle of the night. And Grisha, she knew, shed tears at night and was forever running off to his room on Bashilov Street. For him she bought a leather coat in a special second-hand store on Nevsky Avenue.

In the theater everything had changed. *Ignat Timofeyevich* had been nominated for an award, and the new season began with a promotion and raise in salary for Lyalya. Nikolai Demyanovich bought himself a car and moved into a new apartment. The canvas bag lying on his trunk in the entryway bulged with letters, many of which came from soldiers. After Lyalya's portrait appeared on a magazine cover, Smurny started playing up to her and she sensed a secret, malicious jealousy on the part of her girlfriends, some of whom simply disappeared, unable to come to terms with her success. In the meantime, her poor father was languishing in Botkin Hospital. He'd been sent there again at the end of the fall, after his third heart attack.

Once again it was December, and once again there was snow. But this December was completely different from all the others. Lyalya had gone to the hospital to visit her father, bringing with her some tangerines and the new book *Moonstone*, which everyone was trying to get a copy of. During her long visit she also managed to slip fifty rubles to the elderly nurse to make sure that she took good care of her father. And now, emerging from the hospital yard, she made her way slowly along the darkening side street which lay wrapped in a frosty mist. People kept passing her by—people with string shopping bags and bundles, all running toward the nearest streetcar stop—but she walked along without hurrying. A car was waiting for her. And for some reason it was right here outside the hospital, in a moment of fatigue and grief for her father, that Lyalya suddenly experienced for the first time the comforting and unaccustomed sensation of being a *wealthy woman.*

All these people ahead of her, equally weighed down with the misfortunes of their dear ones, went hurrying about their business, as endless and dreary as the hospital fence. Yet she walked along slowly, breathing in deeply, calmly, and sadly, as befitted a woman of *wealth.* This sensation was a complex one, on many levels, and had little to do with the amount of money in her pocket—money was one thing she did not have, it disappeared so quickly. Rather, her sense of well-being was reflected in other things: in the fact, for example, that in cold weather she was warm. In this luxurious merino lamb coat with its fresh, lovely fragrance, she had no fear of the cold weather—perhaps for the first time in her life. It was also reflected in the peace of mind she felt with regard to that which is most important in life and without which one has no sort of life at all. For now no one would dare to say anything bad about her or even to think it. She had proved herself beyond all doubt, as could easily be seen by the crestfallen faces of the other actresses whenever she walked into the rehearsal room or whenever she... but one could go on forever, the examples were endless. Her sense of well-being also arose from the fact that men liked her, that she was a fa-

vorite, and that they suffered because of her. And it arose from the fact
that she could buy certain things which before had seemed inaccessi-
ble—a Chinese tea service, for example—and that she could go out in
the evening, drink red wine, and order her favorite dishes, such as
chicken *tabaka* and *suluguni* cheese. And finally, it arose from the fact
that she was meeting all sorts of new and exciting people.

After the first premiere there had followed a second, then a radio
performance, then an invitation to the Moscow Film Studio, then re-
views, articles, a portrait, another raise in salary, the promise of a new
apartment, invitations to appear at a conference, at a reception, and
her nomination for an award. And at the fur store on Sretenka Street,
as they were hunting for a fur cap for Grisha, the store manager, an elderly lady with glasses and with allergy blotches on her chin, had suddenly blushed and asked, "Excuse me, but aren't you from the Drama
Theater? Is your name Telepneva?"

The cap had been brought out from the back of the store and
wrapped in newspaper so as not to upset those who had been waiting
in line in front of them. As they emerged from the store with their purchase, Grisha had muttered with a laugh, "Damned if you're not becoming a celebrity! It's almost awkward to be out in public with you,
Madame."

Yes, it was awkward, very awkward. Lyalya could sense how he shriv-
eled up inside whenever he was prodded by reminders of her fame. He
was happy for her, of course, secretly rejoiced, and had even cried on
one occasion—someone had seen him wiping his eyes at a concert
where she had been singing Evdokia's songs from *Ivan Timofeyevich*.
(These songs had become popular and she often sang them at concerts,
sometimes even traveling to other cities for performances.) But inside
something seemed to be eating away at Grisha, something which he
could not control. After all, his own career hadn't moved forward at all,
not the slightest bit. This was a new cause of suffering which, however
much she felt herself to be a *wealthy woman*, stood in the way of her
achieving genuine happiness and perhaps even bliss. And she was not
really very far from a state of bliss. But now this suffering, which was
someone else's and yet at the same time so close to her, got in the way.
Her mother's nervous irritability, loss of weight, and daily anxiety over
her father also got in the way, as did her father himself, whose fate was
still unknown. One day it would seem that he was going to pull
through, the next day they would expect the worst.

Nikolai Demyanovich opened the car door from the inside, and
gathering up the folds of her merino lamb, Lyalya jumped nimbly into

the back seat. In the past she had watched from a distance as ladies gathered up the folds of their expensive furs with casual grace before disappearing into the depths of an automobile. And now here she was, herself a similar object of envy to the women passing by.

As the driver started off, Smolyanov asked about her father. They sped past the Belorussky Railroad Station and Mayakovsky Square, then turned left onto Sadovaya Street.

"Where are we going?" Lyalya asked.

"We're going to Alexander Vasilievich's. He's invited us for supper."

Alexander Vasilievich Agabekov, a friend of Nikolai Demyanovich's, lived near the Kursky railroad station. Lyalya didn't know what exactly he did for a living, but he had some sort of important position. Lyalya had never visited his apartment before, nor did she feel like going there now. On this particular evening she would have preferred to stay home. She was worried and depressed about Grisha. Undoubtedly he was moping about somewhere, feeling bitter. He might be at the library, or at a friend's, or at home, restlessly pacing back and forth, awaiting her return. But what was she to do? How was she to help him? He was, after all, a good man and a capable one. A wonderful man! A man of rare qualities and a genuine intellectual. He had learned Polish on his own in order to be able to read Polish newspapers. Actually, he was good at everything—he drew very well and he loved music. But he never seemed to have any luck. And as a result, time was passing and he wasn't getting anywhere.

Nikolai Demyanovich listened somewhat unsympathetically.

"He has no roots in the soil, that's his trouble," he suddenly remarked. And Lyalya remembered that he had expressed this sentiment once before, using the exact same words: "roots" and "soil."

That summer they had had some sort of evening get-together with the public on the open-air stage at Gorky Park and had acted out scenes from Smolyanov's play. Smolyanov himself had taken part, and for some reason Grisha had been there too. Afterwards the three of them along with Sergei Leonidovich and one of the actors had gone to the Poplavka Restaurant for something to eat. An argument had arisen—something philosophical—Grisha had gotten annoyed and said something sarcastic, and at this point Smolyanov had made his comment about Grisha's having no roots in the soil. Naturally, this was very indiscreet on his part, and he had no right to say it. Grisha had flared up and started shouting, "What soil are you talking about? The chernozem? The podzol? Fertilized soil? My soil is that of historical experience—everything that Russia has lived and suffered through!" And then for some reason he had begun telling about his family background: how one of his grandmothers had been a Polish political exile; how his great-grandfather had been a serf and his grandfather had been implicated in some student disorders and banished to Siberia; how his other grandmother had taught music in Petersburg; how her father had been born into the soldier class and how Grigory's own father had taken part in both the First World War and the Russian Civil War, although he was by nature a peaceful man who had been a statistician before the Revolution and afterwards an economist. And all of this taken together, Grisha had shouted excitedly, was the soil of historical experience, the experience of Russia itself—so you can go to hell with your screwed-up notions. It had been an unpleasant scene, almost a genuine quarrel. Sergei Leonidovich had tried to calm him down by saying that Nikolai Demyanovich had probably been referring to his lack of experience, the fact that he was young and had little experience of life. But Smolyanov had kept muttering with drunken persistence, "No, I definitely meant that he has no roots in the soil, that's exactly what I meant...." Grisha had said something nasty in return, but just at that moment something unexpected had occurred. A vicious fight had broken out at the next table and the police had come rushing to the scene. And by the time they left the restaurant they were no longer talking about "roots" and "soil."

"What do roots and soil have to do with it?" asked Lyalya. "The man needs help."

Nikolai Demyanovich was silent for a moment.

"Well, what if he were to get a full-time job somewhere? It wouldn't be easy, of course, but I could try...."

"No! You know yourself that he's very proud and sensitive...."

"But we could find him a good job."

"No, Kolya, what he needs is help in getting established in his literary career. If you could just give him a hand, open a few doors for him—he'd go the rest of the way on his own. If you could just put in a good word."

Lyalya's voice trembled slightly. She had never made a direct request like this to him before, and if he had done things for her in the past, it had been on his own initiative. But now, for the first time, she was asking. And right away she felt uncomfortable because she could sense his reluctance. And yet he was a kind and goodhearted man. Lyalya knew that he had helped many people—people from his native Saratov, young people, poor people, or people who had had bad luck. She also knew that he couldn't bring himself to leave his wife even though he didn't love her and was continually having to put up with her foolishness and bad temper. No, he couldn't leave her; she was mentally unbalanced and he felt sorry for her.

But Grisha's case was different. Lyalya sensed that here she would meet with resistance and she decided to meet it head on, unpleasant as this might be. Undoubtedly he hadn't forgotten that outburst in the Poplavka, but he had never once said a word about it to Lyalya. Only on one occasion had he observed rather timidly, "I just don't understand how you can live with such an adolescent." Lyalya had taken offense. No, that she wouldn't tolerate! Grisha was no adolescent but a real man in the best sense of the word. "And how can you live with that hysterical wife of yours?" But he managed to justify himself by saying, "Marta isn't a hysterical wife—she's a sick woman. And I don't have any feeling left for her except, perhaps, a feeling of obligation and a fear of inflicting a fatal blow. But as for you, you'll never break away from your Grisha." That was true. Why should she deny it? Grisha was Grisha, and that was all there was to it. Somewhere in Chekhov there was the line: "A wife is a wife." And the strange part of it was that Grisha was not even her "wife," that is, not her husband. They were not officially married, and he still kept his own room on Bashilov Street, which he would regularly flee to after the two of them had quarreled or on days when he felt particularly depressed. He didn't support her, as a husband was supposed to, he didn't pay for her clothes, and yet, nonetheless—she didn't understand why, it was impossible to explain!—she didn't have the strength to drive him from her heart. He had become an integral part of her; she was bound to him even by the ills of his childhood his measles, scarlet fever, lisping, rashes, sweating spells....

Nikolai Demyanovich laid his hand on Lyalya's and said, "Okay, we'll think about it...."

Agabekov's other guests had already arrived. They were seated at the table in the living room in a formal, stagelike manner. The room itself must have been well over 100 feet long—Lyalya had never even seen such a large room—and above the table was a magnificent chandelier. The meal was already well under way, and there was a great deal of food of the choicest variety. One could tell immediately that it was not homemade but had been brought up from some restaurant.

As soon as he could do so unobtrusively, Nikolai Demyanovich whispered in Lyalya's ear, "I forgot to tell you, it's his father's birthday today."

The little old gentleman was seated at the head of the table. He had unusually bright and rosy cheeks, almost like those of a mannequin, and was dressed in a black Circassian coat.

The toasts and speechmaking had already begun. One lady suddenly and enthusiastically raised a toast to "the lady who is here with us this evening and such a splendid representative of..." The men gazed at her in delight and exclaimed, "To you, Lyudmila Petrovna! Bottoms up! Everybody drink to Lyudmila Petrovna!"

Someone shouted, "I'm warning you, anyone who doesn't empty his glass for Lyudmila Petrovna...."

In their excitement and eagerness to clink glasses one sensed a certain joyful admiration and perhaps even devotion. Although Lyalya realized that this was the usual sort of nonsense brought on by alcohol and that most of these people probably hadn't even heard of her, much less seen her on stage, still, she found it pleasant—extremely pleasant. A guitar appeared, and Lyalya was asked to sing. She was reluctant at first, but gave in after they pleaded with her and after Nikolai Demyanovich, squeezing her knee under the table, softly entreated, "Please don't refuse." After a while, when she had already finished her second glass of wine, she herself was in the mood and enjoyed singing "Up in the Firmament, among the Glimmering Stars," along with some gypsy songs and "Raising the Dust along the Street," which her mother had taught her and which had been one of her favorites since childhood. As she sang, Alexander Vasilievich kept staring at her with unblinking eyes. It was a strange look, directed straight at her mouth, and because of this—because he did not look at her eyes but only at her mouth—she felt uncomfortable. There was something cold and lifeless in the gaze of this man with his small mustache and high, prominent forehead. His gaze grew glassier and glassier, even terrifying for a moment, but finally his eyelids fluttered and the glassiness disappeared. The Georgian guests went on to sing some of their own songs in their characteristic manner, which was really quite beautiful, and Lyalya tried to accompany them on the guitar. Then one of the guests suddenly jumped up and, clapping his hands, began to sing in a strong Georgian accent:

We'll drink, drink, and have a good time!...

The others joined in, singing and clapping, and dragged Lyalya with them as they moved into the other room. Already somewhat lightheaded, she felt like being silly and, for that matter, playing along as the belle of the ball. She plunked herself down on the floor with her guitar, and seated there on a bearskin, she began to sing with feeling and so loudly that she drowned out the music coming from the radio-gramophone:

> Bold Khas-Bulat!..
> Poor is your mountain hut....

And why was she suddenly in such a gay mood? Because they used to sing "Khas-Bulat" at home. Her father would sing bass, and Uncle Misha, Aunt Zhenya's husband, would strain to sing tenor. Yet half an hour later, when they returned to the large room with the chandelier, Lyalya felt a sudden stabbing pain, like that of a sore rib that has accidentally shifted position. It was the thought of Grisha flashing through her mind. By now there were only men sitting at the table in the large room. They were arguing, and Nikolai Demyanovich wasn't among them. Lyalya was told that he had gone off in the car to pick up a friend and would soon be back. Lyalya remained in the room, listening to their conversation—something about the American president and about Germany and Yugoslavia—but none of this interested her, and she was utterly bored.

Two hours later, Alexander Vasilievich and Lyalya were sitting at a small table in his study. There were three candles lighted in the gilded wall bracket overhead. They both felt warm from the heat of the radiators and from the wine they had drunk, and Alexander Vasilievich had loosened his tie and unfastened the top button of his white shirt. They were talking about music. In her childhood, Lyalya had attended music school for three years. She was found to have absolute pitch and a good voice, but her parents would have had to buy a piano and her father could somehow never raise the money since he spent every extra penny on his garden. It was only just before the war that they finally managed to buy one, but in 1943, when they didn't have enough to eat, they sold it. True, her mother did buy her a guitar by way of compensation. Alexander Vasilievich said that he loved Italian songs and opera and that he had a lot of German recordings of Caruso, Gigli, and Toti dal Monte. Lyalya's eyes lit up—she was dying to listen to them. They went into the other room and sat down on the sofa. The guests had all left by this time, and there were just the two of them. The records were so beautiful that Lyalya forgot about everything—about the fact that she was expected at home, that Nikolai Demyanovich had disappeared somewhere, and that Alexander Vasilievich hadn't really appealed to her earlier in the evening. She had suspected him of being a Don Juan—a type that she absolutely detested. Not that she had any real evidence of this; she just sensed it instinctively, and in the most foolish details: his trim, little mustache and his overly delicate treatment of her, as if he were taking pains not to lay so much as a finger on her.

As one a.m. drew near, Lyalya became extremely agitated: "Where can Nikolai Demyanovich be? What if there's been an accident?"

"Kolya will be back soon," Alexander Vasilievich firmly reassured her. "He'll definitely be back."

"But in the meantime I'm keeping you up."

"Oh, don't worry about me. I never sleep at night, that's when I get my work done. And if I yawn, that's my heart acting up. I just have to take something for it." He took a small glass receptacle from his pocket and shook several tiny, red capsules into the palm of his hand.

"Can I bring you some water?"

"Please do, if it's not too much trouble."

She ran into the kitchen and turned on the light. It was an enormous room—more like a public cafeteria than anything else—and from behind a cloth partition she could hear someone snoring. She poured some water from the cold teakettle into a cup and returned to the other room. Alexander Vasilievich was lying on the sofa with his eyes half closed. His face, which had been flushed from wine just a short time before, had gone pale and his cheeks were sunken. None of this boded well.

After swallowing the water, Alexander Vasilievich took Lyalya's hand. "Don't go away, Lyudmila Petrovna."

"I'm not going anywhere," said Lyalya, at the same time thinking to herself: "Where would I go? It's after one—too late for the subway. There's something wrong with him, and Grisha's expecting me...." "Sit closer, right next to me. That's it. Here, please...." He didn't let go of her hand, but continued to hold it tightly. It was as if he were afraid to let her go, as a sick man might cling to a nurse. But for some reason Lyalya felt no pity for him. Suddenly the phone rang in the living room. It was Nikolai Demyanovich, reporting in a weak voice—she could barely hear him through the static of a pay phone—that they had gotten stuck in the Zamoskvorechie section of town. They had landed in a ditch, and there were no cars around. No one would be able to get them out until morning.

"Please forgive me, and spend the night there, at Alexander Vasilievich's. I'll pick you up in the morning. Only behave yourself, you hear? Behave yourself!"

"Are you all right?" she cried in alarm.

"Yes, yes, I'm all right. Please forgive me!"

She couldn't understand why he should ask her to forgive him.

"Nikolai Demyanovich won't be coming," said Lyalya, returning to the room where Alexander Vasilievich was still lying on the sofa. "I'm going to be off, Alexander Vasilievich. Maybe I'll still be able to catch a trolleybus. Goodbye. Oh, where did I put my handbag?"

It suddenly swept over her: she had to leave right away, she mustn't stay a second longer. That was the way it was sometimes—she wouldn't know why, but all of a sudden there would be no power in the world that could hold her back. Her host tried to dissuade her and even jumped up from the sofa with unexpected vitality. Where was she going? What had happened? He refused to give her back her handbag. No, no, she definitely had to go. But it was almost two a.m! Never mind, she'd find a taxi. But what about calling her family? No, no. No, no, no! No, that was impossible, completely out of the question. He'd keep her handbag as a souvenir. Excuse me, but I'm leaving, I'm on my way, thank you very much. But why the big hurry? What on earth is the matter?

He looked at her with a certain haughtiness mixed with incredulity.

"What did Smolyanov say to you?"

"He said that I should behave myself. What do you think he meant by that?"

"He meant... I think that...." He seized her hand and pulled her toward him. "He's an idiot! What do you need him for anyway?"

And right then and there she was struck by the chilling realization. It always happened that way with her: at first a feeling or intuition, then the realization. For the first second she couldn't believe it herself, but then—yes, perhaps that call had not been the result of any accident. For if there really had been an accident, why would he have felt the need to apologize? A person who is drunk isn't capable of dissembling. He had given himself away involuntarily by asking her forgiveness.

"There's a lot we need to talk about. We didn't have a chance to...." This man with his high forehead and somewhat pompous look was speaking very sternly now and tightly gripping Lyalya's hands. She tore them loose, though not with all her strength, since he did have some sort of heart condition and she was afraid. He started talking about the Academic Theater and about how he was going to have her transferred there and appointed to a permanent position, with a promotion and a raise in salary, and how he would arrange for any concerts she wanted to give or any trips she wanted to take. And if she refused, she should realize that a woman with such lips.... Well, that did it! No one had ever gotten anything from her using that technique. Suddenly she asked disarmingly, "Tell me, is Nikolai Demyanovich terribly afraid of you?"

"What? He certainly is!"

Lyalya burst out laughing. Easy, easy does it. You should take it easy and not tire yourself out this way. It's bad for your heart. And now she felt both sadness and contempt for Nikolai Demyanovich, that petty liar who had suddenly been transformed in her own mind into a pitiful nonentity. As for herself, she vowed never to say another word to him or even glance in his direction.

She flew through the snowstorm along the enormous and now empty Sadovoe Ring. Where was she headed? After running a long way she suddenly realized that she was going in the wrong direction. The subway was closed and she needed to head toward the center of town— toward the inner ring of boulevards and Masha's place on Clear Ponds Boulevard. Half an hour later and by now thoroughly exhausted, she finally reached the inner ring. Here it was as quiet and deserted as a forest: no tramps, no policeman, only the benches in their thick, snowy armor. And now, wandering along one of the boulevards with tears running down her face, she thought to herself: "Lord, what a fool I've been! What have I been doing with my life? ... And Grisha, my own beloved Grisha...."

V

Rebrov managed to earn a little money by answering letters for two editorial offices and by writing radio scripts. Besides this, he sometimes published short historical sketches in popular magazines. All this brought in next to nothing but it was at least a way of staying afloat. At best he would earn about 1,000 rubles a month; sometimes 700, sometimes 300, and at other times, nothing at all—a big, fat zero. Now that Lyalya was earning good money and all sorts of unexpected bonuses kept flowing in, things should have been easier for him. But instead, this improvement in their financial situation only made him feel all the more frustrated and depressed. Before when they hadn't had money, well, that was all there was to it. He was no aristocrat, he could get along with a simple cup of coffee when he went out in the evening. Nowadays Lyalya might hand him a 30- or even a 100-ruble note. Still, he hated being in the position of having to ask. Then there was his mother-in-law, who only made matters worse. It seemed to her that he was forcing Lyalya to run around and make extra money from concerts and other special appearances—or in other words, that he was exploiting her. Irina Ignatievna did not come out and say this in so many words, but she let her feelings be known, and Rebrov was very much aware of them. Moreover he sometimes came across her epistles to her daughter—Lyalya would carelessly leave them lying around—and there were times when he felt that he was beginning to hate his mother-in-law. In the evenings she would complain to Lyalya directly, "He came into the kitchen and didn't even say hello.... Three times I've asked him to chop up some firewood...." All this was irksome and impossible to put up with, and he was dying to escape to his room on Bashilov Street. But Lyalya begged him to stay, since otherwise she would have had to go with him. This was what had usually happened in the past, but right now she didn't feel that she could run off and leave her mother alone. So she begged and pleaded with him, but never had the courage to take her mother firmly in hand.

He kept silent, put up with it, and every day he would sneak off to the library early in the morning and return home as late as possible.

On this particular day, as luck would have it, he had come home early and rather upset. For in one of the editorial offices, where for three years now he had regularly been assigned to answer correspondence, he was suddenly told that the new editor-in-chief had been looking through the list of part-time employees and that his future there was in jeopardy. Why? Why should it be? One of his acquaintances in the office shrugged his shoulders in embarrassment: "I don't really know anything about this. I suppose the situation will be clarified before long." And a female acquaintance remarked ironically, "It seems you're not so hard up anymore. Your wife is doing very well, isn't she? And there are people whose only source of income is these letters."

He should have stood his ground, complained, and appealed to their sympathy, since the matter did not seem to have been definitely decided. But his old fear came to the fore—wouldn't he have looked foolish and pathetic in the role of supplicant?—and he gave in. Of course, there were people who were more deserving, he couldn't deny that. Everything they said was true. Nevertheless, this was terribly unpleasant news. But rather than let his feelings show, he even joked with them, told a humorous anecdote, and walked off with proud composure. His income had been reduced by one third. He didn't want to see or talk to anyone, he only wanted to go home, to Lyalka. Only she could make him feel better by telling him something silly and reassuring.

Lyalya was to have visited her father in the hospital at six and to have arrived home at about seven, since there was no performance that day.

But she didn't come home at seven, or at eight, or at ten. Her mother began to get worked up, which, as usual in her case, took the form of all sorts of pointless flailing around. First she wanted to run off to the subway station, then she thought of calling the hospital from a public pay phone, and finally she was simply going to head out there on her own. It was only with difficulty that Rebrov dissuaded her. Did she want to upset Lyalya's father—how foolish that would be!

Tamara Ignatievna, Lyalya's Aunt Toma from Alexandrov, had already been living in the house for several days now, having come to give his mother-in-law a hand with the housework. She was a tall, quiet old lady with a very unhappy fate: all her immediate family, her husband and children, had been scattered and killed during the war. Although she was registered as a permanent resident of Alexandrov, 100 kilometers away, she usually spent a good part of the year in Moscow, living with her sisters Zhenya and Veronika, with her brother Kolya in Izmailov, or less frequently here, with her sister Irina. She was a private seamstress, and not a very good one, having learned to sew in order to support herself. In connection with her work she often had to live for weeks at a time in the homes of complete strangers. His mother-in-law didn't really like her sister, and in fact, Lyalka and her father treated Tamara more kindly than did Irina Ignatievna, who seldom invited her sister to visit. Her most common excuse was that she was afraid of being fined for having an overnight guest who was not officially registered in Moscow. And considering the fact that their neighbor, police lieutenant Kurtov, had it in for Pyotr Alexandrovich, such a fine could easily come about.

But the heart of the matter lay elsewhere—in an old woman's foolish jealousy, whose underlying causes reached back some quarter of a century. Yet when Pyotr Alexandrovich had gone off to the hospital for the second time, Irina Ignatievna had herself written to Aunt Toma, asking her to come and stay with her. And all of her pent-up anxieties and frustrations—her fear for her husband's life, her irritation with her son-in-law, her apprehensions about her daughter, the pain from her ulcer—all of this had been unleashed on quiet, lanky Aunt Toma. And she had been patient and long-suffering, she had forgiven her sister and tried to calm her. Right now too, she was trying to pacify her, or at the very least to dissuade her from setting off for the hospital. But for this her only thanks was the cruel retort, "You've been without a husband or children for so long, you can't possibly understand how I feel."

As it got close to eleven, Rebrov himself began to get nervous. He ran out to the pay phone to call Lyalya's girlfriend Masha, who acted as their telephone go-between—Lyalya sometimes leaving messages with Masha for him. Masha was at home—but no, no one had called. Perhaps—yes, most likely a concert had come up. It seemed that they had been planning to give some sort of concert in Krasnogorsk.

"How come you didn't go with them?" asked Rebrov suspiciously, though he already felt somewhat relieved.

"It wasn't our theater's concert, it was the group from the Moscow Variety Theater," Masha explained. "But I don't know for sure. It's just a guess."

When Rebrov told his mother-in-law about the concert, she seemed somewhat reassured and the three of them sat down for a late evening snack. But Lyalya didn't appear either at twelve or at one. The Moscow Variety Theater usually traveled by bus when making outside appearances, and on the way back the bus would drop Lyalya off right at her door. Nonetheless, at half past twelve his mother-in-law grabbed her fur coat, put on her scarf, and ran off to the Sokol subway station in order to meet her. Whom did she think she was going to meet? Rebrov tried to explain to her that this was absurd, a complete waste of energy. Irina Ignatievna was already in such a distraught state, however, that logical argument had no effect on her.

"Of course it's not very pleasant to be out walking the streets late at night. It would be much pleasanter to be sitting inside, where it's nice and warm," she muttered.

"Well, I could go instead, I'd be happy to. Only what's the sense?"

"Sense, sense! Everything has to make sense for you. You just can't seem to understand that when a person is terribly upset—I just can't sit here doing nothing...."

From the yard Kandidka gave a thin, joyous yelp. Irina Ignatievna must be untying her and taking her with her, which meant that he, Rebrov, didn't have to worry: Kandidka would tear any would-be assailants to pieces. But there was something offensive in this whole scene—in this senseless running off just to make a point. For it wasn't to meet Lyalya that she had gone running off to the subway—not even she herself had any hope of that. She had gone in order to insult and reproach him, and so that her sister might see how horrible and unfeeling he was, staying at home while an old woman went out alone in the middle of the night. But he for his part couldn't bring himself to perform some senseless act just for the sake of proving her wrong.

Tamara Ignatievna came quietly out of Pyotr Alexandrovich's room. There was a guilty look on her face. She shuffled about in her felt boots for a while, then she said, "I wanted to go with her, but she chased me off.... She's angry with me because I stood up for you. Well, what does she think—that I don't have any right to express my opinion? I say exactly what I think...."

Rebrov was sitting at the table, smoking.

Continuing to shuffle about, the lanky old lady droned on in a plaintive voice, "I'm not a sponger or a beggar of some sort. I have my own house. And I have hundreds of friends in Moscow. There's Natalya Alexeyevna Mikhnacheva, for example, a general's wife—she has begged me to come and live with her so many times, she's even sent two telegrams. But why did I come here? Because I felt sorry for Irina. She's going crazy without Pyotr—she's lost her bearings and is a nervous wreck. And I understand her only too well. She hasn't been through what some of us have been through.... And I felt sorry for Lyalka and wanted to help.... But why should I have to listen to her telling me that I don't know how to do this or that I don't understand that? Or that I'm always playing up to you? As if I were playing up to you! Well, if that isn't a foolish idea! Why on earth should I play up to you? Are you going to give me a pension or feed me chocolates?"

"Your sister likes to humiliate people," said Rebrov.

"It's true, Grisha, it's true! She likes very much to humiliate people. You're absolutely right. Even when we were still students at the gymnasium, she was like that. She once made our youngest sister Veronika eat chalk before she would show her some letter that Veronika was begging to see.... No, Irina was not the kindest member of our family.... And yet she's turned out to be the happiest! All the rest of us have suffered some family disaster—or at least something has gone wrong in our personal lives. Zhenka's Mikhail Abramovich is her second husband—her first died before the war. Veronika doesn't have any husband at all—or rather, she had one, but he was a drunkard and she kicked him out. Then there's my own case, which speaks for itself. And even in Kolya's case—you can't say anything good about his marriage. Olimpiada is so greedy and materialistic. She actually shortened our mother's life. No, none of us is happy, only Irina—and now, as you see, life's misfortunes have caught up with her as well. But I didn't say anything special on your behalf. I merely told her that I always sympathized with you because you're all alone in this world. You have no father or mother or sisters or brothers—no one at all. Isn't that true?"

"Yes," said Rebrov, "but you don't have to feel sorry for me."

"Grisha, it's not a question of feeling sorry for you. I was simply pointing out that she should be more understanding. I reminded her that she has Lyalka, Petya, us, and all sorts of relatives—enough to fill a whole village—but whom do you have—no one at all."

"You really don't have to sympathize with me. I'm not interested in that."

"And she tells me that I'm playing up to you. Or that being alone is not a reason for praising someone. And she points out that I'm alone too. Well, I gave up trying to talk to her—never mind, I thought, life hasn't taught you anything yet, but you'll learn soon enough. Yes...."

She sat down at the table, under the lamp, which immediately illuminated her large nose and heavily lined face. It was the face of a useless old woman, but at the same time it was strangely reminiscent of the weatherbeaten face of a sailor. It bore the traces of time, the many places she had been, and the many sufferings she had known. Suddenly, turning to Grigory, she said gently and even entreatingly, "Still, please don't be angry with her, all right? You have no idea how beautiful she used to be, and how many men proposed to her in 1923! She was simply spectacular. She was, after all, a ballerina. She studied with Polyakov in his studio on Bronnaya Street, and the whole family would turn out to see her perform. Polyakov invited her to join him when he emigrated to Riga. But she didn't go. She felt sorry for Mother. Father had just died and Kolya was having a hard time.... Petya had already appeared on the scene by that time, but no one had any idea what was going to develop there.... No, it was only because of Mother, only because of Mother.... I say that she's been happy. But what sort of happiness has she had—squatting in the soil and manure, planting potatoes, sawing and chopping wood like some peasant? We've all kept telling her over the years that she and Petya should sell this house, the garden, and buy a small, convenient apartment in the center of town, where they could start living like other civilized people. After all, what does one need with a house and garden in Moscow? But no, Petya couldn't do that. He couldn't live without his garden. And here you have to give her credit: she's always been devoted to her family. After all, her youth, all of her hopes, and whatever talent she had—and she did have quite a bit—all of it has gone into tending this house and garden. There's her happiness for you, Grisha, and what has she got to look forward to now? Heaven forbid that anything should happen to Pyotr Alexandrovich! She wouldn't survive it.... Oh, how silly and naive she can be. If I were to tell you...."

As Tamara Ignatievna mumbled on, Rebrov strained his ears for the sound of a dog or of voices, but he heard nothing. It occurred to him that the human face, when seen through a magnifying glass, must be repulsive, with all its pores, little hairs, and surface irregularities. But that's exactly what we do in life, we see everything through a magnifying glass. Every minute, every second, is magnified a thousandfold. And yet, one should always look at the years, the whole... then there wouldn't be any hatred. It would be impossible to hate a woman who had given birth to that other woman who was his very life. It would be impossible because they were, after all, one whole, one continuum. They were like a tree and its branches. You couldn't separate the pain of the one from the other. She had wanted to be a ballerina and instead led a poor, kitchen-garden sort of life. And so? And so one shouldn't hate her. A person doesn't notice when he gradually changes into something else....

Irina Ignatievna returned after an hour and burst into tears as soon as she learned that Lyalya hadn't arrived. Rebrov himself began imagining various accidents, assaults, catastrophes. There wasn't any possibility of his sleeping, of course, but to remain in the same room with his sobbing mother-in-law was beyond his strength. He went upstairs to his and Lyalya's room and tried to read, but was unable to concentrate. So he lay down on the bed, smoked, and felt miserable. Sometimes he would be overcome by drowsiness, and the next few minutes would pass in a sort of delirium. Then he would suddenly jump up and reach for a cigarette. At some point or other Irina Ignatievna appeared at the door. Her face was swollen and wisps of matted hair protruded from under her kerchief.

"All this extra money be damned! All the money in the world isn't worth an evening like this! Why do you send her out to earn extra money for you? You should be ashamed of yourself!"

Rebrov felt a choking sensation in his throat. "*Who* sends her out to earn extra money?"

"You! Don't you have any conscience?" And her tearful eyes expressed not spite but a genuine belief in what she was saying and genuine despair as she confronted him, the villain.

"No one sends her out to earn money! It's you who... I...," he began shouting, gasping for breath. "You are the one who's destroying our life together! You, not me! You! You!"

"But you, you send her out to earn extra money...."

"Don't lie! You've already destroyed our family—yes, yes! You forbid Lyalya to marry me! You force her to have abortions!"

"But you're not a real husband to her, so why should she have children by you?"

"Yes, I am a real husband to her, but you're not a real mother, because you make her life miserable, simply miserable!"

This was followed by another fit of sobbing and a scream through her tears, "Don't you dare say such things to me! I love my daughter more than life itself!" And after blowing her nose and wiping her mouth with tidy precision she added, "You're no husband, you're nothing but a pitiful failure, and my daughter is unhappy with you."

He ran downstairs, grabbed his coat and fur cap, pulled on his felt boots, and ran out into the snowy yard. As he circled around in the dark, he was oppressed by a nasty sort of feeling—a fear of himself, of what he might have done in that moment of hatred, almost insanity. How had it happened? Why, just a short while before he had been thinking about the old woman quite calmly. He was going out of his mind and turning into a nasty, spiteful person. He had to do something. Perhaps he should apologize to her? No, that wasn't it—he had to do something about *himself!* Sometime after two and completely numb from the subfreezing temperature, he came back into the house, went upstairs, and collapsed on his bed.

Lyalya arrived in the morning, her cheeks rosy from the cold. She kissed Rebrov passionately, with a certain greedy impatience, while simultaneously expressing concern for her mother.

"My God, you haven't slept at all! Oh, my poor dears! Aunt Tomochka, and you didn't sleep either? How awful of me, what I've put you all through...."

"Lyalya," her mother asked tearfully, "why do you wear yourself out with these concerts?"

"I wasn't at a concert at all. I stupidly got stuck at a certain person's place, Smolyanov promised to come and pick me up, but his car broke down and I ended up going to Masha's on foot at 2 a.m. The whole thing was a nightmare...."

"Oh, Lyalechka...."

Her mother sighed, but one could tell that she was immediately relieved upon hearing Smolyanov's name and the reference to a "certain person's place." Rebrov could guess what she was dreaming of.

But now he was overwhelmed by a new anxiety: where *had* she been? Had somebody been forcing his attentions on her? Here was Smolyanov cropping up again. Yet despite his anxiety he was happy with the fact that she had been so genuinely upset at his suffering and had kissed him passionately and without embarrassment in front of her mother and aunt.

Lyalya sensed the tension between her mother and husband right away, and after she and Rebrov had gone upstairs to their room, she asked him if everything was all right at home. He replied that everything was the same as usual.

"Grisha, I'm begging you—please!" Lyalya whispered urgently. "Be as gentle as you can with Mother. She's going out of her mind on account of Papa..."

"Okay," said Rebrov.

Lyalya threw off her dress and heels, put on a bathrobe, and lay down. The frosty glow had disappeared from her face and as she lay there with her eyes closed, she looked pale, her cheeks sunken with fatigue.

"Well, where were you actually? Before Masha's?"

"Oh, Grisha, it's a very dull story. I was at somebody's apartment, they were celebrating some old man's birthday... I'll tell you about it later. Right now I want to take a nap."

"Did some cad try to proposition you?"

"Of course... and not just one! All sorts of people were trying to proposition me...." She turned over on her side, with her face to the wall. "Please wake me in an hour. I'm being picked up at 11:30. And please put the blanket over me. Thanks, Grishenka."

Rebrov left the room. In the hall he ran into his mother-in-law and said to her quite unexpectedly even for himself, "I shouted some foolish things yesterday, Irina Ignatievna. Please don't pay any attention...."

"Yes, yes, I understand. We were both upset. It's that naughty girl in there who's to blame. Grisha, would you please run out and get some milk?" On her face there was a sweet, pleading smile, as if the previous evening had never happened. "She's coughing and I want to give her something hot to drink."

Rebrov ran off to the store with a light heart and returned with two bottles of milk. Then he went upstairs to his "study."

Next to his and Lyalya's room was a tiny little room, a mere cubbyhole with a slanted ceiling and sloping walls formed by the eaves. A table and chair were all that would fit into this "study," but there was a small window and one could work there. Rebrov began laying out his folders and thick notebooks. The notebook which he now took in hand had on its cover the words: "Outline for pl. on P. W.," which meant "Outline for a play on the People's Will movement."[7] He had been working on this play for the past few weeks, actually almost a month, ever since he had become interested in Nikolai Vasilievich Kletochnikov, a People's Will agent who had operated in the Third Section.[8] He had first learned about Kletochnikov four years ago when the Academy of Sciences published a new edition of Morozov's[9] memoirs. Later on he had read about him in other books, such as Figner's[10] *Records of a*

Life's Work. But the idea of writing a play about Kletochnikov had come to him only recently and, as was usually the case, it had come all of a sudden. He had begun working on it with great enthusiasm—with the same sort of enthusiasm that he had begun his novella about the Decembrists, then about the uprising of the exiled Poles in Siberia, then about Ivan Pryzhov, and finally about the poet Mikhailov. All of this unfinished muddle lay heaped in draft notebooks inside innumerable folders, awaiting the right moment for completion. A day would suddenly come, however, when he would be forced to ask himself what all of this was for. The question would present itself timidly at first, only slightly cooling his ardor, but promising to return full force later on, with predictably chilling effect. And when this happened, his creative impulses would become stalled, he would feel fed up and depressed, and his mind would turn to the more urgent matter of earning a living.

He took out a thin stack of paper from the folder. On the top page, along with several handwritten paragraphs, were ink drawings of faces with sideburns, of swords, and of horses. Rebrov loved to draw horses, though this was not out of any particular love for horses. Actually, these shaggy monstrosities were not really drawings at all, but the offspring of his nervous tension. They would come to life on their own, spontaneously, the moment he plunged deep into thought.

A large quantity of ugly horses on a crossed-out page was a bad sign—it meant that a period of creative paralysis was close at hand. Well, he knew what the problem was. And it was his own fault! Three days ago he had talked about Kletochnikov to one of his magazine acquaintances. After hearing him out, his acquaintance had said that no, probably no one would be interested. Rebrov had guessed as much himself, but still, it would have been better not to ask. Poor Nikolai Vasilievich Kletochnikov, this police department chief who had quietly died from a hunger strike in the Alexeyev salient of the Peter and Paul Fortress after a quiet, short, and heroic life—what could he hope for now, seventy years later? He had been incurably ill, doomed to death. And doomed to oblivion. There was absolutely no future for a play based on his life, even a fool could see that. So Rebrov had come to a decision. Maybe he should go off somewhere, to a different city, heaven knows where. But Lyalya wouldn't be willing to go with him, not now when things were going so well for her.

With his customary dexterity—the product of his despair—Rebrov kept fashioning horses at lightning speed, one after another, one after another....

Two years ago he had been offered a job in Barnaul, with the local newspaper, and Lyalya had applied for a job with the Barnaul Theater. They had been just on the point of leaving when at the last moment his mother-in-law had managed by superhuman efforts—tears and demagoguery—to spoil their plans. But his mother-in-law was beside the point. The one thing she was afraid of, of course, was that Rebrov and Lyalya would become firmly united forever. And Barnaul would have meant precisely that—forever! For Rebrov the move would have involved a tremendous sacrifice—the loss of Scholars' Reading Room No. 3, old books and antiquarian bookstores, and the popular magazines in which his historical vignettes were published (could he send them in by mail? probably not, and besides where would he get his material?)—but nonetheless, he was prepared to make this sacrifice. Temporarily, of course. He was even eager to do so, in order to break with the past and start afresh. After all, one lives a long time.

Yes, his mother-in-law had protested with all her strength, but Lyalya was not the most exemplary daughter and she had often acted against her mother's wishes before—she had left music school against her mother's wishes, she had had an affair with that lame poet and had run off and lived with him against her mother's wishes, and now for the last five years she had been living with him, Rebrov, against her mother's wishes. What this meant was that she couldn't make up her mind about moving to Barnaul and being with him forever. He had to go through some sort of trial period in order to show what he could do and to provide her with a guarantee. His mother-in-law spoke about this openly, while Lyalya thought the same thing—he was convinced of it—only subconsciously, without even being aware of it herself.

But if one were to probe deeper, to the very heart of things, then probably even Lyalya was beside the point. The crux of the matter lay in himself. He could not say either to himself or to her that it was forever. Not because he didn't love her enough, but because he loved her too much. His love constricted him and weighed him down. It was as if he were in an overloaded boat that was about to capsize and he was afraid of falling into the open sea. Yes, he first had to prove to himself what he could do and to provide himself with a guarantee. And Lyalya sensed this too: "Grisha, now that we don't have to worry about where the next penny is coming from, you can sit calmly and work...."

At breakfast Lyalya hastily told about her visit to her father and about how he might be able to come home by the beginning of February. Then she said something about the theater, about Smurny's intrigues, and about the conflict that had arisen between Sergei

Leonidovich and Smolyanov because Sergei Leonidovich didn't want to stage his new play. Bob agreed with him, but the executive director was insisting that they go ahead with it. Bob was in danger of being fired, and Smurny was already playing up to Smolyanov. Irina Ignatievna was eager to know more, but Rebrov kept silent. He didn't like to discuss theater matters with Lyalya in his mother-in-law's presence. Suddenly, however, he blurted out in spite of himself:

"And he's right in not wanting to stage it! He's finally come to his senses."

"Why is he right?"

"Well, because his plays are no good. No one needs that sort of...."

"Grisha, you're wrong, and excuse my saying this, but I think you're a bit envious. Some of Smolyanov's plays are quite good, and the public likes him."

"The public likes him! As if that were any criterion! Well, just put two fools on stage and let them start punching each other in the face, and naturally the public will.... But what really gets me is your saying that I envy him. What do I have to envy? His money perhaps? In that case I might as well envy our neighbor, that young shoemaker Arkashka."

"You know, Grisha," said Aunt Toma, now entering the conversation for the first time, "I don't agree with you. I liked that play of his that Lyalya was in. I laughed a great deal."

"Don't distract her with idle conversation, or she won't manage to eat her breakfast," his mother-in-law said sternly.

Rebrov burst out laughing. "Well, the three of you really surprise me! Don't tell me you take all this business seriously? His so-called success—all this uproar and publicity?"

For some reason he had gotten stirred up and said more than he should have. His mother-in-law immediately asked, "And you don't think he is a success?"

"You know, Grisha, Smolyanov is kinder than you are. You speak about him so spitefully, and yet he wants to help."

"I'm not being spiteful at all. And who's this he wants to help?"

"I was talking to him yesterday. About you."

"What about me?" He looked at her in astonishment. She began to blush. Lyalya rarely blushed, and if she did, it meant that she had good cause. "Well, what could you be discussing with him about me?"

"Well, it was stupid of me. He's not very reliable, and I shouldn't have...."

"But what was it you were discussing?"

"Well, about how he might be able to help you. With your work...."

"That's really ridiculous!" he muttered. "How could he possibly help me?" And with an impatient wave of his hand he got up and left the room. He was infuriated by her lack of tact—talking about this in front of her mother! Besides, he wanted to question her right away, this minute, about Smolyanov, so that he could either dismiss or confirm the suspicions which already rankled like a wound. But of course he could not speak of such things in front of the two old ladies, so he waited impatiently for her in their room. Finally, Lyalya came running upstairs—the car from the theater had already arrived and was parked out front by the gate. As she hastily began collecting her things and throwing them into her little suitcase, he asked her how the conversation with Smolyanov had happened to come up. Lyalya said something in reply. Suddenly he seized her by the shoulders, and looking her straight in the eye, he gasped in despair, "You're having an affair with him!"

For a second she gazed at him in bewilderment, then once again she began to blush. "Of course, what do you expect! After all, he's our playwright and we all depend on him. No, Grishenka, it turns out that he's a stupid man. And as you know, stupid people don't exist for me. Well, I'm off! See you later!"

Watching from upstairs, Rebrov caught a glimpse of her merino lamb coat as it flashed against the white background of the garden, amidst the bare trees. Nothing had been settled. Of course she had been joking about Smolyanov. It was inconceivable that she was having an affair with him. She knew that he wouldn't be able to live with that.

An hour later he set off by streetcar to Bashilov Street. He needed to pick up some books which he was planning to sell, having torn them from his heart long ago and already adjusted himself to their absence. Upon arrival, he was told by his neighbor Kanunov that someone from the housing administration had come around, asking to see his employment certificate. And he had better come up with it in a hurry, or his residence permit would be cancelled and he would be forced to leave Moscow. This neighbor was not a very nice man. He had seized his own one-room apartment right after the war, and rather highhandedly, under the guise of being a disabled veteran. The room had previously belonged to some good people, Rebrov's original neighbors, but when the war came to an end, they were still stuck in some evacuation camp and thus were in no position to prevent Kanunov from settling into one of their two rooms. Once he was there, parasite that he was, neither boiling water nor kerosene could flush him out.

He repeated the business about the certificate three times, barging into Rebrov's room to do so.

"The man said, Grigory Fyodorovich, that if you didn't present it by the first, they'd inform the police."

"Okay, okay, I'll present it."

"And you'd better make sure you do, since I'm now the official housing representative for our section of the building."

"How nice...." And having to exert a certain amount of force—since his neighbor refused to back away—Rebrov pushed against the door and closed it.

A minute later there came a knock and Kanunov's voice, now much harsher and more demanding, "And please seal up that window! You live somewhere else, nobody knows where, and you make the rest of us freeze. So please, seal up that window right away."

"Go to hell," Rebrov muttered inaudibly. Right now all he felt was irritation and fatigue. Nor was there any point in starting an argument with someone like Kanunov. He was supposed to produce a certificate? Okay, he'd do it. Without wasting any time he began rummaging through his bookcase and shelves, looking for the books that he wanted to sell. He came across some old school notebooks, some albums with clumsy, schoolboy drawings, and then he stumbled upon his Polish grammar and an *Italian Self-Taught* book—good Lord, how many worthy undertakings! His books were in a chaotic state, and it took him an hour and a half to set aside enough volumes to bring in the amount of money he needed—some 120 rubles. In the meantime he enjoyed poking his nose into these dusty notebooks and other old things, immersing himself in this aimless reading and forgetting about everything else. Finally, having stuffed his briefcase to overflowing, he left the building—this building which at one time had been dear to him, his only home, but which later on, after his parents' and brother's deaths and the beginning of his new life with Lyalya, no longer seemed habitable, more like a barn than a place to live.

The editorial office that had given him his certificate for the housing administration for the past two years just happened to be the one that had crossed him off their list of freelance employees the day before. He would have to find some alternative, and quickly too! Kanunov would follow through with his promise. Apparently he wanted his, Rebrov's, room for himself. Well, it was understandable; he had a family, they were overcrowded, and when he could see that the room next door was empty for months at a time, it struck him as unfair. The housing administration had perhaps forgotten about the certificate—he had presented one last year—but Kanunov would remind them. What did he do there at that meat-packing plant of his, anyway? Was he a foreman, engineer, rate-fixer—damned if Rebrov knew! At any rate, he made sausage. Before you could bat an eye, he would slap you into the machine and you'd come flying out the other end as a roll of Favorite Choice, wrapped in cellophane and neatly sealed at each end. If the film studio would take his scenario or some theater would accept his play—even for use at some future date and with revisions, but just as long as there was a contract—then the certificate would be in the bag. But in the meantime he was an absolute zero, a purveyor of air. At the brick factory they always needed unskilled workers and they'd give him a certificate. After all, he wasn't even the husband of a well-known actress. Kanunov had sensed something, and it was not accidental that he had asked him several times, "Well, why don't you register yourself at your wife's place? Aren't you a member of some sort of professional union?"

It was all very clear: Kanunov had swung into action. Last time he had very politely tried to find out Lyalya's address under the pretext of wanting to forward Rebrov's mail, so that it wouldn't lie around and perhaps get lost. But Rebrov had sensed some kind of danger and not given him the address. Never mind, it was all right if his letters lay around. Otherwise this character might show up at Lyalya's some day and announce, "We've come about your certificate, Grigory Fyodorovich."

Rebrov glanced around involuntarily, but the street was deserted. The wind was sweeping the snow along the narrow little sidewalk.

Down the street from the Moscow Art Theater, in Bookstore No. 14, where he happened to know the sales manager, he received ninety rubles for his books. From there he went straight to the editorial office on Gogol Boulevard where they sometimes published his "Historical Curiosities" and "Forgotten Facts." Here he was told that they couldn't give him a certificate because he wasn't on their official staff list. There was absolutely no point in going to the other editorial office, since he had worked for them—answering letters—only sporadically.

He wandered on to the Hotel National. And the first person he ran into in the hotel cafe was Shakhov.

"A-ha!" said Shakhov with would-be amicability. "Well, young fellow, how are things going? Sit down and have a shot of brandy. You look about as cheerful as a frozen fish."

"Everything's going fine with me," said Rebrov, taking a seat and pouring some brandy from Shakhov's decanter into a wine glass. He was putting up a brave front since he had already decided to order 200 grams of vodka right away. "Listen, you had something in mind for me, remember?"

"What? Oh yes, I remember. But I forget what it was," Shakhov burst out laughing, at the same time giving Rebrov a wink. His purplish-red cheeks, puffy from the brandy he had drunk, shook with laughter, and his eyes had a seemingly drunken look, though at the same time there was something piercing and attentive in their gaze. "We'll discuss it right now. You just have a good meal. Order the carp. It's tremendous today...."

His proposal was the following: there was a certain person who could help him. He would have to submit everything he had, show him both the scenario and the play, and then this individual would tell him what, where, when, and how much. He was an extremely important person with a great deal of experience. What would this be—some sort of co-authorship? Why should it necessarily be that right away? But who knows—time will tell. It's not out of the question. Yes, it is out of the question! God damn it! Who *is* this extremely important person, anyway? Sh-sh, don't get so upset, especially with that carp in your mouth. It has too many bones.

"As the saying goes, it's ours to propose, yours to dispose...."

With his red and always moist little eyes he looked like an old setter suffering from conjunctivitis. He was close to seventy, but everyone addressed him familiarly as Kostya. In his day, it seems, he had even had something to do with *The Stock Market Gazette*. Or he might have been working seventy years ago, or a hundred or more, for that matter. Perhaps he'd had something to do with Krayevsky's *Voice* or Katkov's *Moscow Gazette* in the previous century.... But my dear Kostya, this is sheer effrontery, unspeakable effrontery—it simply won't do! Why do you say that, I'd like to know? And exactly what opinion do you have of yourself, young fellow? Well, okay, order yourself another 200 grams and we'll forget about this whole conversation. But just in case you need me, I'll be here on Tuesday after six. What's going on in the theater these days? And how do things stand with Sergei Leonidovich? I hear that he's having problems—some sort of conflict with the executive director.

It was about 3 p.m. when Rebrov left the cafe and set off for the theater. He hadn't been there in a long time—he always hated going there. But now his back was against the wall, and he felt he had to make one last effort to be heard. After all, Marevin never had given him a proper answer regarding his plays, nor had he even discussed them with him.

And both manuscripts were still there. Besides, he wanted to see Lyalya and question her right away. Whatever she told him would decide his fate.

He slipped through the empty lobby, tossed his coat on a hook in the cloakroom, and headed straight for the small, smoke-filled office of the theater's chief literary consultant.

Marevin sat slouched on the office sofa, with one short little leg tucked under him and the other hanging loose. Beside him was a lean, skittle-shaped lady who sat decorously erect on the edge of the sofa. They were talking in subdued tones, and Marevin was fingering his worry beads. He always had them with him, as if he were some ortho-dox Muslim. He glanced up at Rebrov with a tired look, at the same time showing some surprise.

"Excuse me, Grisha, but it seems to me that we did discuss the mat-ter. Didn't we? I think you're mistaken about...."

"Nothing of the kind! It was through Lyalya that...."

"Yes, we did discuss it, we did. It's just slipped your mind. You were asking me over the phone about *A Many-Storied Building*—or whatever the exact title is—and I conveyed Sergei Leonidovich's opinion...."

"And where's my official, written reply?"

"I don't understand, Grigory Fyodorovich..." The look of displea-sure in Marevin's black eyes grew more intense. There were bags under his eyes, like dark sores, as if he had been drinking too much. And this pygmy, this pathetic creature with his ulcer, was God and Tsar in this theater!

"What is it you want from us? An official discussion? We wanted to spare you.... What would you gain from it? Our actors and the mem-bers of the theater council are rude, tactless people. They might say something unpleasant—and there you'd be, so discouraged that you wouldn't be able to get back to work for six months. It was in your own interest.... But as for an official reply, that I'll be happy to give you—right this minute if you wish."

It seemed that Marevin was mocking him. But probably only on pro-fessional grounds. Apparently he considered him a third-rate writer. His head was throbbing with pain, as if someone had twisted a towel around his skull and were drawing it tighter and tighter. Oh, to hell with it! And suddenly, in an unrecognizable, vulgarly aggressive tone—the sort of tone one would expect from a third-rate writer—Rebrov said, "Boris Mironovich, I'd like to have a certificate to the effect that I'm your author and am working on a play for the theater. I've got to have it...."

The phone rang. The pygmy lowered his little legs from the sofa and got up to answer it.

"for the housing administration," Rebrov finished his sentence.

While Marevin was muttering into the phone, the lady bent her lean torso in Rebrov's direction and whispered, "Did you know that Boris Mironovich has suffered a terrible blow. His wife has just died. And now he's completely alone. He has no children, nor any close relatives...."

Marevin continued to mutter into the phone, "My resignation, yes, yes, on Monday, and please have all my papers in order, yes, yes, yes, it's vitally important...."

"What did she die of?" asked Rebrov, now with genuine interest.

"She'd been sick for a very long time," the lady replied with a sorrowful and deferential nod. Tremendous respect for Boris Mironovich was written all over her face.

Marevin was trying to grasp what certificate Rebrov was talking about. Once he understood, he advised Rebrov to have Lyudmila Petrovna discuss the matter with the executive director. He probably wouldn't refuse her. He, Marevin, could talk to Roman Vasilievich himself, but there wouldn't be any point in that now that he was leaving the theater. Roman Vasilievich wouldn't do anything for him—in fact, just the opposite, but if Lyudmila asked, perhaps he'd do it. She was in his good graces at the moment. As Marevin returned to the sofa and began rubbing his worry beads, Rebrov shuddered at the thought of losing the one person in the world one felt close to and of being left *completely* alone. Scrutinizing Marevin's small, wan face—he could see now that it was wan—he realized that this man was in a bad way. He wasn't the type who'd be able to live completely alone. Nor would prim ladies like the one sitting here on the sofa be able to save him. Suddenly Rebrov was struck by the frightening thought: "Bob is going to die soon! Without the theater...."

"And perhaps you should drop in on Sergei Leonidovich," said Marevin. "Discuss the matter with him. Go and see him, go and see him right now. I happen to know that he's in his office."

Rebrov felt like telling him: never mind. Never mind all this business about plays and certificates. It's all nonsense anyway, and not worth discussing. It really is nonsense. He'd get around this situation somehow, and life would go on. After all, one lives a long time. And what they should be discussing was something else: death and loneliness. But that was the one thing which it was impossible to discuss. So he merely shook Marevin's hand, gazed into his eyes—there was a defenselessness about them, but at the same time a certain haughtiness—and having hesitated while squeezing his hand, he walked out of his office without saying anything at all.

Why, he asked himself, should he bother to see Sergei Leonidovich now? After all, everything was perfectly clear and there was nothing to be gained by it. But at the moment—as was often the case with him—he was acting from inertia and didn't have the strength to do otherwise. The artistic director knew Rebrov fairly well as Lyalya's husband, but they had never sat down and had a serious conversation. Everything had been casual and in passing—chitchat over dinner or a few words exchanged at the railroad station, in the cafeteria, or in the cloakroom.... And now, to Rebrov's utter astonishment, this stout, gray-haired individual suddenly began telling him all his troubles and innermost thoughts. No sooner had Rebrov said something to him about the certificate than Sergei Leonidovich declared that he was mad at the whole world, that he was in an extremely negative, misanthropic mood, that mankind had not acquitted itself honorably, that hypocrisy would be our downfall—and more in the same vein. He paced furiously back and forth as he spoke, while Rebrov remained standing by the window, his back pressed against the high windowsill.

It seemed that a meeting of the theater council had adjourned just half an hour ago and the old man had lashed out at all of them—at the executive director and his assistant, and at the assistant artistic director! The previous night, while suffering from insomnia, he had suddenly realized that the only possible way to save the situation was to tell people the truth to their faces. Of course, someone would go and tell Smolyanov right away what he'd said about him, since it was Smolyanov who had sparked the whole controversy in the first place, when Boris Mironovich had tried to block his third play.... And as for that third play of his, that, you understand, was a subject in itself. Its action jumped back and forth between Chicago, Belgrade, and the Volga-Don Canal....

"And why is it that I'm telling you all this? Probably because your Lyudmila was the only council member who tried—even timidly—to help me save Bob."

He gave Rebrov a long, searching look, then his voice suddenly changed and he went on in a dry, unfriendly tone, "Well, now let's talk about you. But I've warned you—I'm feeling merciless today. Is that all right? Can you take it? Well then, when I read your plays and those of other young playwrights—including Smolyanov—I can't help wondering why it is that people make things so difficult for themselves. Why do they write about things about which they have only the vaguest notion? After all, each one of us has something which lies close to our heart and can move us to tears, just as Chekhov had his Uncle Vanyas and his Doctor Astrovs and Gorky, let's assume, had his petty bourgeois—his Bulychyovs and Dostigaevs. But you—whom do you have? What do you have? Here you've written a play about the Korean War, and yet you don't know Korea, you haven't had the slightest exposure to the war there, and in general you've probably never been farther east than the Kazan Railroad Station, right? Am I right?"

"The play isn't meant to be completely realistic... it's more a fairy tale," mumbled Rebrov, unable to hold back a smile, which probably made him look all the more foolish. "Or perhaps even a parable...."

"A parable! Listen, it's very presumptuous to say that I've written a parable! Parables are written by peoples, not by authors. Now, regarding your other play, the one about the construction of a university. Just be patient and listen to what I have to say—this is just one of those days. Well, my dear young friend, for God's sake, have enough sense to start off by writing about normal-size houses—about workers' barracks or the cozy little rooms with flowered wallpaper where our Pyotr Ivanoviches and Maria Ivanovnas live. Later on you can tackle your university skyscraper with its forty-five stories! Take Smolyanov, for instance, a man not lacking in ability. Some time ago he submitted his first, straightforward little play about forest conservation. It had something fresh about it, something true to life.... He didn't know much about writing, but he was trying to do something worthwhile.... I hesitated, but the others managed to convince me that his theme was an important one that needed to be dramatized, so I went ahead and produced it. But now in this new play of his he introduces elements of myth and even some sort of theory of mythology...."

Rebrov was unable to concentrate sufficiently to take in everything Sergei Leonidovich was saying. It was something about Smolyanov, something incredibly long and complicated, and expressed with a great deal of emotion. But after all, all of this was trivial, a lot of silly details. Why did he have to go on about it for so long and with such heat? Well, one thing was clear: Smolyanov had managed to cause him a great deal of trouble. He was feeling lonely and hurt, and there was no one to complain to, no one to pour out his feelings to. Apparently he had come to some sort of decision and it frightened him. A few other fragmentary sentences managed to reach Rebrov's consciousness: "Herman Vladimirovich, that master of hypocrisy, is dying to become artistic director.... While previously, you remember.... They were both my productions—but it was my own fault, all my own fault. I was the one who gave birth to this golem...."

"But Sergei Leonidovich," said Rebrov, "what's your answer to my question? What am I to do?" As in Marevin's office he felt once again that vulgar compulsion to hammer away at the same point. Well, what else could he do? He had come here as a supplicant, so he might as well behave accordingly. "If I could just have a certificate."

"A certificate? What sort of certificate?" the artistic director asked in surprised. "Oh, the certificate you were telling me about. Well, you should speak to the business office about that."

He turned on the desk lamp and began shuffling the papers on his desk. In an instant his face had turned into that of a tired, crotchety old man. Suddenly Rebrov sat down on the armchair near the lamp and said, "Listen, could you spare me ten minutes? I want to tell you about something. No, it has nothing to do with those two plays of mine. They don't count. And please understand that I don't resent any of the things you said about them...."

"Well, just don't waste my time. I've already given you seven minutes."

They remained in his office for two and a half hours. Rebrov told him about Nikolai Vasilievich Kletochnikov—about everything that had been burning inside him for the past few months but which a few days before had begun to cool and turn to ice. Now he found himself getting fired up again: after all, Nikolai Vasilievich's life was an example of how one should live, not worrying about the eternal questions and not thinking about death or immortality. It wasn't even clear whether he had been a genuine revolutionary—that is, whether he had been fully aware of the goals and purposes of the revolution. This ailing, bespectacled, mousy-looking provincial official had appeared unexpectedly, from out of the blue, and offered his help to the revolution. No one knew him and there were doubts, hesitation—after all, there was nothing heroic about him! Neither Alexander's steel-like muscles, nor Sergei's pistols and daggers, nor Lev's erudition, nor Nikolai's Carbonarist romanticism. He had nothing, nothing at all. He was an instrument. He carried out the will of others, which some called the people's will. He planted himself in the gendarmerie, penetrated its armor and infiltrated into its very core, into the heart and entrails of the Third Section. And from here he was able to help, save, and kill. In so doing he was also carrying out the demands of his own conscience. And that was all. It is almost impossible to explain his actions, for conscience is a nebulous concept, almost as nebulous as the fourth dimension. Just try to explain the concept of the fourth dimension—nothing will come of it, and you'll start stammering and groping for words. Nonetheless, conscience is a tremendous force. Of course, at certain times it grows stronger, at other times weaker, depending on—who knows, perhaps on certain explosions of solar matter. At his hearing he made all sorts of absurd statements, slandering himself by pretending that the revolutionaries had paid him for the information he had given them. He had to give the authorities some sort of explanation, and what was he to tell them? Well, of course, he was sick, suffering from consumption, and would not have lasted more than two or three years. But sickness only intensifies that which is in a person to begin with, and in this case what was intensified was conscience.

When he played cards with his fat landlady, a police informer, trying to please her so that through her he would be able to get a job in the desired institution...

Sergei Leonidovich was listening with all the eagerness and enthusiasm of a child. There definitely was, in fact, something childlike about this stout old man. And every once in a while, as Rebrov proceeded with his story, Sergei Leonidovich would spontaneously interject a few words on the subject of "worldly hypocrisy." Finally he said, "It's amazing how many splendid and forgotten people have lived on this earth. And this really was only a short time ago! My father was a contemporary of your Nikolai Vasilievich, and also a resident of Petersburg...." And struck by Rebrov's story, he went on to make some comments of his own. Rebrov was almost touched. It seemed that this was the first time that the artistic director had ever heard the name of Nikolai Morozov, much less that of Lev Tikhomirov.[11]

"How funny it is: for you 1880 means Kletochnikov, the Third Section, bombs, assassination attempts on the Tsar, while for me it's Ostrovsky, *The Female Captives* at the Maly, Yermolova in the role of Yevlalia, Sadovsky, Muzil....[12]Yes, yes! Lord, how terribly interrelated everything is! When you think of it, the history of a country is like a many-stranded cable, and when you rip off one of the strands.... No, you can't look at things that way! Historical truth is interaction through time, everything taken together: Kletochnikov, Muzil.... Oh, if one could only depict on the stage this flow of time which carries along everything and everyone! But today I announced that if Boris Mironovich goes, I'm going too. So the management will have to decide. Usually this office is packed after meetings of the literary staff; there's a lot of noise and joking around. But today they all hurried off, I have surprised and upset them...."

When Rebrov left the theater it was twilight and the streetlights were already on. He was completely worn out from his long conversation with Sergei Leonidovich, and yet for some reason he felt happy—which was really absurd, since he hadn't accomplished a thing, not a single thing. In this strangely happy frame of mind he wandered from Pushkin Square to Trubnaya Square and from there down Neglinnaya Street and up Pushkin Street, back toward Pushkin Square. By now, however, his happy mood had faded and he was beginning to feel depressed. It was not so much because one more day had been wasted— he hadn't even managed to get to the library—but because it suddenly occurred to him that he himself, like the old man, Sergei Leonidovich, had no desire to go home. The thought saddened him, and when a few minutes later he happened to run into an old friend, Tolya Shchyokin, by the entrance to the health food cafeteria, he was already feeling utterly depressed. Rebrov had studied with Shchyokin at the institute and was always running into him on the street. His friend had been disabled during the war and received a pension from the government. He had no family and led an incredibly frugal existence. He didn't drink, he didn't smoke, he ate in public cafeterias, and he always wore the same thin coat with the same checked scarf.

For some reason, whenever they ran into each other, Shchyokin would smile condescendingly at Rebrov and adopt a patronizing air. Yet Rebrov always enjoyed running into him. The very sight of this individual who had given up all attempts to get ahead in life was enough to improve one's mood. Usually they talked about women. Rebrov would ask whether Shchyokin had gotten married. Shchyokin would roar with laughter, "Are you kidding? Never!" There was always a ruddy glow on his cheeks, and his gold-filled teeth would sparkle. His girlfriends were sales clerks, waitresses, dishwashers, shoe-repair and dry-cleaning attendants with whom he would spend a few scheduled hours each week. He would invite them up to his modest room, treat them to a modest supper and a bottle of wine—or sometimes simply to tea and sausage—and rejoice at his modest catch. But about the "catches" themselves they spoke only briefly as a rule, on the run. On this occasion Rebrov was too tired and depressed to feel like jesting, and with a sullen look at Shchyokin he asked from sheer force of habit, "Well how are things—have you gotten married yet?"

"Never! Not on your life!" replied Shchyokin, laughing heartily and giving Rebrov a friendly, if somewhat patronizing, slap on the shoulder. He was almost at the head of the cafeteria line—there being only three old ladies in front of him. Behind him stood some twenty people.

Apparently they had been standing there a long time. They were frozen, and now, noticing Rebrov entering the line ahead of them, they became angrily alert. Rebrov was in fact hungry. He had had lunch around twelve and it was now after six.

"I hear that your wife's doing very well for herself," said Shchyokin. "Are you planning to buy a car?"

"Who told you about Lyalya?"

"All of Moscow is talking about her..."

"Citizen, the line begins back here!" came a rasping voice from behind.

Shchyokin announced in a booming voice that Rebrov had been standing in line in front of him. The line swayed slightly forward, and someone shouted, "We didn't see him!" The atmosphere became charged and tense, but Rebrov didn't turn around. And when the door opened, he managed under false pretenses—as friend and protector of the disabled—to wedge himself inside behind the three old ladies. Over soup and a casserole Rebrov told Shchyokin his problems. He realized that he needed to confide in someone, and Shchyokin was a good listener. He would nod, inject some trite but sympathetic remark, and smile condescendingly.

Suddenly he said, "The trouble with you, old man, is that you've got too much pride! That's why you keep writing all these plays and stories...."

"What are you getting at?" Rebrov asked in surprise.

"Your vanity has gotten the better of you. You're making all these efforts for nothing. As for me, I'm content to teach literature at night school, six hours a week. And it's so enjoyable: Fonvizin, Pushkin, Derzhavin...'' 'I'm a king—I'm a slave, I'm a worm, I am God!' If you want, I'll get you a job there. You can teach history. And they'll give you the certificate you need."

Rebrov shook his head. "No thanks. At least not for the time being."

"Well, okay, keep trying a little longer. But usually it's pointless. Shall we have another helping of the fruit-juice dessert?"

Rebrov was too despondent to answer.

There was a certain naive but deadly accuracy in what his honest, well-meaning, and not very bright friend (for some reason Rebrov was convinced that Shchyokin was not very bright) had expressed so openly. Here it was, *truth* staring him in the face. And Sergei Leonidovich's specific criticisms of his plays were really quite beside the point. And actually, wouldn't it be better to take the easy way out? Teaching history at the night school. Six hours a week. A certificate, a job, a means of support. Shchyokin was hobbling toward him with two glasses of the dessert, and saying something about the brunette behind the counter, whose name was Rita and who came from a good family. "I could give you her phone number. Do you want it?" But Rebrov was so deep in thought that although he heard the question, he didn't reply.

When they went out onto the street, Shchyokin said, "Don't take it all so hard. Twenty years from now everything will be reversed. You and that director, Sergei Leonidovich, will have changed places—that I promise you." He began to laugh. "And I'll be the only one who's stayed in the same spot."

"Twenty years from now! Who needs that? I'll be an old man by then, almost as old as he...."

"That's just my point: you'll have changed places. And he'll no longer exist—almost in the same way that you don't exist now. Ha-ha."

"Thanks a lot, you've really cheered me up."

"Just don't be depressed, old man! Give me a call. And don't forget about the night school. There's also an opening for a club director in the First of May District. I could get you the job. You're not done for!"

And the playboy of the health-food cafeteria set moved on down Pushkin Street toward the subway. Rebrov set off in the opposite direction. Shchyokin's last words, seemingly so well-meant, had utterly disheartened him. It was hard to believe that he had spoken without malicious intent. "But of course he's right, the scoundrel—I don't exist...."

He wandered around for a long time, pondering the matter.

If he were suddenly to give up the ghost, who would mourn for his death? Who would even stop and take notice? Lyalya would mourn for him. She wouldn't have anyone else to feel sorry for. But in three months she would be introduced to some consumptive—a physicist and lover of symphonic music—or to some other splendid man—a surveyor and hard drinker. It wouldn't matter who or what he was—Irina Ignatievna would be happy all the same and would be sure to discover his good qualities. And one thing you could say about a consumptive or a hard drinker: they *did* exist.

Snow was beginning to fall, but it was still too early to go home. And now, drawn toward the inner ring of boulevards, he proceeded down Trubnaya Street and then over toward Sretensky Gate. He knew what was drawing him: their old house on Sretensky Boulevard. The "A" streetcar was making its slow ascent of the hill. The passengers with their winter-pale faces could be seen swaying back and forth inside its cozy, heated interior. Barely quickening his pace, Rebrov caught up to

the streetcar and jumped on. Suddenly he remembered a similar moment which had occurred long ago. It had been winter, snow had been
falling, and the trees stood skeleton-like on the ascending boulevard.
And right here, in this very spot, where the dark brick wall of the ancient fortress rose on the right, he had jumped onto the streetcar,
hitching a ride. Holding his school satchel in his left hand, he had
walked briskly and precisely, trying to get in rhythm with the streetcar
wheels. Then a valiant jump and—there he was, with his feet on the step
and his right hand on the door rail. Thus it had been every day until
that March, when one icy afternoon his foot had landed in empty
space, his satchel had fallen, and some strong hand had grabbed him
by the collar and dragged him onto the streetcar. At Sretensky Gate,
which was the goal of his short, stolen ride—it was only one stop away!—
he heard a shout and saw the figure of a man waving his arms as he
came running downhill from Trubnaya Street. It was his father, and he
was carrying the satchel which Rebrov had been planning to run back
for. He came running up to him, white-faced and breathing heavily,
and without saying a word, gave him such a slap in the face that Rebrov
landed hard on the sidewalk. No sooner had he gotten up on his feet
than his father hit him again, proclaiming in a frightening, hate-filled
voice, "I saw you, you rascal, trying to sneak a ride!" And for a long
time afterwards his father secretly kept an eye on him. Just like a real
spy he would take cover behind a house on Rozhdestvensky Boulevard,
waiting to see if Rebrov would try to hitch a ride on the streetcar on his
way home from school. The trouble was that his father had nothing
better to do. He was no longer working by that time and had become
peevish and irritable, often picking quarrels with Rebrov's mother. But
she felt sorry for him, and whenever Rebrov would complain to her
that his father was spying on him and that the other kids had noticed
and were teasing him about it, she would tell him not to pay any attention. "Let him do as he pleases," his mother would say. "After all, he is
suffering and there's nothing we can do to help him." Rebrov couldn't
understand why his father, who was an economist, couldn't find another job and stop suffering. He was unaware that his father was already ill. At the end of the summer he was taken to the hospital, never
to return. Rebrov's mother would go there to visit him, but she never
took Rebrov or his brother Volodka with her. Once she returned from
a visit in a cheerful mood, saying that their father had recognized her.
He had been sitting up in bed, piecing together a quilt out of scraps,
and when she entered the ward, he had suddenly looked up at her and
said in his usual querulous tone, "Vera, we have a lot of old scraps of

cloth at home. Why didn't you bring me any?" His mother had been so
flustered and overjoyed that she couldn't think of anything to say, and
she burst into tears. Later on, when the war broke out, the hospital was
evacuated to Kirov Province. Rebrov's father died of pneumonia at the
beginning of 1942, but Rebrov didn't learn of his death until two years
later. His mother probably found out right away, since she was in correspondence with the hospital. She was living in Kuznetsk, where her
plant had been evacuated. Before her own death from a heart attack in
1943, she had written to Rebrov expressing her anxiety over the fact
that she had had no news from his brother Volodka in almost a year.
When Rebrov returned to Moscow toward the end of the year, after his
stay in the military hospital, he began making inquiries. He wrote to
every place he could think of, but the answer was always the same: we
have no information on this individual. Later on, by putting two and
two together—the historical facts plus certain information supplied in
Volodka's last letters—Rebrov concluded that his brother's unit must
have been trapped in the Nazi encirclement of Kharkov in the summer
of '42.

There it was, the two-storied house with its stone columns and
chipped lion faces. The best years of his life—up to the sixth grade—had
been spent here, on the second floor, third and fourth windows from
the right. When his father had had to stop working, he couldn't bear
living here any more—he suffered from insomnia and said that the
street noise kept him from falling asleep—and they had moved to quiet
Bashilov Street, which was almost in the suburbs. How Rebrov had
protested at the time! How he hated having to leave his school, his play-
mates, the boulevard, the Clear Ponds skating rink, and the stamp shop
on Kuznetsky Bridge Street where he and his friends would run after
school and where, in the covered passageway next to the shop, vicious
fights would take place! On one occasion his mother had given him six
rubles to buy the French colonial series, and no sooner had he happily
emerged from the shop than someone pushed him into the passageway. Three boys began twisting his arm and trying to grab his newly ac-
quired stamps. He fought back desperately and finally managed to
break loose. He went running off down the street, and only when he
had reached the subway did he notice that the whole front of his new
spring coat was hanging in shreds. It had been slashed with a razor. But
his pride in having fought them off and having saved his precious
stamps far outweighed this minor annoyance. After all, what was a
mere coat?...

The snow was coming down harder now, covering everything in

sight: the snack bar, from whose slamming doors warm air would escape, the sidewalk, the people trudging along it, their caps, their faces, and his own memories—memories of himself as a little boy in a black sheepskin coat, which was first too long and then too short. Four people had lived behind those windows on the second floor, and Rebrov was the only one of them who remained. And here he was, standing and looking into his prewar past.... Where had they disappeared to? They were neither here nor there—nowhere. This was the way it had turned out. He was their only representative on earth, where the snow was now falling and the trolley buses crawled along with their headlights turned on....

Later that evening Lyalya asked, "Why did you show up drunk today?"

"Where did I show up drunk?"

"Bob told me. He said that you came in completely smashed and started demanding a discussion of your plays—and that you wanted some sort of certificate. But you do know, don't you, that Bob is going through a terribly rough time?"

Rebrov waved his hand. Yes, he knew, but he didn't have the strength to discuss it. All he said was, "You can thank Smolyanov for that!"

They got into bed and Rebrov told her that he had walked to his old house on the boulevard today. Rebrov's prewar life always intrigued Lyalya, and she loved to ask him about his father and about the times when he was very little—before the seventh grade, when the two of them had first met. And now she lay very still beside him and listened. He was telling her how a long time ago, around 1933, his father had bought two children's wicker chairs and attached them to the rear of his and their mother's bicycles. On Sundays the four of them would go riding together, with Rebrov and Volodka seated in their chairs in the rear. Somewhere there was a photograph of this; he'd have to find it. Lyalya's hand touched his hair and forehead in the dark and began to caress him. He took her hand and pressed it to his lips. He told her that someone had offered him a job today—to teach history in a night school for adults. He could also get a job as director of some club in the First of May District. Lyalya caressed his face without saying a word, and he went on to mention still another proposal. He could bring his two plays to a certain individual who had connections and would be able to help him. He'd probably have to make this person a co-author, but that would be better than standing still and getting nowhere as he was now. Still, he hated to do it.

"And you don't have to," Lyalya whispered and began kissing him. "You don't have to, my sweet. You don't have to, my love. Don't think about any of these things. Everything's going to turn out all right for us. We'll get that certificate and you'll be able to work undisturbed. You're going to get everything that's coming to you. After all, you're talented, so please, don't give up. Who was the idiot who offered you the club director job?"

He lay perfectly still. He was listening, drinking in her every word— her sweet, whispered murmurings which enveloped him like some ethereal mist.

"You know what I think?" she whispered. "That I'm... you understand?"

"Really?"

"Yes, I think I am.... And this time I want to have it."

His heart was pounding, and all his strength seemed to return. Joy and fear, both mixed together. Equal portions of good fortune and bad—yes, that was all that one needed in life. And this warm, beloved being beside him was the only proof he needed of the fact: I exist.

And at that moment, as often happens in dreams, he was struck by a truth which seemed age-old and self-evident: it was not *cogito ergo sum*, but *amo ergo sum*. And that was all one needed to know. Why was it that people didn't guess this? Why did they refuse to realize it? After all, it was terribly obvious. "And I exist too! I exist in spite of you all," he thought with a fierce and angry tenderness, not feeling anything but the taste of love on his lips and a great surge of strength.

At about eleven the next morning two men arrived from the telephone service center and began checking to see where they could hook up a telephone line to the house. No one had called them and everyone thought they must have come by mistake, but the workers showed them their order slip, which indicated the name L. P. Telepneva and bore the signature of the head of the service center. At this point Lyalya realized what had happened and said, "Oh, I know what this is!" She was obviously embarrassed, however, and didn't seem very happy about it. When Rebrov demanded an explanation, Lyalya told him that the theater management had been trying for a long time to get her a phone, since it was inconvenient for them to have to send a car around every time they wanted to relay some message. But nothing had come of their efforts—there was no underground cable nearby, and it was expensive to hook up a special above-ground line. Now it must be that Smolyanov had interceded with the telephone people. He had connections there too.

"What a wonderful surprise, Lyalechka!" Irina Ignatievna exclaimed joyfully. "Please thank Nikolai Demyanovich for us and tell him how grateful we are. And you can tell him he's a wonderful man, an absolute dear..."

"Mama, I don't like getting favors from people."

"Don't be silly, Lyalya! And how can you talk about getting favors when all of our friends and relatives have had phones for ages! Why, you'd think we were living in some backward village...."

There was something in all of this sudden fuss, in Lyalya's discomfort and her mother's excessive rejoicing, that put Rebrov on his guard. Though damn it all, a telephone—that really was something! He had never had a phone in his life before, not in their Sretensky Boulevard apartment nor on Bashilov Street. Still, there was something strange in Lyalya's embarrassment over the matter—as if she were stumbling on a perfectly even surface.

The car from the theater arrived shortly afterwards and Lyalya left in it. Within an hour his mother-in-law had managed to call Uncle Kolya, Aunt Zhenya, Uncle Misha, and all the remaining horde of relatives in order to relay their new telephone number and the latest news regarding Pyotr Alexandrovich, who was to be released from the hospital in another week.

Two days later, as Rebrov was returning from the subway station and had almost reached the Telepnevs' yellow fence, he saw something that took him completely by surprise. The policeman Kurtov and his own Bashilov Street neighbor Kanunov were standing and conversing by Kurtov's gate. Kanunov, who was dressed in a long, black coat and stood with his back half turned away from Rebrov, pretended that he hadn't seen him. Rebrov likewise pretended that he hadn't recognized Kanunov, though he had walked right past him and they had almost touched shoulders.

It was a nasty experience, and so unexpected that it left Rebrov feeling weak in the knees. Nor could there be anything pleasant about discovering that someone was trying to dig out the ground from beneath him. Here he was, just leading a normal life, going about his business, while this someone was snooping around, thrusting his nose where it didn't belong. "Well, I'm in for it now!" thought Rebrov. And as he reached his own gate, he involuntarily burst out laughing. Glancing back, he saw that the policeman and Kanunov were watching him.

VI

Smolyanov's lucky star, which had risen sharply over the last four years, suddenly slowed in its course. Actually, nothing terrible had happened in his professional life, there had been no catastrophes, but he had lost momentum—which might be taken as a bad sign. And however much Nikolai Demyanovich tried to persuade himself that even the best soccer team—the Red Army team, for example—occasionally loses points and that it's impossible not to make some mistakes or to suffer some losses, still he lacked the wisdom and self-restraint to wait things out. Instead of proceeding coolly forward, without reacting to the groans and insults from the sidelines, he let himself be provoked and ended up behaving in scandalous fashion. Somewhere on the theater stairs, right in public, he began answering Sergei Leonidovich's shouts and rude remarks in kind. He shook his finger and threatened him, and he called the former literary consultant Marevin a two-faced hypocrite, and, like a fool, completely exposed himself. His nerves simply gave out on him—which was perhaps understandable since that January he had been beset by one misfortune after another. In Saratov his mother had suffered a paralytic stroke and lost the use of her legs and her powers of speech. Now he didn't know what to do with his little girl or where he was going to place her. For the time being he had hired an old lady to look after her, one of his mother's neighbors. Ten days later his wife Marta had pulled a stunt of her own and had tried to jump out of the window of their new, sixth-floor apartment. His sister-in-law Frosya had seen what she was up to and had pulled her down from the windowsill. This was the second such attempt, the first having been in October, in their old apartment. Naturally he had to report his wife's attempted suicide, and she was taken off to the Kashchenko psychiatric hospital. He didn't tell a soul about his troubles, especially anyone in the theater. What would be the point? No one was going to feel sorry for him, and they might even try to make things worse for him.

As a result of all this Nikolai Demyanovich was in the worst possible mood, and to add insult to injury, Lyudmila had been avoiding him for the last two weeks. Whenever they ran into each other in the theater, she would return his "hello" with a cold nod and walk right past him. There were moments when he thought about starting things up between them again, but well, to hell with her and her hurt feelings! He didn't know for sure, but he could guess the reason for her resentment. Apparently she had decided that he had tried to set her up with

Alexander Vasilievich. It was true that Alexander Vasilievich had requested this, even demanded it, and there had been no way that he could refuse. But if only she knew, the little fool, how he had suffered because of her, what nightmares he had lived through in his imagination, and how he had counted on her independence of character, which had so often irritated him in the past. He hadn't slept a wink that whole night and had been tormented by fantasies and hallucinations. First, he had imagined that Alexander Vasilievich was yelling at him and pounding his fists on the table, looking right through him as he knew how to do. Then, he had pictured Lyudmila with Alexander Vasilievich in some insufferable pose and sticking her tongue out at him, Nikolai Demyanovich. Yet, despite all this he had believed with all his heart, with his very bones and marrow, that no, no, a hundred times no, not for anything in this world! He was almost one hundred percent sure and would have bet a thousand rubles to one that Alexander Vasilievich wouldn't get a thing from her. My God, no, not on your life! Not this time. And when Alexander Vasilievich had telephoned him the next morning, his deep bass voice had sounded angry as the devil— so angry, in fact, that it was impossible to understand what he was saying. Nikolai Demyanovich had jumped for joy right then and there by the phone. "Oh, dear, you poor man! Heartburn, you say, and shortness of breath—well, 1 *am* sorry," he mumbled sympathetically, while at the same time making comic faces at himself in the mirror.

He had gotten used to Lyudmila, had become attached to her—there was no denying it. And so quickly too! True, she wore him out, irritated him with her hurt feelings, and sometimes alienated him with her foolish Grishenka and with her whims and arbitrariness. What a fuss she had made about Marevin! And how foolishly she went on defending the old man! Sometimes she drove him to the point where he felt like breaking with her for good. After all, did she think that she was the only desirable woman around? There were others even more desirable, and as a matter of fact he had endless opportunities—all he had to do was beckon. Yet, although he had been introduced to all sorts of women and had taken them here and there—to his dacha, or to Khimki, or to visit friends—still, after an hour or so he would feel bored and depressed. For these new acquaintances were empty and shallow; all they wanted was fun and good times. And he had known more than enough of such people. His own life had been difficult, and he was not the easiest man to get along with. It was not every woman who could understand him.

But Lyudmila did understand him. All in all, she was extraordinary:

she never asked him for anything, never abused him, and never took any money from him. He had offered her some two or three times, but she had flatly refused it, telling him that he ought to be ashamed of himself. This pleased him, not because he would have begrudged the money, but because she was such a wonderful woman and—she loved him. His total expenditures had amounted to 380 rubles—for the rubber-soled shoes that he had bought her a long time ago. Well, of course there had been their evenings out, but these went without saying.

Nikolai Demyanovich tried to be patient, to wait things out. But he grew tired of waiting, and one day when he didn't have the strength to wait any longer, he stopped her in the corridor, and taking her hand, he said, "You know, Lyudmila, something terrible has happened."

She looked up at him. "What is it?"

"My mother's had a stroke. She's in the hospital, and I don't know what I'm going to do with Galka..."

Whether out of concern or out of pity, Lyudmila's eyes gleamed with their old, familiar kindness. "You should bring Galochka here to Moscow. It'll be the end of your mother if she starts worrying about..."

"Things are bad here in Moscow too. Marta has...."

He gave her a brief account of all that had happened. Things seemed to be pressing in on him from every side. There was a full-scale war going on at the theater, and that swine Marevin had turned both actors and critics against him—thank God, they had at least gotten rid of him! At home he was barely keeping his head above water. And those whom he felt close to were turning away from him, not giving any comfort or assistance.

"I feel sorry for Marta, terribly sorry for her. She's only thirty-eight, not even middle-aged, and yet her central nervous system is utterly shattered. She's going to have to undergo treatment for at least a year, and no one knows what the results will be. It's terribly sad. And she was such an excellent teacher—she taught gymnastics in an elementary school. What happens is that she has periods of insane raving, and it seems that she's obsessed by certain ideas. It was terrible, the way she used to behave with Frosya—screaming and attacking her with her fists—well, you already know about that. And now it turns out that she's been mentally ill all along, and there's nothing one can do about it. It's just so sad...."

As Nikolai Demyanovich quietly droned on, he noticed that Lyalya's dear face grew pale and her eyes filled with tears. Suddenly it occurred to her to ask, "Is there anything I can do to help?"

He nodded. "Come home with me right now!"

But then he stopped to consider. Frosya might disapprove and the plates would start flying. Oh well, to hell with her. He could send her off somewhere—to his dacha in Tarasovka. Ah, but the dacha would have to be heated—it hadn't been heated in months.

"Where's the nearest phone? I'll just make a call and then we'll leave."

"No... we won't."

They had left the corridor and were standing next to the window on the broad staircase landing. One could see the courtyard below with its patches of muddy ground and trampled snow. The executive director's car was parked by the entrance to the car repair shop with its hood up. Next to the brick wall between the theater and the building next door hulked some stage sets completely covered with snow.

"I must remember to stop off at the repair shop and have my battery checked," thought Nikolai Demyanovich.

"It's all over between us, Nikolai Demyanovich," he heard Lyalya's voice. "I've made up my mind."

"Why?"

"Just because...."

A door slammed below, and someone started heavily up the stairs, wheezing and panting. Lyudmila broke off in midsentence. The old man, one of the theater's retired actors, greeted them, and Lyudmila returned his greeting. Then, when he had passed through the door leading into the corridor, she repeated more firmly:

"Just because!"

"Couldn't you have found a better time?"

"I didn't know about your misfortunes."

"But you know now."

"Yes, and I do sympathize...." She stopped for a moment. "But that doesn't change anything."

Her eyes were distant and cold. "I thought you were... but you see, you're not what I thought you were! I'm used to weak men.... I thought at first that you needed me too...."

"And what is it you see in weak men?"

"At least they don't do despicable things, they don't go around hurting people."

"You don't think so? Of course they do!"

"No, they don't have it in them."

"You're wrong! You don't know what you're talking about, you're simply talking nonsense," he muttered, feeling an unpleasant agitation, a sort of feverish chill, pass through his body. "Well, and what have I done, for example, to hurt anybody? Whom have I killed or strangled?"

"You'd be up to killing or strangling anybody, if the situation required it. You've already strangled Bob, and now it's Sergei Leonidovich's turn—I can see what you're...."

"Well, what of it? You see correctly. But my role in all of this is really beside the point. His day is past, do you understand? He's made a mess of things, he's not up to the job—he's fallen hopelessly behind."

Lyalya burst out laughing. "Behind whom? Behind you, I suppose."

"Behind the *times,* my dear!"

"Oh, my God..." she continued to laugh.

Suddenly he realized that the feverish chill that had gripped him was fear—fear because the end had come. He could see it.

"Well, if that's the way you feel, why did you play along in the first place?"

"I didn't realize, Nikolai Demyanovich, I really didn't. I'm just a stupid female—what more can I say? If I'm guilty, then punish me. Grisha's not a strong person; actually, he's a rather weak person, and without me he'd never make it.... Still, he would never do anything despicable...."

"You're wrong, completely wrong, you're just talking nonsense," he repeated in a barely audible, birdlike voice, not having the strength to speak any louder. "Your Grisha is an ordinary man, just like me. Do you think he doesn't know what's been going on between us? Of course, he knows, but he puts up with it."

"He doesn't know."

"He does so, he knows perfectly well, only he has more brains than character."

"He doesn't know!" Lyalya suddenly shouted, her eyes flashing so angrily that Nikolai Demyanovich recoiled.

"You're wrong," he whispered despairingly, then watched as she nodded, made a parting gesture with her hand, turned, and walked away.

Two days later Kostka Shakhov brought this very same Grisha to Nikolai Demyanovich's apartment. As Grisha began showing him his precious scribblings in their frayed, string-wrapped folders, he seemed terribly tense and kept repeating in the wrong places, "You see, the point here is that.... Nikolai Demyanovich looked at him with a certain sad amazement and thought: "What *is* it she sees in him? And how did all this come about?" Grisha had a scared, dumbfounded look on his face and started babbling incomprehensibly about some sort of certificate for the housing administration. Kostka in the meantime was thoroughly enjoying himself as he sat at the small magazine table, impudently downing one brandy after another in anticipation of his commission. Nikolai Demyanovich had asked Kostka to keep Grisha in the dark as long as possible, not letting him know to whom he was being taken until today, when Kostka had arranged to meet him at the subway stop nearest to Nikolai Demyanovich's apartment. And even when Kostka had told him their destination, Grisha had not protested or cried out in indignation, "Ah, so that's the story!" Nor had he gone running back to the subway. No, he had come along as nice as you please, and now here he was, sitting decorously on the sofa with his legs crossed, a cigarette in his mouth, and looking for all the world like a worthy, honorable man. Was it possible that he hadn't guessed? Good God, no! He knew, the dog. Of course he knew. Lyudmila had told Nikolai Demyanovich how Grisha had stumbled upon the shirt which she had bought for his, Nikolai Demyanovich's, birthday and which she had left in their bureau. Grisha had asked her about it at the time, and she extricated herself by saying that it was a collective gift for one of the musicians in the theater orchestra. Nikolai Demyanovich had put on this shirt today and purposely let it be seen from under his lounging robe. And Grisha must have noticed the shirt right away, though he didn't say a word or even ask about it; instead he merely stared at it. In the meantime they had discussed everything there was to discuss, including the critics and the theater's artistic director, who should have retired long ago and allowed someone else to take over. But of course Sergei Leonidovich didn't want to retire and was kicking and thrashing in protest. And in this connection Nikolai Demyanovich suggested that something ought to be done about the situation: someone ought to get up at a meeting and talk about the disgraceful things that were going on and about how young authors were being held back: "You could even bring up the matter yourself, Grigory Fyodorovich."

All the while Grisha's eyes had remained glued on the shirt. He was obviously beside himself, and finally when he could stand it no longer, he asked, "Tell me, Nikolai Demyanovich, where did you buy that shirt?"

"Oh, this one? Lyudmila Petrovna gave it to me."

"Ah!" said Grisha.

And that was all. Apparently it was true that weak men never made a fuss. They didn't punch you in the face or even cry out, "Wha-at?! What's going on here?!" And in fact, the two men parted on peaceful terms, with the understanding that Nikolai Demyanovich would look over the manuscripts, think about them, and let him know in three or four days.

"You have a phone now, I know, I know," he said with a benignly superior smile and an amiable wave of the hand as he accompanied Grisha to the door.

He read through the compositions in the worn folders that very day and consulted with various people about them. Then Kostka gave them to Levka and Alinka to read. Nikolai Demyanovich always listened to what Lev's wife Alinka had to say. She was a smart woman—with a degree in sciences. Alinka said that the stuff wasn't badly written, but that it could have been put together with a lot more imagination. If one just shifted things around a bit and served it up in a different way, they might just have something. But there was no reason for both names to appear on the title page. Anyone would be happy, of course, to be a coauthor with Smolyanov, but Rebrov—who was he? How would you package him? "You'd package him," thought Smolyanov and even burst out laughing, "together with his wife. He and his wife come in one package!" Well, it's just a joke, nothing to get upset about. Don't worry, my dear, we're going to help you, but not because of your beautiful eyes and not because of what was, but because of what *still is to be.* And here Nikolai Demyanovich was overtaken by a compelling image: imagine a small bird suddenly flying onto your porch on a summer evening. If you shut the porch door and all the windows, the bird will beat its wings against the glass—flap! flap! flap!—until it finally becomes so exhausted that it falls to the floor and you're able to pick it up in the palm of your hand.

Nikolai Demyanovich pictured the whole scene very clearly, and his mouth even went dry as it usually did whenever he thought about a woman. About five days later, having settled some other business matters, he called Lyudmila's number and asked to speak to Grigory Fyodorovich. A woman's voice replied that Grigory Fyodorovich didn't live there anymore.

VII

Lying on his wooden upper berth, Rebrov had been tormenting himself for the past three days, endlessly turning everything over in his own mind. On a sheet of paper he had written the words: hill—hall—hole—mole—mope—dope—dupe.... This saving diversion had been handed to him by the man in the opposite berth, a certain Modest Petrovich, as soon as they had left the outskirts of Moscow behind them and plunged into the deep snow and dark picket fences of country dachas. Whenever Rebrov put down his piece of paper and stopped mumbling "loop—lop—loss—moss," his gaze would fix on the ceiling or slip down to the dull whiteness that lay beyond the window (it was the beginning of March, but winter and its snowdrifts still reigned supreme) and he would hear the voices and see the faces which he was tearing himself away from forever, as he flew off into the unknown. Pyotr Alexandrovich would smile with his withered, yellowed lips, "You know best, Grisha. Do as you think best...."

The old man was indifferent to everything. Even the garden, which had once been his whole life, no longer excited him. For days at a time he would sit in his chair by the window, listening to the radio, or dozing, or reading *Ogonyok*. And frozen on his face would be a smile of indifference to everything that was unrelated to his sickness—that is, to death. He spoke only about the state of his health, about his medicines, his doctors and nurses. One of the nurses was good with the needle and spoke to him in a pleasant manner; the other was rather morose and inserted the needle painfully, not always finding the vein on the first try. He hated this woman and called her "the jabber." "How a man's whole personality can change!" Rebrov had reflected in amazement, not yet knowing that *his own garden*, which had once been his whole life too, would soon be abandoned—and abandoned forever.

"My advice, Grisha, is not to pay any attention. Just forget about it, forget about it! Oh, my God...." The old man gave several faint gasps—not out of any onrush of feeling for Rebrov, but because he was overtaken once again by thoughts of his illness. "You don't know women... they're made differently from us. Irina, for example, can never understand that when she opens the door to the kitchen...." Suddenly he went on to ask in a whisper, "But why did you go to see Smolyanov?"

"What difference does that make?" Rebrov exclaimed with irritation. "I felt I had to, so I went."

Of course, his going there had been a stupid move. No, actually, a cowardly one. He had suddenly been overwhelmed by fear and desperation—a feeling that he had to do something right away, had to earn a lot of money so that they could start their family and have a place of their own. No, that wasn't it; probably the main reason for his going there had been some sort of base, masochistic urge to satisfy his curiosity, to subject himself to a particularly humiliating experience. After all, he had long since guessed that Smolyanov was the "certain person" Shakhov had in mind, the "certain person" who would be able to help him.

For two whole days after this nauseating visit Rebrov had not asked

Lyalya for any explanation. He had not wanted to believe any of Smolyanov's insinuations or to get to the bottom of them. For what would the point be? This wasn't the sort of thing that could be proved. The fact that she had given him the shirt as a present and that he had smiled insolently when telling about it didn't necessarily mean a thing, especially since he was such an insolent brute to begin with. Three days after their meeting, however, the situation changed. That morning Rebrov accidentally came across one of Irina Ignatievna's epistles to Lyalya on the floor of their attic room. Rebrov had gotten used to these compositions written on the pages of school notebooks and sometimes placed in an envelope, sometimes not. The fact was that his mother-in-law became a graphomaniac whenever she quarreled with her daughter. And Lyalya, with her usual negligence, would leave her mother's epistles lying all over the place—so that you couldn't help but pick them up and start reading them. Obviously something had happened between the two women—they hardly spoke to each other—but Rebrov hadn't asked what it was all about. One thing he knew: it had begun with them, but it would end up involving him. For Lyalya couldn't endure long quarrels with her mother. Still, he shouldn't have picked up that letter. He should have said the hell with it!

Characteristically, the letter was written in the most avant-garde prose, like something from Dos Passos, without periods or commas: "You're a fool a real fool life doesn't seem to have taught you anything you're a complete idiot why do you need this? Just remember I'm not going to take care of it so don't count on me I don't have the strength it's enough for me to try to get your father back on his feet you work like a mule for him running around all over the place now with a baby in addition you'll be completely tied down you'll get old very soon you'll be a wreck like Aunt Zhenya's Mayka she's completely lost her looks her children have worn her out and yet you have talent but you're such a fool you're willing to waste it children don't bring joy only grief and disappointment there's a lot you don't understand you're as naive as a child he exploits you like nobody's business he sits around the National eating and drinking at your expense while you're out working like a horse if he were a real husband to you I wouldn't be so upset Nikolai Demyanovich was courting you but you've rejected him—and for what? If you don't call Alexei Ivanovich I won't have anything to do with you you two can do as you please just don't count on your father and me you can start paying half of the ground rent and house taxes and your share of the utilities the telephone will be your expense we don't need it you can eat out I refuse to cook for you And I want the 240 rubles back that I lent you for the fur coat...."

In all this semi-delirious rambling Rebrov was struck by one sentence: "Nikolai Demyanovich was courting you but you've rejected him." That evening he could stand it no longer and asked Lyalya, "Well, what's the story, are you going to call Alexei Ivanovich or not?"

Alexei Ivanovich was an elderly gynecologist who had once been Irina Ignatievna's doctor and who had performed two abortions on Lyalya in the past. Rebrov could see that Lyalya was tense and worn out from her mother's hostility—this being the fourth day that her mother had given her the silent treatment. The situation would have resolved itself somehow, so he should have kept his mouth shut—but he lost his self-control. One word provoked another, and this seemed to be all that was needed for the volcano to erupt. Lyalya and her mother started accusing each other, and her mother, as always, proved to be the stronger of the two. Lyalya burst into tears and suddenly began to feel faint. They gave her some medicine, and her mother, now thoroughly frightened, began babbling as she sprinkled Lyalya's face with cold water, "Dear child, I won't leave you." An awkward silence followed, and after a while the two women went off to their separate rooms. Rebrov was left alone with Pyotr Alexandrovich, who had stood there throughout, leaning on his cane and not saying a word.

"Grisha, I want to tell you something," the old man suddenly began as he slowly walked up to Rebrov. "It's all the same to me.... You'll be taking off tomorrow and I'll be dead the day after tomorrow. So it doesn't make any difference to me. But fifteen, maybe sixteen years ago there was this Valentin...." He glanced around and then went on in a whisper, "Valentin Ivanovich Skobov. He was foreman of the forge in our factory—a good man. A very good man, quite impressive in fact. We used to go fishing together, visit each other, do this and that together. And suddenly I sense that there's some sort of hanky-panky going on between him and Irina—the woman was pining away, falling in love, you understand...."

Rebrov smiled, "If...."

"Well, maybe it wasn't love, I don't know. Who knows what it was, call it anything you like. But the point is that there came a moment when I thought I'd leave her. I'd definitely leave her. I'd take little Lyalya with me and simply leave town...."

"Well, what happened?"

"Nothing happened. I was just being foolish, don't you see? Such foolishness doesn't last, whereas life goes on for a long time."

"No," said Rebrov. "This is a different situation. I'd be happy to...but

I can't. I can't because...." And without finishing his sentence, he gestured despairingly and ran off upstairs.

He left the next day. And leaving, he realized that this was not at all like the other times when he had rushed off with hurt feelings to Bashilov Street. It was a sunny winter day and the sky was clear, bright blue. The old man sat with a smile on his face, looking out the window at the blinding snow. He bit his lips and said, "Do as you think best, Grisha..."

Three nights later Lyalya arrived with her suitcases—to move in with him. She had broken off with her mother for good. Couldn't he forgive her and trust her? After all, how could he treat a person this way—without pity or compassion? He was dying to understand and to forgive her. But still—how had it happened? Crying and repentant, Lyalya told him something so shameful, so base that he couldn't bear to listen. Yes, yes, she said, somewhere deep inside and perhaps only half-consciously she had probably wanted to further her career. Rebrov felt like shouting, "My God, how can you slander yourself this way? That couldn't have been the reason!" It could, it could so. She refused to yield on this point. He hoped that she would, but no, that was the way it was. And this truth, this whole, *naked truth* was wilder than the wildest, most naked passion. And now he began pressing her, wearing her down and forcing her to tell him everything: about this man and that, about all of her old loves. And when she had told him everything down to the last detail, including this last, pathetic truth, it was as if they both had gone mad. Looking back on it, he could see that that night had been the end. But they hadn't realized it at the time, imagining only that this was an opportunity to begin anew.

The next day, however, when Lyalya went off to the theater and Rebrov was left alone in his room, he felt so empty and depressed that it occurred to him that perhaps he should just drop her a note in the mailbox and take off for some faraway place. A little later the same day, Shakhov arrived and said that Smolyanov had long been expecting him. Rebrov replied that he wasn't interested. Then one evening a few days later, Smolyanov himself appeared, bringing with him Rebrov's folders, a bottle of brandy, and a cake for Lyalya: "If the mountain doesn't come to Mohammed...."

He reported that he had found Rebrov a job at the theater as chief literary consultant in place of Marevin. He had reached an agreement with the executive director and with the central theater administration as well. Lyalya was in a performance that evening, and Rebrov felt ashamed of his cramped, messy room, of Kanunov's crying children who could be heard from the other side of the wall, and of his own slovenly appearance—dressed as he was in slippers and an old pair of pajamas. He vaguely sensed that what he ought to do at this moment was either to punch Smolyanov in the face or else go to the director's office and accept the job. He was deterred from the former by the thought that the man had, after all, come with good intentions and was trying to help him. So, why should he suddenly start punching him in the face? He did refuse the brandy, however. Of course there was still the problem of the certificate, since Kanunov kept pressing the matter, but he felt a certain strange lack of urgency in all of this, as if it were happening in a dream. And even his feelings of shame seemed to be part of this dream, as did his sense of surprise.

"Why hasn't Lyalya said anything about this?"

"She doesn't know about it. So far I've discussed the matter only with the executive director and with Herman Vladimirovich.... Herman Vladimirovich, as you may already know, is probably going to be the new artistic director.... Sergei Leonidovich was taken off to the hospital yesterday. He's had a heart attack, apparently a very serious one. But then, what can you expect? He's been pushing himself too hard.... The salary is 1,500 a month; you won't have to be at the theater until one, and there'll be some days when you won't have to come in at all...."

For the past several days Rebrov had had the distinct feeling that something inside him had changed irrevocably. This change had taken place back then, just before his departure, and was of such magnitude that it seemed to him that he had become an altogether different person, with a different blood type and a different chemical makeup. And this different person—this new self—had the right to behave differently from his old self, just as his old self did not have to be held responsible for the acts of his new self. In response to Smolyanov's job offer Rebrov said that he would have to discuss the matter with Lyalya.

"What's there to discuss?" laughed Smolyanov.

But he never did have a chance to discuss it with her. Lyalya fell ill that very day and stayed in bed at her mother's where he subsequently went to visit her. Two days later they sent for him by telegram and when he arrived he was told that Alexei Ivanovich had come and gone and that everything had been taken care of. Lyalya was still weak and confined to her bed, but there was a bright, happy, and as it seemed to Rebrov, guilty look in her eyes. The old Rebrov felt like rushing to her and pressing his forehead to her white hand, for the happiness which shone in her moist eyes was that of suffering overcome. But the new Rebrov said in a calm voice, "How do you feel? I'm glad that it's all over with."

His mother-in-law smiled at him in conciliatory fashion and whispered, "Just don't upset her now, all right? And Grishenka, would you please run to the market and buy her some fruit?"

"She'll be in her power forever—until one of them dies," Rebrov thought to himself. An hour later, when he returned from the market, Lyalya was asleep, and Rebrov went back to Bashilov Street.

The following day, Friday, Shakhov came to see him. They went out to a restaurant for dinner and from there hailed a cab to take them to the theater. They had drunk so much that Rebrov's legs would barely move, but his mind was working clearly. There's nothing worse, he thought, than a long goodbye. At Mayakovsky Square he ordered the driver to stop. Then he opened the door and put Shakhov out on the sidewalk. He was experiencing a fantastic sensation of lightness—something both delightful and absurd. If he hadn't been afraid of making a fool of himself, he would have taken off from the ground and winged his way above the buildings. The train was leaving at 9 p.m. Right now Lyalya was probably wandering around her room in her bathrobe, having an evening snack, and here he was flying off without saying goodbye, soaring through the winter sky above the rooftops, vanishing without a trace.

Modest Petrovich swung his gray, wool-clad feet over the edge of the berth, and dangling them above the man sleeping below, he asked, "So, Grigory, my boy, have you just finished college?"

"No, dear fellow. I'm almost thirty, thank God," said Rebrov. "I've just finished life."

"Ah, so that's it...."

Modest Petrovich burst out laughing. Outside the window the sky had already turned a deep, bluish black, and someone switched on the lights. One life had finished and the other was just beginning. Actually, every man, including even this prospecting geologist Modest Petrovich, lives not one but several lives. He dies and is born anew; he is present at his own funeral and watches his own rebirth, as once again life slowly starts up with all its new hopes. After one's death one can look back on one's past life, and this is what Rebrov was doing now, as the train carried him eastward through the ever deeper snows and harsher frosts.

On the morning of the fifth day there was a loud commotion in the corridor outside their compartment. In a strange voice which boded no good, a woman was wailing loudly, "Oh-oh-oh-oh!" Their compartment door burst open and a red, crumpled, jellylike face thrust itself forward and gasped, "He died... at 5 a.m...." Rebrov stepped out into the corri-

The Long Goodbye   *169*

dor. In one of the compartments sobs could be heard, while in another
the door was wide open and people were playing cards. One individual
was running along the corridor with an enormous Chinese thermos in
his hand, pushing his way through the rapidly assembling crowd.
Rebrov returned to the compartment and climbed up onto his berth.
Unable to fight back the tears, he turned toward the wall, and with his
face buried in his pillowcase, now dampened by his tears, he thought
about the life which he had led so far and wondered what it had all
added up to.

"But the real question," he muttered through clenched teeth, "is will
I have another one...."

A week later Rebrov witnessed the following scene from the window
of his hotel room on Great Siberia Street, where he was awaiting a visit
from the local Party leader. A fight had started on the pavement below.
One man had stabbed two others in the stomach and taken to his heels.
Several bystanders had run after him, knocked him down, and were
now starting to beat him. Three people had grabbed him initially: a
worker in white, flour-covered overalls (he had been unloading flour
sacks from a truck on the corner), a soldier who happened to be passing by, and a woman. By the time Rebrov managed to run downstairs,
however, a crowd had already gathered around the assailant. One of
the men he had stabbed was lying on the pavement, groaning, while
the other was still reeling on his two feet, half doubled over, and clutch-
ing his stomach. Several people kept raising the assailant up to a sitting
position and then bashing his head down on the pavement. They were
trying to finish him off in a hurry, before the police arrived. Five minutes later a police car came rolling up. The crowd made way, and the
assailant remained lying on the pavement, his face lifeless and as black
and grimy as the sole of a shoe. It was clear that justice had already
been done. The two policemen picked him up, and holding him under
the arms, began dragging him to the open rear door of the police car.
Suddenly, however, the assailant straightened his cap, pulled it tighter
on his small, childlike head, and climbed into the car on his own two
feet.

Rebrov went back into the hotel and up to the second floor. It is so
easy to kill a man, he thought. And so impossibly difficult. The Party
leader Balashov arrived soon afterwards. He was a native of Tomsk and
a nice fellow. By now the pavement below was deserted and all that remained was a powdering of white in the spot where they had been unloading the flour sacks from the truck. Balashov was informing him of
the latest employment opportunities. There were office jobs available

in the city through the middle of April, then from the twentieth it
would be off to the taiga for five months. And on his way back from the
taiga, Rebrov decided, he would be able to stop off in Petrovsk-
Zabaikalsky, formerly the site of the Petrovsky Ironworks, where Ivan
Pryzhov had died in exile, yet managed to keep "one leg kicking" up to
the very end. Rebrov wanted to see what the place looked like and what
changes had been wrought by the passage of time.

    Lyalya sometimes took a trolleybus to a quick-service dry cleaners on
Karbyshev Boulevard, and as she rode past the eight-story building with
the butcher shop on the first floor, she would suddenly recall something from her old life of eighteen years before: Grisha, the theater, the
old director Sergei Leonidovich, the scent of lilacs in the springtime, or
their dog Kandidka, clanking her chain along the fence. And whenever
she thought of these things, her heart would momentarily and painfully
contract, and she would feel a strange mixture of joy and sadness that
all of this had once been part of her life. Sometimes, however, she
would ride past the building with the butcher shop without feeling a
thing—so preoccupied was she with her present cares and concerns.
And of these she had more than enough. There was her husband and
her eighth-grade son to think of, and all sorts of complications at work:
the Director of the House of Culture would load her down with all
sorts of extra tasks because she was as strong as a horse and would take
everything on herself. Then there were her local trade-union committee obligations and, in addition, her activities with the physical education group at Dynamo Stadium, where she jogged on Saturdays with
other middle-aged colonels' wives. Lyalya's husband was a military
man, a university graduate, who taught at the Officers' Academy. Her
father, her mother, Aunt Toma, Uncle Kolya, and even the unhappy
Mayka, who was five years younger than Lyalya, had died during the
past eighteen years. Her old theater friends had all disappeared, nor
did she feel like seeing any of them. She had fought a long legal battle
when they fired her. She fought desperately and had even developed
asthma in the process, but all to no avail: she had been forced to give
in. And now she had a new circle of friends—military people, engineers,
and automobile enthusiasts. Vsevolod himself was crazy about cars,
and every summer they and their friends would take off in two or three
cars for the Crimea, or the Carpathians, or the Baltic. But as for her old
theater friends, she only felt uncomfortable whenever she happened to
run into them.
    Once she bumped into her old friend Masha in line for pillows at

GUM. How Mashka had changed! Not only had her face aged, but she had become affected and a bit spiteful. For some reason Masha began telling her about Smolyanov. As if she, Lyalya, were interested in hearing about him. Actually, she had trouble remembering what he looked like—whether he was fat or thin, and whether or not he wore glasses. Apparently he was hard up now and suffered from poor health. He was no longer writing plays and had to live off the income he got from renting his dacha to summer people. Well, so what—who cared? She really wasn't interested in hearing all this.

"And your Rebrov is having an affair with the daughter of one of my girlfriends."

"Really?"

Though she assumed a look of indifference, Lyalya listened with interest as Masha began telling her about Rebrov. The girl in question had acted in one of his pictures, and the two of them had traveled together to some film festival in Argentina or Brazil—or one of those countries—and some common acquaintance had traveled with them.... But here Masha's account was broken off, for by now the two women had reached the counter and were quickly swallowed up in the surging crowd. Nor did Lyalya make any effort to find her friend after completing her purchase. Actually, she already knew from others that Rebrov was doing well—that he was earning good money from his movie scripts, that he lived in the southwest section of town, also had a car, and apparently had already been married twice. That was the extent of her knowledge. And she was happy for him. After all, she had always had good feelings about him. There was one thing she didn't know, however, and which she wondered about. Did he often think about his life, evaluate it from every angle as he used to do—this had been one of his favorite pastimes, especially when he was traveling—and did it seem to him now that those years when he was poor and discouraged, when he envied, hated, suffered, and lived almost like a beggar were actually the best years of his life, since to be happy one needs equal portions of....

In the meantime Moscow was spreading out farther and farther, beyond the circumferential highway, across fields and ravines. It was throwing up building after building, stone mountains with a million lighted windows; it was laying bare the ancient soil, traversing it with giant concrete pipes, strewing the land with foundation pits, laying asphalt, building up, tearing down, destroying without a trace. And every morning the subway platforms and bus stops would be swarming with people, more and more of them crowded together with each passing year. Lyalya would wonder in amazement: "Where have they all come from? Either there are an awful lot of newcomers or else everyone's children have suddenly grown up."

1971

Translated by Helen P. Burlingame

GAMES AT DUSK

We knew them all by name and not one of them knew us. We were simply, "Hey, little boy! Bring the ball!" Or else we were, "Thanks, little boy," or "There it is, behind the bush! Over to the left, the left!" They played from four until dusk, while we sat on a bench carved by knives—my friend Savva and I—turning our heads from right to left, right to left, right to left. Our necks hurt. This continued for hours. Neither hunger, nor thirst, nor any earthly desire could distract us from this remarkable occupation. From right to left, right to left darted the small, right to left white, right to left, tennis ball together with firm resonant strokes which were evenly, right to left, right to left, hammered into our brains, made us dizzy, cast a spell on us, and hypnotized us, we were like drunks, unable to leave, to stand up, even though at home a bawling-out awaited us, we continued to sit stupefiedly, turning our heads from right to left, right to left, right to left.

From the other side of the court—if someone happened to glance at us!—we resembled two little bowing Chinese idols, so tirelessly and smoothly did we move our almost crew-cut heads. And truly, we were like little Chinese idols. But really, not little Chinese idols, not at all Chinese, but very real, suburban Moscow, eleven-year-old summer residents, idlers who wasted their July evenings turning their heads from side to side.

Nearby was the river, a sandstone slope, a sandbar, barges—the odor of the water and yells of the swimmers reached us without penetrating deep into our consciousness. These were the odors and noises of a distant and superfluous world.

At dusk our chance came. The first player to give up was a lanky spectacled guy whom Savva and I called "The Trembler." The Trembler was very nervous on the court. At each unsuccessful stroke he would yell, "Oh hell!" seize his head, look around with amazement at the rim of his racket, shake his head and mutter something like, "What's going on? What's the matter with me?" But nothing particular ever came out of it. He always played the same. The best player, Tatarnikov, an aristocrat, the owner of an Erenpraiz bicycle, a model in everything for Savva and me, who played almost at the same time as The Trembler, would stop the game. He was silent and ironical, and wore elegant striped shirts, his hair sleekly slicked down in the "polit-cut" style.[1] Tatarnikov treated his partners so scornfully that he could get away with stopping the game whenever he felt like it, even in the middle of a game—if he had fewer points. He would suddenly raise his racket with the words, "That's it, folks! This has no class—an eyesore," and would walk off the court, and no one dared to argue with him. Everyone swallowed this boorishness silently as if in their minds they thanked Tatarnikov for the fact that he came to play at all. After all, Tatarnikov had once played with Henri Cochet himself and the latter had said about him, "A fine fellow."

Tatarnikov would get on his Erenpraiz and ride away, and immediately Anchik would get ready to go also. She wouldn't throw down her racket right away, but it was clear how uninteresting everything became for her. She would stop trying, miss the ball, and bicker. Anchik was dark-complexioned, like an Indian. Sometimes she could be very merry, laughing loudly and lifting everyone's spirits, but sometimes she was gloomy and irritable. Poor Anchik! I pitied her. And Savva did too. Although Savva once said he didn't like coquettes, I saw that he was lying. I noticed how he would tense up and how his face would flush in spots when Anchik addressed him in her soothing though completely indifferent voice. "Little boy, would you mind..." With sullen haste he ran after the ball much faster than usual. I, on the contrary, sat silently and haughtily. Just as soon as Anchik stopped her game, the Professor and Gravinsky usually accompanied Anchik to her dacha on Line 3.

A small, dark-faced little man in square glasses, the owner of a Japanese racket, would remain playing longer than the others. Savva and I suspected him of being a spy. A husband and wife, a disgusting pair for whom tennis was necessary only to lose weight, would hang around the court even longer than "the spy." They played very badly, but long and persistently, until dark. I noticed that the worse the players, the more avid they were for the game. Savva and I detested them. They deprived us of the last, precious seconds because the real players did not permit them, like us, on the court. But late in the evening they didn't permit us, insolently using their prerogative as adults. "Children, children! You've been hanging around here all day...." But finally they, too, would clear off. I would take my twelve-ounce Dynamo racket from its case and Savva his marvelous German one—with steel strings—

and we would run out onto the empty court. There were no people happier than we at that moment.

The court was cement. It turned white in the dusk, like an open and spacious meadow. We really hurried. In the dark we often missed. We wanted to serve with all our strength. Every now and then the fast balls we missed would strike against the wooden wall with a drumming noise. The back line and the serving courts were no longer visible. The flying ball would fly out from the dark so unexpectedly that I instinctively held up my racket in self-defense. We enjoyed ourselves for twenty minutes, until Nikolai Grigorievich, the net manager, returned from swimming and took it down and left. We continued to play for a while without the net; actually, in the dark, it made no difference whether there was a net or not.

And then for a long time we would talk about all sorts of things and meander home along the bank. On the other side of the river, in the meadow, hung layers of fog. Someone was swimming in the river and someone stood on the bank and yelled, "How's the water, eh?" Someone would run, warming himself after a swim, along the smooth, sandy strip by the water. The patter of bare feet along the gray sand resounded clearly and softly, like the slaps of palms on a naked body. One could hear this person with his patter of bare feet saying, "Br-br-br!" And the superfluous, starry July world lie around us amidst the pines and beyond the river, where on the horizon, the fires of Tushin shimmered through the warm air. That was a long time ago. It was back when people used to wade across the Moscow River, when people used to ride a long, red Leiland bus from Theater Square through Silver Forest, when people wore silk tolstovkas, pants made from white linen, and canvas shoes which were rubbed with tooth powder in the evenings so that in the mornings they looked freshly white and with each step released a cloud of white dust.

***

It is difficult to say now who these people were or how old they were. They disappeared from my life and at that time I didn't pay any attention to such things. I only knew that Gravinsky was the son of some worker of the Comintern. The Trembler and the Professor may have been students, but perhaps not. Tatarnikov worked somewhere, but it is possible that he worked nowhere at all, because he often came to the court during the day. Anchik was a high-school senior; that, how-

ever, is also not certain, and it's quite possible that she was a college
student. I knew that her father drove a black Rolls Royce. Once I saw
the black automobile stop outside a house on Line 3—there was a terrible downpour and I had been sent to the corner for milk; I was soaked
to the skin and plodding along the street, hurrying nowhere—when
Anchik jumped out of the car, took off her shoes and, squealing,
splashed along in her bare feet toward the gate. Right after her came a
man in a black hat. Suddenly he stopped right in a puddle, took off his
hat, exposing his bald head to the rain, and stood several seconds
strangely pensive, looking at the ground.

Anchik was tall and slender, *with a wasp's wisp of a waist,* with *jet-black
hair* and big black eyes, as black and deep *as the night.* I liked her very
much. Of course, not in the same way I would like a girl, for example,
Marina, my classmate. I liked Anchik platonically—as a woman. I liked
her husky voice, her clothes, sarafans and *maikas,* which apparently
were last year's—a little too small and tightly cutting her body. I liked
the way she walked, swinging her arms and swaying like a sailor. I liked
her habit of joking about everything and talking in a haughty manner. I
liked the way she picked up the ball from the court without stooping,
but deftly and quickly by the rim of her racket and foot. I could pick up
the ball like that too, but only with the help of my left leg. Anchik did it
with ease with either leg. The ball seemed to stick to her racket. And
she never dropped balls on the court. But Savva and I dropped them
often.

I don't know, maybe it was because of Anchik that we dragged ourselves to the court each evening. That didn't occur to me then, but now
I think that that's the way it was. Because of Anchik and because of
Tatarnikov, whom we also liked. After all, we could have come during
the day, in the heat when no one was playing, but the empty court and
the empty benches didn't suit us—we wanted the public, noise, passions, struggle, beautiful women—and we wanted to see it all, as in the
theater.

in the middle of summer Savva's father died, and his mother took
him to Leningrad. He left me his racket with the steel strings. He
promised to return at the end of the summer, but he didn't. I never
saw or heard anything about Savva after that. And he didn't see me
when I played doubles with The Trembler or see what happened the
following summer when the Moscow-Volga Canal was opened: the
river was made navigable and ships began to go up it. New players appeared on the tennis court, but Tatarnikov remained the champion of
Silver Forest and its environs. He played some people for money. He
would spot them four games and still win.

At the beginning of that summer—when the first ships came—it was very hot, but later it rained constantly. It was a kind of light, fleeting rain which broke out suddenly and did not last long. But we had to wait half an hour or an hour for the court to dry. The tennis players would gather under an awning built next to the court, play chess and other games, or simply sit, telling jokes. I loved to sit on the bench among them and listen. One day we're all sitting together, me, Tatarnikov, the Professor with Gravinsky, Anchik and someone else—when this Boris came and said that an acquaintance of ours had drowned. Boris had appeared at the court not long ago, he didn't play badly, but a bit flashily and arrogantly. He argued about every ball. His father was the director of a factory and they used to live in Tbilisi. So, he came and said that an acquaintance of ours had drowned. It later turned out that no one had drowned, he had cooked it all up, but, of course, at first everyone was alarmed. Anchik even screamed and then this Boris stepped up to her; he was stocky, not tall, shorter than Anchik, with unforgettable, round, knee-like cheekbones. He always spoke clenching his teeth, and this made his cheeks move. And he said, clenching his teeth, "Take this, you trash," and hit Anchik in the face with the edge of his palm—a violent back-handed blow. At this point everyone began to shout.

"Hey! What's that for?"

Boris didn't answer and looked angrily at Anchik while she stood covering her face with her hands. She neither cried nor moved. The way Anchik was struck and the way she *took* the blow was so unbelievable that in astonishment I froze on the bench, while everyone else was jumping from their places, jostling one another and yelling. The Professor or Gravinsky or perhaps both of them seized Boris by the chest. But he brushed them off and quietly said:

"Butt out! Get away! I'm telling you, get away! Or else...."

"Wait," said Tatarnikov. "Did anyone drown or not?"

And at this point Boris again struck Anchik on the hands covering her face, but with such force that she was knocked off balance, staggered back like a branch, and almost fell. Then she started walking quickly, almost at a run, and Boris kept up with her. They went through the pines and the bushes, not glancing at each other, paying no attention to where they were going, businesslike and straight, and each was isolated, but something terrible and simple bound them together. They were like one person, flashing for a moment amidst the pines, going away from us.

The court dried and someone came out to play, but I couldn't stand to see the pale face of Tatarnikov with his "politcut." The tennis players

were filled with indignation and, as I heard, agreed not to play again
with Boris, with that beast. "Striking a woman! Sinking so low! It's a
pity that he left. We'd have stomped on him!" But I felt they were indignant at something else.

After this, life on the court somehow began to quickly and irretrievably change. Some people completely vanished, stopped coming, others moved away. New people came. Many new ones. They say that
Anchik with her younger sister, brother and grandmother, was living at
Elk Station. But Tatarnikov came just as before on his Erenpraiz; sometimes The Trembler and the man whom Savva and I considered a
Japanese spy would come. They built a volleyball court next to the tennis court and in the evenings a noisy crowd gathered there to play.
There were forty people who waited to play, the losers yielding to those
left and the winners staying on. The hubbub was like at a bazaar.

The beast Boris came once on a Sunday with a friend as if nothing
had happened. Both were wearing jockey caps. Boris asked, "Who's
next?" We didn't answer him. There was a foursome on the court and
another foursome was waiting in line. Boris and his friend sat waiting
for half an hour, then began to make a scene. There would have been a
real fight had there not been a strange noise from the riverside. The
woods crackled under the feet of a hundred people. A huge crowd was
moving in our direction with music and songs, and in front ran little
boys who informed us that a ship had docked, that the crowd was coming from there, with a tin-pan band behind them. The tennis players
continued to play coolly. In a moment the horde surrounded the court;
several of them were noticeably tipsy and sat down on the grass. Some
danced, others played leap-frog, an accordion was playing, several people entered the court and started to demand that the tennis players
take down the net. They understandably refused to do so and said they
were going to call a policeman. The Trembler became particularly excited and yelled,

"We're going to complain! Tell us where you work!"

A thickset man in a panama also yelled, swinging his arms:

"You want to play foursomes, while four hundred people watch you,
right? Is that what you want?"

"You're disturbing us!"

"Comrades, where's a policeman...?"

"We have an arrangement with the resort administration!"

The band came out onto the court and made themselves comfortable by the wooden wall while they argued. Someone had already
stripped off the net and the first couple began to shuffle along the ce-

ment, even without music. But then a waltz broke out: "The blue globe
spins, turns." I saw how Boris, his cheeks puffed out, dragged along a
thin ugly woman, a total fright in a shawl, and began to dance with her.
The tennis players were still fuming and trying to break up the band.
Tatarnikov was the only one who wasn't fuming. He got on his
Erenpraiz and rode off.

The wooden fence was broken down and burned for heat during the
war. Once, decades later, I went back there and walked up the hill in
order to see the spot where so much of what my life later consisted
began. At that time there were only promises. However, several of
them were fulfilled. On the top of the hill I stumbled across a majestic,
summer movie theater with glimmering thick white walls. All that remained of the court was a cement area on which people were bumping
into each other, arm in arm, men and women from the dachas waiting
for the beginning of a performance. How could you call them people
from the dachas! This was Moscow. It smelled like Moscow, with gaso-
line and dusty foliage. I asked a man in a red pullover made half of
leather, half of wool if he knew where the cement square had come
from. "It's from the war," he answered with confidence. "There was
some sort of fortification here. When the Germans flew to bomb
Moscow, it was from here, over Silver Forest, that they were shot down.
Yes, it's from the war."

I went up to the river and sat down on a bench. The river had remained. The pines also creaked as before. But dusk was somehow different. I didn't want to swim. In the days when I was eleven, dusk was
much warmer.

1968

Translated by Jim Somers

A SHORT STAY
IN THE
TORTURE
CHAMBER

In the early spring of 1964, when I was still suffering from an insatiable love of sports, when I kept charts on the champions, knew by heart the best players of the Fiorentina and the Manchester United, when I believed that you could write as seriously about sports as, say, about the tomb of Lorenzo di Medici in Florence, when I had just released my legendary film about hockey and didn't feel at all embarrassed by it, I arrived in the Tyrol with a group of sports writers, lived in a mountain village not far from Innsbruck, and each morning took the bus to the games. The Olympics were being held in Innsbruck. Who won there, who lost, I don't remember. All that nonsense has been forgotten. I don't remember the name of a single athlete from that time—what I remember is the blinding snow on the slopes, the sharp blue of the sky, the freshness in the air, the smell of coffee, and my landlord, who would squint and squeeze out, *"Morgen,"* through his dry lips.

Sometimes when I didn't feel like going to town I would stay in the hotel and watch the games on television. On a table in the empty hall lay thick books in antique-looking leather bindings: *Gästebücher.* Guest books. Having nothing to do, I leafed through them, relishing the examples of German ingenuousness. The books had been kept since 1929, when the hotel first started up in the village of Stubental. All of the comments were the same: gratitude to the proprietor, praise for the mountains, the snow, the view, the girls, the selection of records on the jukebox. I reached the Anschluss: nothing was changed, the same delight about the snow, the air, the girls. And then the war: judging from the comments, wounded German officers took time off here, but it was impossible to find out anything from them, either, except raptures over nature, girls, Italian wine, Spanish oranges. Once there flashed a patriotic entry: *"Alles wagen, England schlagen!"* that is, "Give it your all—beat England." Someone had written above in pencil in small letters, "But England really trounced you." And then still later, with a green felt-tip, *"O Sie gute arme Idioten!"* But it was unclear to whom this was addressed: to the beaten Germans or to those who rejoiced in the victory. And that was all about the war. The same comments continued: skis, sun, happiness, *Erlebnis.* The proprietor didn't care for us. We paid him money; he tolerated us. He did not enter into conversation. The only thing we heard from him through his clenched teeth was: *"Morgen!"*

But still, I liked the snowy mountains, the valley, the huge bridge across the gorge, the smell of coffee in the morning, and I liked what I was, so madly and senselessly carried away with then, what filled the newspapers, what I wrote about at night, and at noon shouted by telephone to Moscow, and only one thing spoiled my mood: the presence of N. in our group. He had emerged from my distant past. Of course, I knew that he existed and I would come across his name in the newspapers, and from time to time would run into him one place or another. We both would act as if we were scarcely acquainted or, indeed, if we did bump into each other head-on, we would barely nod and would pass on by, although at one time we had been on friendly terms and had liked the same girl. But she was incidental. The girl had nothing whatever to do with the whole matter, which took place fourteen years ago—the point was this: we had lived separate lives all those years. He worked for the radio; I sat working at home. I thought I was done with him. And suddenly, he turned up in Innsbruck. N. was always far removed from sports. How the hell did he turn up in our group? The first minute we saw each other in the group gathering in Moscow, I noticed something waver in his face, like a momentarily repressed impulse to be glad, or, maybe, to nod in a friendly way, but he couldn't read this weakness in my face. I met him with a cold look and barely discernible nod which signified nothing on my part but an icy memory. That kind of relationship, I assumed, would become established between us, and somehow I would get through the twelve days.

Sometimes, when my friends would go to town and I would stay at the hotel, it would be partly because I didn't want to see the rosy-cheeked, dried-up, old-mannish N. There had been a time, I remembered, when he wore an army jacket and boots, smoked a handmade pipe and looked like a staid, patrician youth, deeply absorbed in something. Later, I found out in what. But at the time it seemed to me that his unhurriedness, his quiet, indistinct voice, and his gloomy look concealed something significant. I was engrossed in reading Blok[1] then, and it seemed to me that this line was about him: "Let us forgive the gloomy look,/For not here lies the hidden moving force." True, he did not resemble the lines that followed: "He was all a child of love and light,/He was all a celebration of freedom." N.'s moving force had to do with something else: N. himself alone.

But when we arrived in the Tyrol and settled in the hotel, something strange began: he behaved as if nothing had ever happened. In the morning he would greet me from afar with happy smiles, raise his hand in greeting and nod earnestly, and the nods conveyed not only the old amiability, but also a genuine esteem, the kind expressed to people you sincerely respect. I tried not to pay attention. Then it started to annoy me. Once we ran into each other in the pressbox at the stadium, face to face, and in passing he grabbed my arm above the elbow, squeezed it rather familiarly, and said, "Hi!" I pulled my arm away and muttered, "What is it?" But my mutter sounded more frightened than hostile. He winked at me and passed by without saying anything else. Another time in the presence of two journalists, an Italian and a German, he launched into a conversation with me about hockey, after introducing me as an expert, the author of an excellent film, *The Hockey Players*. That's the way he said it—"excellent," and his voice sounded honest and simple, without the slightest touch of envy or irony, and, like it or not, I had to respond and talk with him. But I cut the conversation short and left.

Later, the German found me and asked me to give an interview about how the games were going, observing, "Mr. N. reads all your dispatches with delight. He said that they are genuinely *Spitze!*" I didn't know how to take this. I didn't understand him and I didn't understand myself. Can it be, I thought, that a person has completely forgotten *how he behaved fourteen years ago?* But that's impossible. It doesn't happen. He didn't forget, probably, but looks at his own past cold-bloodedly, as something natural, trivial, and worthy of oblivion. If he had acted differently—had not greeted me, had scowled, passing by without a glance and wearing a haughty look—this would not have bothered me. I would have accepted it as the way things should be. A person who has done something evil to someone else always looks at his victim with a scowl or passes him by with a haughty look. That is the nature of things. But here he was pretending *that nothing bad had ever happened!*

And the more I thought about it the more I boiled with rage and just waited for the opportunity to vent my rage on N. A fuss started about awarding the Rolex Company's "Golden Pen" award to the best journalist from each national group, and N. nominated me. This was ridiculous. I am not a professional journalist and had not earned the "Golden Pen." Someone else was nominated, and N. began to insist on me. It became so intolerable that I left the room. Our meeting was taking place in the restaurant. I was beside myself with anger. I waited for him in the hall. As soon as he appeared, I went up to him and said: "What the hell makes you keep hanging on to me? I'm not bothering you!" I probably had a malicious look on my face, for he was silent for a second, looking at me in bewilderment, and then, seemingly flustered, shrugged his shoulders and said, "Me, hanging on to you? You're off your rocker. You've lost your mind, buddy."

"I'm asking you to stop bugging me."

"You're sick," he said. "You should get help."

It was a starry night. I walked along the asphalt road in front of the hotel, breathing in the warm night air of the mountain valley, now empty and silent, and thought: is it true that I'm sick? Occasionally the headlights from cars rushing past would flash over me. I reached the turn onto the bridge and looked at the range of darkening slopes; there, far in the depths, where the now-invisible road led, Innsbruck shone weakly with a handful of lights. It flickered below like a small forest campfire that hadn't been doused. I am sick, I thought, like a person who hasn't shunted his memory aside. I remember too well: the May evening before the meeting when he came without calling, on the pretext of returning some books because he was leaving for Berdyansk. He went to Berdyansk every summer to see his relatives. But I felt that something else had caused him to come. From the start his actions were unnatural: he didn't put the books on the table, he didn't say "Thank you," or "I'm returning these," or "Here are your books," but from a distance threw them on the bed without a word. There was nervousness, a lack of decorum, and decisiveness in this gesture. He was tossing aside not books, but something which had burdened his life. As soon as the two of us were left alone, he said, breaking into a little laugh, "Want to hear a joke? Tomorrow I'm going to speak out against you!"

"Against what?" I asked stupidly, not understanding a damn thing.

"Against you. You, you!" he smiled and poked a finger at me. I thought he was drunk. Something like that could happen, I supposed, but why come and warn me? I said people play dirty tricks without giving warnings. He mumbled something about having understood the "conscious necessity" of it. And I mumbled something meaningless. Suddenly I shouted, "Why did you come here?" He said he came not of his own accord. So Nadya had made him come. She demanded that either he not speak at all, or that he go to the person and honestly warn him. "You don't know what she's like. She actually went into hysterics on me."

I had forgotten about Nadya. Nadya was the girl we both had liked earlier. She had survived the Leningrad blockade; she was pale, fragile, and anemic, with straw-colored braids and a thoughtful look; she was soft-spoken, wrote poetry, and to me as an admirer of Blok, she seemed like the mysterious stranger in Blok's poem. Her whole family had perished in the blockade. Nadya lived in a domitory. Once I had dreamed passionately of her. The summer of '47, when we moved up into the third-year class, the three of us—Nadya, N. and I—went on summer assignment to write articles about the hydroelectric stations at Lake Sevan. This was arranged through the Komsomol organization. We set out in July. At first everything was fun, poignant, intriguing, enveloped in the opiate of uncertainty and love. We had the girl right there beside us and we expected a struggle for her. We kidded around, sang songs, didn't sleep at night, and endlessly recited poetry. We had to transfer four times to get to Yerevan. In Sochi, I swam in the sea for the first time in my life. I remember how N. and I swam far out, while Nadya stayed on the shore and N. asked, "Shall we cast lots for Nadya?" That caught me off guard, and I almost choked on the salt water and blurted out, "No!"

He said, "Watch out, then, you'll have yourself to blame." This threat seemed absurd to me. I had blurted out, "No!" precisely because deep down I thought that if she had to choose between us, Nadya would choose me. I, too, wrote poetry, but N. composed articles for the Sovinform Bureau.

Our journey was becoming more and more tiring. From Sochi to Samtredia we traveled by a local train that was stifling and cramped, where all around people were shouting in a strange language. Some men made passes at Nadya. N. and I defended her, and the matter almost ended in a fight. Because of the closeness and heat everyone stripped down to his undershirt. We sat Nadya in the corner and blocked her from view with our backs. Samtredia seemed to us the Promised Land—it was quiet, peaceful, and people were selling pears and corn flat bread. But later we came to hate Samtredia: we couldn't get out of there.

As soon as the ticket counter opened, a bellowing crowd rushed over, and while were were making our way to our goal, using our elbows to help, the cashier said, *"No teekeets!"* and slammed the window shut. We went to the station guard on duty. He ignored us. N. got into an argument with him and threatened to write about him to the newspaper. He waved our assignment orders, which, signed by the provost of the institute, looked impressive, though they actually didn't mean a thing.

"Your papers mean zilch to me!" the guard said and swept them onto the floor without reading them. Then he said, "You won't get out of here alive!" We had to spend the night in Samtredia. We were afraid to spend the night in the station: that was the guard's territory and he could harass us there. N. proposed that we sleep in the square at the base of the Lenin monument, which was illuminated all night.

"Here they won't dare touch us," N. said. We were afraid that they would attack us and abduct Nadya. All this time N. kept quietly humming, "Enemy whirlwinds swirl above us . . ." He had begun to annoy me. Nadya calmly lay down on my raincoat, covered up with his jacket, and went to sleep, and we guarded her, and grumbled and argued all night. I remember we swore at each other over Akhmatova. But no one attacked us.

The next day we managed to get on a train by evening and we left for Tbilisi. There our quarrels grew bitter: our money had melted away catastrophically, and I thought that we simply had to go on without delay, but he took it into his head to stay a few days in Tbilisi. He had a friend there who had served with him at the front. I objected strenuously. Suddenly, he said that if I was going to be stubborn I could go on ahead, and they would catch up with me at Lake Sevan. Something stirred up inside me and burst. As if a trench had been dug out, a mine laid, and now it exploded.

I asked Nadya, "Do you really want to stay with him in Tbilisi?"

"I don't care," she said. "I'm not rushing anywhere."

An unusual honesty set her apart. But for some reason, her honesty burst like a bomb and inflicted contusions on people. The friend from the front couldn't be located, and we went on together. In Yerevan a hundred-degree heat wave was raging—we just had to dream up a trip to Armenia in July! The heat turned us into half-corpses: our energy sapped, we lay around in a room that an old woman had offered us at the station. On the third day N. advised me to look for a room for myself.

"Somewhere nearby," he said. "Not far from us." And I left them that very evening. Just that suddenly everything ended. It was my first disappointment: in friendship, in women, and mainly, in myself. To be so self-confident and blind! But I didn't suffer for long. I was twenty-one.

Later, my relations with N. recovered, although our previous friendship was no longer possible. We became distant, but not hostile to each other. Without half-trying, I noticed that he and Nadya were going together, then they split up, and about the time we finished the institute they got back together, and for good it seemed. But this didn't affect me. I was busy with something else. I was writing a book. Other women with straw-colored braids came and went. Suddenly, I got married. Life flew by in youthful impatience. My second-rate book became famous, a fog obscured my vision, and then a mountain collapsed on me.

For four years N. had not once come to see me, and suddenly he turned up. This didn't scare me: he was only a small part of the mountain. But what was puzzling and what I cannot understand was why did he come and warn me? Although I cannot understand it now, at the time, suprisingly enough, when I heard that Nadya had made him come, for some reason I *understood* and *agreed.* The matter involved a threat of expulsion. I had finished the institute, but had remained a member of the institute Komsomol. The second-rate book suddenly received a prize. Therefore, it was sweet to expel me. And there was a reason: in my entrance application I had concealed that my father was an enemy of the people, which I had never believed. What N. had said when he came to see me at night was sheer madness. And what Nadya had demanded from him, which implied honesty and openness, was also sheer madness. Everything was sheer madness; the month of May, the prize, the expulsion, the applause, and the animosity. And perhaps the plea for remission of sins was also madness. They would have liked for me to say to them, "Go ahead!" and maybe they heard the words "Go ahead!" for I muttered something incoherent, as in a dream, yawned, and shook hands on parting. Sometimes dreams such as these do occur. All the absurd things that happen during the dream seem incredibly logical and perfectly reasonable, but when you wake up, you can't for the life of you figure out why all that hocus-pocus seemed so clear to you. So, all the speakers talked only about the entrance application. They needed more, something concrete that would confirm that I was *rotten inside,* that the case of the application was merely evidence of a general *rottenness,* the way feverish lips are evidence of a breakdown of the whole organism with a cold. N. spoke with difficulty, as if it was painful. It was hard for him. After all, he had been on friendly terms with me. He could barely put words together. He said that he had a torturously dual relationship with me: on the one hand this, on the other hand, unquestionably, that. Details are important in such things: well, for example, what I once said about Akhmatova. This was long ago, but so much the worse for me. That is, already at that time I had some faulty ideas. Once I praised so-and-so. Another time I was all upset about something. Once I teased him when he wanted to sing revolutionary songs. But I was not a hopeless case, however. Therefore he was against expulsion, and for a severe reprimand and warning. After long arguments the meeting decided just that way. But the Regional Committee expelled me; the minor details of N.'s testimony were good enough for that. Later, the City Committee reinstated me with a stiff rebuke, or as people used to say then, half-lovingly—a "stiffy."

In the Tyrol all of this seemed ancient; by now it had receded into such a biblical antiquity that you suddenly thought: did all this happen to me? Maybe I dreamed it. Maybe someone told me a pack of tall tales, and in my mind everything got turned around and upside down? Someone said that in Russia a writer has to live a long time: and it is true, you can come upon many surprises and marvels. Time darkens the past with an ever-thickening veil, and you won't see through it, for it's pitch-dark. Because the veil is in us. And the surprises also disappear behind the same veil. Chekhov could have lived to see the war. As an old man, he could have sat as an evacuee in Chistopol, have somehow lived on ration cards, read the newspapers, and listened to the radio. With a hand growing weak, he could have written something important and necessary for that moment. He could have reacted to the liberation of Taganrog, but how would he have viewed his own past, remaining behind the dusk of days? His own *Uncle Vanya*? His own chopped-down orchard? How would he have viewed Olga, who dreamed, "If only we could know! If only we could know!" As soon as we find something out, it vanishes into a fog. Indeed, Anton Pavlovich would have been able to find out before Chistopol about things that poor Olga wouldn't have dared to dream of. So, he found out—and so what? He couldn't find out the main thing—how the war would end. But we know this.

Strolling at night along the highway in front of the Stubental Hotel, I suddenly decided: I have to have it out with N. Why I had to was unclear. But I was possessed by the idea. Now, when it's all stopped hurting, and we're both free of those days, and the waves are rolling us in different directions, it's easy to ask: why did you do it? I began to wait for a convenient time. While the games were going on, we rarely met: I was watching hockey; he, figure skating. And then it was all over. The hotel proprietor smiled for the first time as he said good-bye to us, and we left by bus for Vienna, stopping along the way to have a look at this and that. The weather was warm. We were tanned, as if we had been in the south. In the bus he looked friendly and again nodded amiably, as though nothing had happened. Sometimes he would ask me something insignificant in passing: "Do you know what the next stop will be?" or, "Did you happen to notice where the bathroom is?" I always answered dryly. I thought: "Just wait, I'll ask you something altogether different. You'll stop smiling!" On the second day after lunch in Salzburg, we went on an excursion to a castle which housed a medieval torture chamber. I thought: "Here's the very place!"

Everyone was feeling a little high after lunch—we wandered through the huge castle laughing and joking, and lingered in the passages and halls of the dungeon, where in the semi-darkness, as luck would have it, instruments of torture stood on end and the two of us turned up alone in one of the rooms. I asked him, "Listen, I've been waiting a long time to ask you, just out of curiosity, why did you try to do me in then?"

He didn't understand. "When?"

"You know, during those years, the devil knows when. They were expelling me. Remember?" We were standing in front of a huge tub into which they used to place a criminal and then, with a windlass, lower him into a well of putrid water with snakes and toads. There the victim was either drowned and his corpse dragged out, or he was kept half-drowned, then tortured and forced to tell his secrets. This information was conveyed on a plaque inscribed in beautiful Gothic letters. This occurred in the sixteenth century. We looked into the depths of the well. It was now dry, but had no bottom. Our voices disappeared in a rumble below.

I knew what he would say. "I swear to you, old man, I acted sincerely! We were fools. I believed that you needed to be punished, that your father was an enemy, and that mercy shows weakness. If you like, one should feel sorry not for you, but for us sincere fools."

I would answer: "But the difference is that you fools weren't threatened by anything, but I was, of being without work, without money, and maybe, without a home, without a family. Times were grim, but that didn't trouble you fools. What could one expect from you? You acted sincerely. There's nothing nobler and more remarkable than sincerity!"

"Are you calling that into question?"

"If it means sincerely forgetting about conscience, about other people's suffering—then to hell with sincerity! You didn't give a thought to what your sincerity was turning into. You didn't give a damn what was happening to the people who ran up against your sincerity, shining with its satanic light! And you know on the day of the damned meeting, my mother..." All of a sudden a crimson cloud of rage sailed into me.

"Your sincerity is villainy." And grabbing the puny N. below his knees, I lightly lift him over the well and throw him across the barrier. He plops into the tub. There's a inhuman scream, the windlass crank begins to turn, faster and faster, the tub crashes below, the scream dies out, the crank turns on and out of control, and I run up the stone stairway. In the bus no one notices that N. is not there. It only dawns on them two hours later. They turn back. Everyone has suddenly sobered up. They run through the castle looking for him, wailing, calling, while I sit on the porch and smoke. Gradually, the terrible truth becomes clear. "Well?" they ask each other with terrified eyes. And someone says, *"But you know, there was something out of kilter with him."*

"Where?"

"In Innsbruck."

"What was it?"

"He stood around a lot on the street reading notices..."

N. looked at me in fright and, shaking his head, whispered, "You've forgotten everything, old man. I didn't try to do you in. I tried to save you."

"Save me?"

"Of course, I shifted the course of the meeting. They wanted to expel you, but after my speech they gave you a 'stiffy.' You thanked me. Don't you remember?"

"I remember something else: you said something about Akhmatova, about my being two-faced."

He stared at me with wide eyes, as if I were a madman, and then grabbed me by the shoulders and shook me. "No way! I saved you! I dragged you out of the fire! Later, I caught it: why, they said, did you go out of your way to defend him? He's scum. I quarreled because of you. How strange that you've forgotten everything."

Yes, I did forget, I didn't remember, I mixed it up, everything disappeared into a fog. He stretched a tentative hand out to me, and I shook it tentatively. We climbed up out of the dungeon into the open air. The snowy white backbone of the mountain flashed in the blue sky. The alpine spring was in full swing. Music floated over from the bus—our driver had turned on Mozart. He liked to doze to music.

I thought about the thick books at the Stubental Hotel: in fact, there really is nothing else in the world but snow, sun, music, girls, and the fog which comes with time.

Fifteen years have passed since our visit to the torture chamber, and it is also covered in fog. N. died of heart disease eight years ago. I don't know what became of Nadya. I haven't been to the stadium for a long time now, and I watch hockey on television.

1986

Translated by Byron Lindsey

NOTES

The Exchange

1. ZHEK. Housing-exploitation office, which is in charge of the material and political well-being of a given group of apartment houses. The Zhek office checks to see if all persons living in a given place are properly registered,etc.

2. Balda. A quote from Pushkin's verse "Fairy Tale about the Priest and His Workman Balda."

3. Red Partisan. That is, partisans on the Bolshevik side during the Russian Civil War.

4. OGPU. Acronym for the secret police.

5. VNESHTORG. Foreign trade.

6. Opel / Zhopel. Adding "zh" makes the car name sound like "zhopa," meaning ass.

7. Red professor. Again, one who supported the right side early.

8. Vasilich. Using just the abbreviated patronymic is both familiar and honorific; thus Lenin is called "Ilych."

9. Nepman. From "New Economic Policy" (NEP), a period in the 20s when limited capitalism was reintroduced.

10. Saira. A popular fish from the eastern USSR.

11. GUM. The state department store near the Kremlin in Moscow.

12. OZHK. Acronym for the General Housing Commission.

The Long Goodbye

1. 650 a month. Before the currency devaluation of 1961 the ruble was worth only one-tenth of its current value.

2. S. G. Nechayev (1847-82), Russian revolutionary, organizer of the conspiratorial student group People's Retribution (1869).

3. I. Ivanov, a student in Moscow and member of Nechayev's group. Nechayev, angered by Ivanov's opposition to his strict discipline, accused him of being a police spy and instigated his murder in 1869. This incident was the basis of Dostoevsky's *The Devils.*

4. Yekaterinburg. Now Sverdlovsk.

5. Lorkh potatoes. A common Russian potato, developed by Lorkh.

6. Collegiate assessor. Lowest of the 14 civil ranks in Tsarist Russia.

7. People's Will movement. A Russian revolutionary organization established in 1879, responsible for the assassination of Alexander II in 1881.

8. Third section. Tsarist version of the secret police.

9. N. A. Morozov (1854-1946), member of the executive committee of the People's Will, editor of the organization's newspaper for several years.

Imprisoned near St. Petersburg from 1882 until the Revolution of 1905.

10. V. N. Figner (1852-1942), populist revolutionary and member of the People's Will. Condemned to death in 1884 for her role in various assassination attempts, but her sentence was commuted to life imprisonment. She was released in 1904.

11. L. A. Tikhomirov (1852-1923), member of the executive committee of People's Will and editor of the group's *Herald,* published abroad. In 1888 he renounced his revolutionary views and was allowed to return to Russia.

12. A. N. Ostrovsky (1823-86), a prolific Russian dramatist famous for his depiction of the Russian merchant class. M. N. Yermolova, M. P. Sadovsky, and N. I. Muzil were leading actors at the Moscow Maly Theater. Yermolova played the role of Yevlalya in Ostrovsky's play *The Female Captives.*

13. Gavriil Derzhavin was Russia's best eighteenth-century poet. The line quoted is from his poem "God."

Games at Dusk

1. A haircut that was typical for government bureaucrats.

A Short Stay in the Torture Chamber

1. The Russian Symbolist poet Alexander Blok (1880-1921).